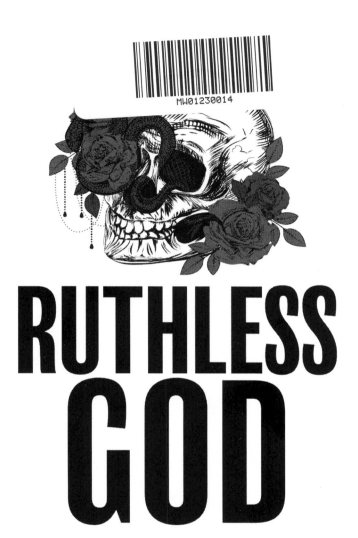

RUTHLESS GOD

J. M. STONEBACK

AUTHOR NOTE

Hey Reader

Ruthless God is a Dark College Romance set in a fictional place called Haven Island, it's extension of New York in United States. Snow is a pitch black character. He doesn't stop killing for anyone and he continues to be pitch black throughout the book. I hope you enjoy his and Lyrical story as much as I love writing it.

This book is not for the faint of the heart and you should head over to my website to read the warnings.

J.M.Stoneback – Dark Romance Author (wordpress.com)

Thank you for taking the time to read this book.
XOXO
J.M. Stoneback

Run, Blue. Pray, I don't catch you.—Snow

RUTHLESS GOD

PROLOGUE

Snow

R AP MUSIC BLASTS THROUGH THE SPEAKERS AS I LEAN against the fireplace with a glass of scotch in my hand. My friends and I are hosting a party at our mansion.

I hate parties.

The music is too loud.

People talk entirely too much, and I'm miserable as hell.

I smooth out the bloodred tie around my neck, flatten out my tailor-made suit, then I sip on Jack Daniel's, ignoring the burning sensation in my throat.

I spot a dude receiving head in the corner of my kitchen and two women making out on the suede couch. These types of parties turn into a big-ass orgy.

I polish off the last bit of my drink, then I set the crystal glass on the mantelpiece above the fireplace.

My best friend, Keanu, pats me on the back with one hand, a bottle in the other.

After he sips his beer, he sets it on the mantel next to mine, then he combs his fingers through his dyed bright red hair. "When are the strippers arriving? I'm ready to get my dick sucked."

He gives out too much information, but he has always been the type to overshare. We've been friends since middle school and he's going to work with me as the CFO of the American Billionaire Club after graduation. There are going to be four of us who will run the club.

I shake my head as my mouth twitches. "I have no idea."

Moments later, a dozen women wearing close to nothing stroll inside, smiling and giggling. I eye Keanu, and he smirks like the Cheshire cat. "That's what I'm talking about."

He strides to a woman wearing blue lingerie, and he whispers in her ear.

When my eyes hover at the front entrance, I spot Lyrical and Bailey at the archway.

What are they doing here?

I told them not to show up, because the men here are dangerous. I don't want any of these bastards to try to bone them, especially Lyrical.

They are always getting themselves into bullshit and I'm the one bailing them out. Last year, they got into trouble at North Haven University for streaking, sprinting around campus while high on weed.

I had to write a fat check to the dean so he wouldn't expel them from college.

Bailey is a handful. Sometimes, I have to act like her father rather than her brother. It's exhausting to keep an eye out on her. If I didn't, my father would blow a gasket and he'll blame me for her behavior.

I spot Lyrical strolling in the kitchen without a care in the world, pouring herself a red cup of spiked punch. As she glances around, her bright blue eyes find mine, and a smile spreads across her face. My gaze studies her body like a map. Her outfit is cute: a white halter top and tiny shorts that hug her plump ass.

My dick grows hard in my dress pants, so I adjust myself.

She's a whole foot shorter than me, stopping to my chest, and her midnight black hair is pulled up into a tight ponytail.

I don't like that every man has their eyes on her, wanting to fuck her. I want to lock her up in a room and never let anyone see what's mine. She's very beautiful and knows it too. I can't wait to take her virginity on our honeymoon. I wonder if she has a dark side the way I do. I love being in control of the women I fuck. I don't like vanilla sex. I like them wanting me to choke them, tie them down, allowing me to have control over them. If she doesn't, then she's going to have to learn to love it.

Someone clears their throat. Glancing down, I see Savannah standing in front of me, her brunette hair falling over her shoulders like a waterfall. She's pale as a ghost, the opposite of Lyrical. Savannah is superficial and only cares about looks and status, whereas Lyrical is creative, full of life, and doesn't care about the finer things unless it's art.

When Savannah smiles, I roll my eyes. We fucked a couple of times, and when she found out Lyrical is one of my best friends, she gave her hell, so I stopped sticking my dick inside of her. Savannah knows we're not endgame, but she wants to be the one I marry. Her father is a member of the American Billionaire Club, a gentleman's club for the richest and most powerful men around the globe, and I'm going to be the CEO once I graduate.

No one knows I'm supposed to marry Lyrical, but they'll find out when we have our engagement ball.

"What the fuck do you want?" I snap.

Savannah stands on her tippy-toes, trying to catch my attention, but I miss what she says, my eyes fixed on my sister and best friend.

I glance at her, crinkling my nose. "What did you say?"

She straightens her spine like a needle, folding her arms across her chest. She hangs around me like an old stench I can't get rid of. "I'm sorry for being mean to Lyrical. I didn't know how important she was to you, and I shouldn't have poured milk all over her and called her a gold-digging whore."

She keeps speaking as I keep my gaze glued to the guy who walks up to Lyrical. Smiling, she places her hand on his shoulder.

She shouldn't be laughing at any other man's jokes. My jealousy is back at full force, and I hate having to get rid of all the guys she likes. It's childish, but I don't care. She's mine, always will be.

My blood boils, and I ball my fist.

I stalk the shit out of her, and I have an app on her phone where I can spy on who she messages and calls. If she saves a man's number, I log into the app and delete it. No one is taking my girl's virginity but me. If she found out I have a tracker on her, she would be pissed off.

The guy is average-looking, a little shorter than me, and has blond hair. I can take him if we go toe to toe.

When Lyrical bends for Bailey to whisper in her ear, I see him slip white powder in her cup.

Oh, fuck no.

That's grounds for death. Growing up, I watched my father kill countless men for crossing our family. I was raised to eliminate anyone who is a threat.

Without acknowledging Savannah, I shove past, and she calls my name, but I ignore her.

This motherfucker is about to take his last breath. He has no idea who he's messing with.

Once I maneuver through the crowd, I snatch the cup from Lyrical's hand, tossing it in the trash can.

When she frowns, her cheeks turn pink. "Hey, what are you doing?"

Her lips are painted bright red, and I want them wrapped around my dick. The smell of her apple orchard scent invades my nostrils, making my dick harden in my dress pants.

She has no idea what I have in store for her on our wedding night. My future wife doesn't know how much I'm obsessed with her.

I stand between her and the guy, and it's taking every ounce of me not to beat the living shit out of him in front of my guests. His death is going to be a slow one.

He sizes me up, probably calculating if he can take me. Lyrical doesn't know I'm a murderer, and I plan to take my secret to the grave. I don't want her to look at me as a bad person—because I'm not. Some things, she doesn't need to know about me.

I grab her by the arm. "Go home, Blue."

Grinding her teeth, she slowly peels my thick fingers from her flesh. Looking up at me, she frowns. "You're not the boss of me, Snow. I do what I want, and we're just having a friendly conversation."

She needs to be controlled, looked after like a delicate flower, and I don't want to treat her like one. Right now, I want her on her knees, covered in her tears and my cum. I want to drag her in the bedroom, tie her up to the headboard, and fuck her until she begs me to stop.

We fight every time a guy sets his eyes on her.

My girl.

I wish she would understand she's mine.

"I thought I told you not to show up here."

Bailey rolls her eyes. "We wanted to have a little fun, Snow."

Instead of replying to my sister, I stand toe to toe with this motherfucker, keeping my eyes glued to him. He doesn't flinch or show fear. He grinds his teeth, staring at me as if he's going to shoot me.

"Sometimes you act like a jealous boyfriend," Lyrical snaps.

When we're married, I look forward to turning her ass cheeks black and blue for being disobedient.

The guy shoves my chest. "You heard the lady. Run along little boy. It's between me and her."

I stumble a little, then undo my expensive cuff links, smiling wickedly at him. It's going to be fun hearing him beg for his life.

"Just because we're getting married doesn't mean you have to cockblock me. You fucked Savannah, but once you get a whiff of another man on my radar, you run them off. I'm not yours, Snow. Not yet."

Oh, but she is. Lyrical can convince herself that she's not, but she's been mine since we were told our marriage is arranged.

Bailey steps into my view, stabbing a finger in my chest. "What's the big issue, Revi?"

She knows I don't like it when she calls me by my real name, so she's doing it to get on my nerves. I love my sister, but she can be a pain in my ass.

I glance down at her, and her wavy dark hair covers her shoulders. She's wearing a floral dress.

I lean down, whispering in Bailey's ear, "He slipped something in Lyrical's drink, so I have to take him out."

She knows what "take him out" means. It's the same phrase my father uses before he's about to kill someone.

Her face pales, and she grabs Lyrical's hand. "We have to go."

"Bu—"

"No buts. This time, we have to listen to Snow."

Concern colors her face, and she swallows thickly. "Are you coming back to our place? There is something I need to ask you," Lyrical asks.

"Of course, Blue."

She stands on her tippy-toes and kisses my cheek, and I'll never get tired of her kisses even though they're platonic. My heart beats a million times in my chest.

I watch the girls head to the front door, and then I knee the bastard in the balls. I grab his wrist, twist it behind his back, and he yelps like a dog.

Leaning forward, I whisper in his ear, "You're about to meet the grim reaper soon. I saw you slip something in my girl's drink."

His brown eyes round in horror, and he shakes his head.

"Let me g—"

"Shut the fuck up."

He tries to break free from my hold, but I keep his hand behind his back as I force him through the crowd, then down to the basement.

Once we arrive there, Keanu and Jameson lean against the soundproof walls. Jameson is munching on an apple, while Keanu grins like the Joker. Keanu gets off on hurting people, but no one suspects that about him because Keanu acts nice and kind, but under the façade, he's as heartless as they come.

Jameson eats the last bit of his apple, then tosses it in the trash can.

They must have seen what happened, which explains why they are here before me. This is the only thing the basement is made for—torturing people.

The faint smell of bleach hits my nostrils. If the FBI knew my body count, they would gladly throw me in prison, but being an American God, I can get away with just about anything and everything. No one can touch me. My father has judges, cops, and lawyers on his payroll. Everyone has a price.

When Jameson tosses me a baseball bat, the fucker tries to elbow my stomach, but he misses, so I slap the bat against his kneecaps and his bones shatter as he falls face-first, slamming his skull on the concrete. He screams at the top of his lungs as blood drenches his face, and he spits out his teeth.

"Please, I d-didn't know she was with someone," he pleads.

It's always the same.

I'm sorry.

I didn't mean to try to hurt her. Or my favorite, *I didn't know she belonged to a God.* People think of me as a god in North Haven University, not just because I'm an American God but because my family is one of the most powerful in the world.

My patience is running thin, so I slam the bat on the backs of his legs, and he whimpers as tears rush down his cheeks.

Keanu chuckles, pulls out his phone, and snaps pictures of the guy. "A pretty sight."

Jameson yanks his cuff links out. He's the only one who seems normal, but he's far from it. He knows how to manipulate people to get what he wants. Plus, he's a genius hacker. "Dude, what did Snow say about pictures?"

Keanu rolls his eyes, tucking his phone back into his pocket. "You two are no fun, I swear. What's the purpose of torturing him if you can't keep a memory?"

I don't have all day to deal with this lowlife.

"Jameson, help me tie this ugly bastard to the chair," I snap.

He grabs his right arm, and I grab the other, and we tie him to the chair, then I place a cloth in his mouth, slapping duct tape over his lips.

I hope the bastard chokes to death.

Gripping his chin, I dig my black-painted nails into his flesh, drawing blood.

"What did you have planned for my Blue? Did you have plans to rape her and leave her for dead? Were you thinking about fucking her while she's unconscious?"

Keanu laughs hard. "You're going to die."

I slam my bat against the guy's chest, and he wails into the cloth. Hearing his bones crush is music to my ears. His dress shirt is drenched in blood.

"What a lovely sound," Jameson says with a sound of delight in his tone. He loves to hear people scream in agony.

"You won't ever rape another woman again." I slam the bat across his face and his skull bursts into tiny pieces, and his head dangles off his neck, creating a pool of blood.

Keanu checks his pulse, and he takes out his phone, snapping pictures again. "He's gone."

"Put that away. What the fuck is wrong with you, Keanu? Why do you need pictures of your victims? What are you going to do? Jack off to them?" Jameson says, annoyed.

Keanu grins from ear to ear. "I might."

"Get rid of the body and all the security camera footage," I tell both of them as I remove my suit jacket, then I head to my room and change into a white T-shirt and gray sweatpants.

Once I leave the mansion, I stop by Lyrical's favorite restaurant and grab her go-to order of meatballs and noodles.

I drive on the highway, and it's blocked off because of an accident. Smoke fogs the clear sky as firemen hose down a car and burning trees.

Paparazzi snaps pictures and a policeman leads me to a detour, so I follow his instructions. When I walk into the penthouse, I waltz to the kitchen, set Lyrical's food down on the counter, and call out her name. But she doesn't respond.

Lyrical should be picking out a movie for us to watch, but when I walk into the open space living room, there aren't any signs of her. She should be home now, unless she stops by somewhere. I grab my phone from my pocket, pulling up the GPS tracker, and the red dot is at a standstill. I zoom in on the map, and realization hits me like a ton of bricks.

The area where the car accident was.

My heart drops in my chest as I rush out the door.

By the time I make it to the scene of the accident, the cops and fire trucks are already gone, so I rush to the nearest hospital which is five minutes away. My heart hammers in my chest as I call Bailey and Lyrical, hoping that there is a mistake and my GPS is wrong.

I don't think I could survive if anything happened to them.

When I pull up to the underground parking lot of the hospital, I throw my expensive car into park. As soon as I unbuckle my seat belt, my phone rings, and my mother's name is displayed across the screen, so I tap the Answer button.

"Revi." My mother never calls me by my nickname. "It's Bailey and Lyrical. They were in a terrible accident."

My heart breaks into a million pieces, and it feels as if I have boulders on my chest. Clenching my shirt, I breathe in deep and exhale loudly.

"Are they okay?"

"Come to the ER."

The line goes dead, and I practically jump out of the car and head inside.

My mother not answering my question tells me enough to know this is bad.

Very bad.

Adrenaline spikes in my blood, and I feel lightheaded as I arrive at the front desk. The nurse directs me to the waiting room, and my mother's face is wet with tears. My father has his arms wrapped around her, then I see Lyrical's parents holding each other, crying, as her mother apologizes to my parents.

I walk up to my mother and pat her on the back, not acknowledging my father's glare. We never got along, and I hate the bastard.

She falls to the ground, continuing to sob, and snot streaks down her nose.

"What happened?"

My father grabs me by the neck, yanks me to the nearest bathroom, telling every man to get the fuck out, then he locks the door.

Stomping up to me, he slaps me across the face. Pain shoots up to my forehead, and I rub my cheek.

I'm not going to back down and he's not about to make me feel even shittier than I already do.

I'm a split image of him and I hate it. We both have the same slender body, our right eye is brown and the other eye is hazel, and our hair is black, but I purposely dyed mine white so I don't look like him. I gave myself the nickname Snow and I refuse to be called Revi because it's also his first name. I hate my father with every fiber in my bones. The only reason why I haven't tried to kill him is because he's protected by the government. There are some things I can't get away with.

His Italian loafers touch my shoes, then he balls up his fist as if he's about to strike me again. "What was Lyrical and Bailey doing at your party with dangerous men?"

I say nothing. I can't say anything, but guilt eats at me like a fucking disease. It's my job to protect them.

Before I can answer, he punches me in the gut, and I bend over as the pain travels through my chest. When I try to punch him in the face, he counters it, placing his hand around my throat and squeezing, effectively cutting off my airway.

"You were supposed to be watching them, you were supposed to protect them. Bailey is dead, and Lyrical barely made it out alive before someone happened to see the fire."

This can't be real.

This can't be real.

My baby sister is dead.

My father lets me go.

I don't understand my father's logic. Why is he blaming me for the accident? But it shouldn't surprise me; he has blamed me for shit that's beyond my control ever since I was little.

I stand up straight as much as I possibly can, ignoring my throbbing stomach.

"How the fuck is it my fault that they were in a car accident?" I say through gritted teeth.

Stepping back, the vein in his forehead throbs, and his face turns tomato red. "Lyrical was driving high and they had Molly in their system, you fucking idiot! How did they manage to get a hold of ecstasy?"

No one knew they had a habit of popping Molly except for me. But this time, they didn't get it from me or anyone at the party. Unless they took it before they showed up.

My father eyes me, frowning. "You're still going to marry Lyrical. You need to be married to run the club."

Typical. My father never cared about anyone or anything but his precious business, and he doesn't care about Bailey's death because to him, she was a business deal, a liability, unless she got married.

Without another word, he leaves me in the bathroom, and I rush to the faucet, turn the knob, and splash icy water on my face. I grab a paper towel and scrub until my skin is raw.

I'm so fucking pissed off at Lyrical for driving under the influence and killing my sister. When are her reckless ways going to end? Why would she pop a Molly and get behind the wheel? I could have driven them home—hell, I could have gotten my driver to take them both home.

When I leave the bathroom, I head to the ER's waiting room, and Lyrical's mother wraps her arms around my shoulders, kissing the side of my temple.

She has always been a second mother to me. Also, she accepted me as the son she never had. I don't like how guilt creeps inside of my chest. Her father pats me on the back, nods, then frowns at me with thinned lips.

When I glance at my own mother, she looks away, casting her eyes down to the tiles, as if she agrees with my father. My mother never had a backbone when it came to my father, always siding with him even when she knew he was wrong.

"It's not your fault," Lyrical's mom whispers in my ear, and her words catch me off guard. Those are the words I want to hear from *my* parents. "Things happen for a reason. I know my daughter, she's reckless, and Bailey was too. I'm so sorry you lost your sister."

It feels like a nightmare that I'm never going to wake up from. I can't believe Bailey is gone. My baby sister that I spent years looking after. No more having Bailey's back and going to her about my problems.

The doctor strolls inside the waiting room, tells us they need to speak to the coroner about Bailey's body, and he lets Lyrical's parents know they are allowed to see their daughter. I have a few words to say to Lyrical myself, and pure rage hums inside of me, waiting to overflow like a volcano.

Lyrical's parents disappear down the hall while I pace the floor like a madman.

What will I say to her?

An hour later, my parents leave without sparing me a glance, and Lyrical's parents tell me she wants to see me.

Once I make it to her room, I suck in a breath as I bang my knuckles on the door.

My gaze snags on her form and her face looks dirty. We stare at each other for several moments, but it feels more like an hour.

Anger burns in my chest at the sight of her, and I look at her in disgust. Tears fall down her puffy face.

"I can't believe Bailey is gone."

She fists the sheets, grits her teeth, and I fight every fiber in me not to choke the shit out of her.

"I'm so sorry, Snow. It's all my fault. I was feeling funn—"

"Why the fuck would you get behind the wheel after you popped a Molly?"

I'm trying to keep my cool, but my sister died because of her. *She* should have been dead, not her. Bailey shouldn't have had to pay for her choices, and neither should my family. The love I had for my best friend quickly goes out the window, replaced with hate.

Confusion laces her face. "What? I didn't take any drugs!" She rubs her forehead and closes her eyes, but I don't give two shits about her. This is not the girl I fell in love with and she's not the person who I thought she was. "Fuck, my head hurts."

I ball up my fists and shove them in my pocket, fighting the urge not to punch the wall. "Just because both our parents turned a blind eye to your foolishness doesn't mean I will. Your and Bailey's bad habit caught up to you tonight."

My sister turned to street drugs when her medication wasn't strong enough to fight the hallucinations she suffered from. Sometimes, Lyrical would get high, too, so she wouldn't feel alone.

I hate the sight of this girl, the girl I was in love with all these years. And, what's worse, I'm stuck with her for the rest of my life. If I don't marry her, I don't get my father's business, and that's the only thing I want right now. To graduate and inherit what belongs to me.

She sinks her two front teeth into her bottom lip as she shakes her head. "Snow. I'm telling you the truth. Bailey and I didn't do any drugs before we came to the party. We made a pact that we wouldn't take it anymore."

She's full of shit and she knows it.

"I don't believe you."

She sits up forward, gripping the rail of the bed. "You're my best friend. Why would I lie to you?"

"So you won't take responsibility for your actions. I knew you were reckless, but I didn't expect you to do this stupid shit. Don't fucking talk to me anymore, not until the wedding."

Thick tears rush down her cheeks like a hose.

My chest aches as if a gigantic hole is in there.

I would have done anything for her. *Anything*. But she betrayed me and what makes it even worse, she lied to my damn face. I don't want to be anywhere near her.

"I was drugged. That's the only explanation. We went to another pa—"

I finally lose my cool, punch the door, and my fist throbs. I'm too pumped up on adrenaline to recognize the pain traveling up my arm. "Stay the fuck away from me."

"Snow, please. I'm sorry."

Without another word, I walk out of the room as she jumps out of the bed, following me down the hallway. She continues to follow me to the parking lot, but I get into my car before strapping the seat belt over my body. I watch her bang on the window, screaming my name. I put the car in drive, leaving her in the parking lot.

Three Months Later...

FIRST SEMESTER

CHAPTER ONE

Lyrical

I SLICE THE RAZOR ACROSS THE DELICATE FLESH OF MY ARM, watching the bright red blood drip onto the bathroom sink. The pain feels like a high I don't want to let go of, and my adrenaline is spiked, so I make a few more cuts. Closing my eyes, I try to get rid of the empty hole in my chest.

The one mistake I made that changed my life forever was killing my best friend in the car accident three months ago. Every day I live with the guilt of getting behind the wheel, because if not, Bailey would have been alive. I've done dumb shit before, but I've never driven high. I may not be the most responsible person in the world, but I have common sense.

I can't bring myself to look at the girl in the mirror because of the shame I feel, so instead I slide on my long-sleeve shirt, ignoring the throbbing wounds, and I wiggle on my leggings. Then I head to my bedroom.

The only thing I remembered about the car accident is that I blacked out, woke up in a hospital bed, and was told Bailey didn't survive.

I remember the pain on Snow's face as he informed me that he doesn't want to have anything to do with me. It hurt more than the headache I experienced right after the accident. It left a gigantic hole in my chest that will never be filled. It's been three months since the accident. This is the longest we have ever gone without speaking to each other. I didn't even see him at the funeral.

Shaking my head, I tell myself I'm going to take it one day at a time. Plus, I have to plan for my wedding right after college. Which I'm not looking forward to.

With my book bag strap over my shoulder, I stride to the living room. I live in an apartment on campus. Tossing my bag onto the wooden floor, I sit on the beige couch, glancing around the spacious room. The flames in the fireplace dance, making the room warm and cozy. I glance out the window, staring at the clear ocean. I wish my emotions were as calm as the sea.

North Haven is where most of the wealthy people in the United States reside when they want to get away from the big city life, and NHU is where the richest people on the planet send their children for the best education. The college tops any Ivy League in America.

My roommate, Lilac, strolls inside, her blue dress hugging her small frame, and her lavender hair pinned up in a ponytail making her light brown skin glow. She looks like a fairytale princess; her beauty as rare as a gem. She's the only person I've gotten close to since the car accident.

She knows the pain I feel, of me losing Bailey, and I can tell her my issues without receiving any judgment. She's truly down-to-earth and a good friend.

Her gray eyes narrow on me and her lips thin, before she asks, "Are you okay?"

I feel fine most days, but today I feel like shit. According to the police report, Bailey died on impact before the car engulfed in flames. My mother and father felt bad, but they never blamed me for the accident, though they did force me to attend a rehab center and seek grief counseling during the summer.

I shrug, biting the inside of my cheek.

She wraps her arms around my waist, squeezing me tight, and I return the hug as her fruity scent invades my nostrils.

Stroking my back, she says, "It's going to get better. I don't know how it feels to lose a best friend, but I do know if you need someone to speak to, then I'm all ears."

She means well, but her words don't do anything to help soothe the ache in my chest, and I try so hard to hold back the tears, swallowing the lump in my throat.

I release her and step back. "Thanks."

Because I do appreciate that she's trying to comfort me in my time of need.

Once Lilac grabs her floral-print bag, she straps it across her shoulders and we head out the door.

The campus is alive and vibrant, surrounded by different colored trees. You can see the crystal-clear ocean from here on the island. The dark towers made out of fiber glass look haunted. I watch as other students stroll to wherever they need to go. Some people are riding on bikes and others are on scooters. I watch the tidal waves roll onto the white sand, the gray sky gloomy, but the temperature is neither too hot nor too cold.

As we walk to the café, Lilac fills me in on her school schedule and we find out that we have two classes together. She tells me about her summer, about her family vacation in Greece. Like me, she comes from a wealthy family. Her mother is a stay-at-home wife and her father owns a national bank.

I'm an art major. When I graduate, I want to start my own museum gallery, a dream Bailey and I shared together. She was an artist as well; she was gifted in making sculptures, whereas my gift is paintings. We had our whole lives intertwined with each other's, and sometimes, I don't know how to pick up the pieces of my life, or if I should continue this journey without her. It's not fair that I get to fulfill our dreams and she can't. Death is one of the cruelest things on this planet.

When we head to the table where Winter sits, she smiles, gets up from her seat, hugs me tight, then she sits back down. She's been my friend since the start of my freshman year. Her sleek bob barely touches her shoulders, and she wears a blue blouse with matching designer jeans. She's into fashion, which is why she majors in fashion design.

"I've missed you two this summer." She takes a huge chunk of her muffin, chewing silently before setting it back on her plate.

The smell of bacon mixed with a burst of blueberry filters through the air, but my appetite is nonexistent.

The waitress places her fresh mug of coffee in front of Winter, the smoke from the hot beverage making her face seem flushed.

Lilac rattles off her order to the waitress, then she asks Winter, "How was it living in Paris this summer?"

"It was fun. I went to a lot of parties, and I had a summer fling," Winter replies, before sipping slowly from her mug.

I'm so envious of other people and their lives. They get to choose who they want to date and have the freedom to go after their dreams. The only thing I have control over is my college degree and my career, though my mother doesn't agree with my life choices because I'm going to be married to one of the most powerful men on this planet. Growing up, I felt like a caged person, not having the freedom to do what I want. My parents were overbearing and strict, but when Bailey came around, they gave me a little bit more freedom.

My friends talk amongst themselves about their summers, while I don't comment.

Everyone's eyes veer up, including mine, as Snow, Jameson, Irvin, and Keanu walk into the café.

My heart drops in my chest and adrenaline courses through

my blood at the sight of Snow. Tears wet my eyes because I miss him terribly. Pain crawls around my heart.

His pure white hair touches his forehead, making his tan skin brighter than the sun. He wears his dark leather jacket with a black T-shirt underneath and a pair of black jeans with rips in the knees.

The butterflies flutter in my stomach every time I'm around him. Yet, I know he won't look at me the same after the car accident.

The American Gods are untouchable, blessed with fame, and have enough wealth to fund a country. They are vicious and people whisper about them like they are the boogeymen in the night. I've only met Snow's friends a handful of times because he used to keep me away from them, said they were too dangerous for me to hang out with. Their families have the mayor, judges, and other powerful people at their mercy; they will soon rule North Haven. No one knows about my arranged marriage to Snow, because we kept it a secret. The public are aware that the American Gods tend to have arranged marriages, but they aren't announced to the world until the engagement ball. I'm not looking forward to it, either. My wedding day will be on every streaming service as if it's important like the Queen of England's wedding was.

Snow's eyes meet mine, and they are cold and distant and filled with anger. When he stalks toward me, his eyes glide over my face as he makes his way to the table. Winter's and Lilac's eyes are glued to him, full of glee, their faces flushed, as they burst into a fit of giggles. None of them know my destiny is tied with his, and, come summer of next year after we graduate, we will be wed.

I'm not looking forward to it, especially when we're not speaking and he hates my guts.

My heart thumps when he stands in front of me, not acknowledging my friends. He grabs me by the arm, dragging me outside, and I don't fight him because I don't want to cause a scene. No doubt everyone on campus is going to be talking about it for the rest of the day.

Once I inhale the morning breeze, I try to snatch my arm away from him, but he grips tighter, slamming me against the cobblestone wall. Pain shoots up my spine.

"Let me go," I grit out between my teeth.

He places both of his arms above my head, and I inhale a heavy dose of his minty breath as I study his facial features. His cheekbones are high, his jaw is sharp like a knife, and his skin is as smooth as marble. He's the most beautiful man I have ever laid eyes on.

"What are you doing here?"

He looks like the powerful American God that he is. Pure rage colors his face, causing me to shrink back. I've never been as scared of him as I am now.

Tears form in my eyes, but I refuse to allow him to see them fall. He will not see me weak, and he will not see how much he scares me, so I straighten my spine and hold my head high.

"I want to finish my last year here. Why, is it a problem? You still believe I popped a pill and drove that night?"

His eyes narrow. "Yes, I do. I looked at the autopsy and your medical records. My father paid off the cops and the judge to get you out of jail scot-free for reckless driving."

"I was drugged," I scream at the top of my lungs, but he places his palm over my mouth, silencing me.

"I don't believe it. I watched you all night and no one drugged you. I even checked the cameras. You may have our families fooled, but not me." He sighs as if he's over this conversation. "Leave this school. I don't want to see you here, not until my ring is on your finger."

I don't care how pissed off he is with me, I'm not going anywhere. He might have a lot of power, but not over me. Plus, I don't have the patience or time to transfer to another school. The only thing I'm worried about is passing college algebra.

I push on his hard chest, but he doesn't budge. "No, I'm staying. You can't run me out of here."

He grips my chin, digging his black-painted nails into my flesh, making me squeal. "Last chance, Lyrical Gina Haynes. Leave here."

I wrap my fingers around his, trying desperately to remove them, but he digs them in harder, watching the tears run down my cheeks. His smile is wicked, as if he's enjoying hurting me.

He wipes each tear, tasting them on his fingers. "You look good when you cry. You look better at my mercy. You would look even better kneeling before me, with my dick between your lips."

My eyes widen at his words; he's never spoken such filth to me. He would say sexual stuff to me here and there, but not like this. His words make my nipples harden like glass.

His eyes glint with delight. "You would like that, wouldn't you?"

I would, but I'll never admit to him what I really want. If he knew the fucked-up things I crave, he wouldn't look at me the same.

"Please, Snow. Let me go, you're hurting me."

He squeezes harder, and I yelp like a dog.

"That's the point. Leave, Lyrical. You're not welcome here."

"No."

A devilish grin spreads across his face. Snow leans down, whispering in my ear, "I'm going to enjoy breaking you."

He lets me go, fixes his erection in his pants, then opens the door to walk inside the building, leaving me stunned with my mouth hanging open.

CHAPTER TWO

Snow

I STARE AT LYRICAL FROM ACROSS THE CAFÉ AS HER FRIENDS say something to her, but she seems zoned out. Seeing her sends me into a fit of rage—I don't want to be tied down to her for the rest of my life. Seeing those tears in her eyes makes me want to shove my dick into her. Hell, the woman breathes in my direction and I'm horny like a teenager. I can't believe I was in love with her. I worshipped the ground she walked on, that's how much I was in love with her. Now, I hate her more than anything in this world and no one knows the deep obsession I have over her even now, after everything she's done, and I can't fathom it. Even when I want to choke her to death, I still want to be around her.

Little does she know I've been stalking her all summer, and I had Jameson plant a tracking device on her new phone that allows me to see what apps she uses. Hoping she would admit she popped drugs before she drove. She claims she was drugged, but I don't believe her.

She didn't do much but stayed at her parents' house. The last time I saw her was at Bailey's funeral, where she cried so badly her father had to carry her away from the gravesite. My father blames me for the accident because I was supposed to be looking out for Bailey, so I haven't spoken to him since the night at the hospital. And my mother, she fell into a deep depression and tried to commit suicide, so my father had her admitted into the psych ward.

"You going to finish that?" Jameson shovels my waffles into his mouth without giving me time to answer.

Jameson loves to eat food. His favorite hobby is restaurant-hopping.

"Are we doing our annual party tonight?" Irvin says, kicking his Italian loafers up on a chair, and he straightens his blue shirt.

I'm not in the mood to party and it has never been my thing, but we do it to allow the rest of the students at our mansion to feel like they can be in our circle. It's crazy how people want our attention, want to network with us, and it can be quite annoying as well. People pretending to like me so they can get into my inner circle. If I befriend anyone, it would give them a boost in their social life. We keep a tight circle because we do a lot of illegal shit.

"Fuck yeah, I need to nosedive into some pussy. My father has been working the shit out of me," Keanu replies, folding his arms across his chest, wrinkling his polo shirt.

"Send out information through IG," I murmur to them.

They pull out their phones, including me, and I make an IG post. I get over two hundred likes in one minute. I tuck my phone back into my pocket.

Savannah strolls over to my table and makes her way onto my lap. She wraps her arms around my shoulders, and I roll my eyes. I don't give a fuck about her. She's a tool I'll use to get back at Lyrical because I know they both hate each other's guts. Even though I fucked her over the summer to get over Lyrical and she was a lousy lay. Her parents have been pestering mine for her hand in marriage. To be honest, I'd rather drag my dick over hot coal before I marry her. She's annoying as fuck, her head game sucks, and she tries to make me talk about my feelings. I would rather be stuck with Lyrical, so I can make her pay for what she did.

I feel the wetness from her pussy leaking all over my pants because she's not wearing any panties, and her tube dress barely covers her tits. When she meshes her lips against mine, her kiss is sloppy as fuck and my dick grows limp, unlike earlier when I was hard as a brick for Lyrical. I pull away from her, wiping my lips with the back of my hand. Even her spit stinks.

Jameson and the rest of the crew talk among themselves, laughing and joking, while Fish Lips can't keep her mouth to herself.

My shoulders go rigid.

"I'm sorry about your loss," she says, giving me a fake, sad face. "You haven't made much time for me this summer."

It pisses me off that she's lying, because she and my sister never got along.

"I've been busy." My tone is flat.

"You ever in the mood to suck my dick," Irvin suggests, "I'm a text away. I heard you gave Jameson head."

I've never liked Irvin because he's egotistic and thinks the world revolves around him, but I have to get along with him because we're going to be business partners soon.

I glance over to Jameson, and he shrugs. "It was bland, and you use too much teeth."

When my eyes veer to Lyrical, our eyes lock, but she glances away. My dick grows hard at the thought of her, and I want my mouth on her pussy as she comes on my tongue with tears in her eyes. I used to have these fantasies of chasing her in the woods, hunting her down, fucking her, or me choking her while my dick is inside of her. I never dared speak those words to her, in fear of scaring her off, but now I plan to use her as my sex blow-up doll. She doesn't want to listen to my warning to leave this school, so

I'm going to get back at her for killing my sister—for destroying my family. I feel the need to control her, own her in every way possible.

Lyrical's eyes roam back to us, and there is sorrow in her bright blue eyes. She holds her head high as if she's not fazed about Savannah sitting on my lap, but tears gather in the corners of her eyes. I stroke Savannah's back, making it seem like I'm into her, and Lyrical balls up her fists, placing them on the table.

Leaning down, I whisper in Savannah's ear, "Come over tonight."

I don't have any plans on fucking Fish Lips, but everyone is going to be there, and this is a ploy to get back at Lyrical just in case she shows up.

A smile spreads across her face as if she won the lottery. "Sure. What are we doing tonight?"

"We're having a party."

Savannah giggles like a schoolgirl, wrapping her arms around my shoulders.

Lyrical looks so beautiful with tears in her eyes, and I want to come all over her face. When she grabs her backpack, she takes one last look at me, then leaves the café. I shove Savannah off me, and she hits her ass on the tile floor, her legs wide open, giving us all a view of her shaved pussy, and I glance away, not giving a fuck if she's hurt. Irvin takes out his phone to snap a picture of it.

"What was that for? Why did you push me?" she whines.

I can't get rid of her yet, so I lie, "I didn't push you off, babe. I was trying to get up, and you slipped."

She smiles. "It's okay."

I can't believe she fell for the lie; she's more dense than I thought.

"You should wear panties," Keanu says. "Your pussy looks gross."

She gets up, yanking down the skirt of her dress, flipping Keanu off. "I'll see you at the party." She bats her eyes at me and walks to the table with her group of friends.

I grab my phone from my pocket, then shoot Lyrical a message.

> **Me: Savannah will be my mistress once we're married. I'm going to enjoy you watching me fuck her.**

She reads my message and sends me a middle finger emoji.

> **Me: You're going to be wearing my ring. Down on your knees, crawling and kneeling before me, worshipping my dick like I'm your god.**

CHAPTER THREE

Lyrical

ATTEND TWO OF MY CLASSES THIS MORNING, AND BY NOON, I'm a little exhausted.

My first day of senior year has been the worst, but at least I'm getting back into the groove of a schedule and still trying to figure out what exactly is my new norm. A few months ago, I was looking forward to graduating, but now, I'm dreading it. I'm not looking forward to marriage and with the way my relationship with Snow is now, I wouldn't be surprised if he locks me up in his home and never lets me out. This past summer, after rehab, I sat in my room, drew, and did not interact with anyone unless I had to. I isolated myself from my old friends—and my family. I held myself in my room because I couldn't face society.

Trauma has a way of making you lose yourself in ways you never thought.

I sit at the gazebo by the oak trees as I remove my college algebra book from my book bag—I failed it for the third time in a row. But no one knows, other than my parents, that I suffer from dyscalculia. I have a hard time reading numbers and understanding math problems. If I don't pass this course this year, I can't graduate, and my dreams will go up in smoke. It's embarrassing because I struggle to count money or do simple math. It was so much easier to hide it because my parents hired tutors to help me and they donated millions of dollars to the schools I attended so they would overlook my disability.

I stare at the math equations as if they are a foreign language, then I yank out my phone and watch a YouTube video to try to understand the concept.

Frustration hits me, so I close the book and slip it back into my book bag.

I asked the director of the disability program who also happens to be my college algebra professor to give me extra time to do my schoolwork, but he told me it will take time to get the arrangement approved, and I even offered him bribe money, but he declined and gave me a lecture about being a snobby person thinking he can be bought.

Lilac sits next to me, while Winter has her literature class right now. I was so glad to get away from them earlier, because they were bombarding me with questions about my relationship with Snow.

Her eyes narrow and concern etches her face. "You haven't answered our group chat. What did Snow say to upset you?"

I put the group chat on mute because I didn't want to answer any questions, but Lilac is persistent. She should become an FBI agent because she knows how to find out people's business. "I don't want to talk about it," I answer honestly. I don't want to carry the pain in my chest of him hurting my feelings.

"Oh, you're the one who was in the accident with her," she pieces together.

"How'd you figure that out?"

"Why else would he be pissed off at you? You used to hang around him since freshman year."

Our car accident made the headlines. Fortunately, our parents didn't reveal who I was to the media.

I nod, trying to get rid of the memory, but I'm pretty sure people who pay attention to Snow know we used to hang out together. If people suspect I was the one in the car accident, no one will dare speak of it.

"Oh, I had no idea. The way he was watching you…" She chews on her bottom lip before answering. "Like you're his prey."

I ignore her comment, and the fact that he had Savannah all over him makes me not want to touch him. If he wants to have her as a mistress while we're married, he's allowed to, as long as he doesn't touch me. He's hurting me out of spite, and it worked. I cried the entire way to my first class that he doesn't believe I was drugged that night. So I have to prove to him that I was.

I've been trying to make sense of Bailey's behavior before her death because she was acting strange, disappearing for hours. It felt like her boyfriend was watching her because she would go into crying spells, though at the time it didn't make any sense. I'm certain we were drugged the night of the car accident.

I need to find out who her boyfriend was because she never told me his name. She was worried he was going to hurt her. No one took Bailey seriously because she was diagnosed with paranoid schizophrenia, but I did. I did everything I could to try to keep her from the dark space. To help her walk a thin line between reality and hallucinations. People usually swept her feelings and thoughts under the rug because of her illness.

Worry mars Lilac's face as she snaps her fingers. "Earth to Lyric. Are you there?"

I slap my palm across my forehead.

"Can you go to the American Gods' party with me?"

"I don't think it's a good idea for me to go."

"Please, Winter won't be able to go because she's hanging out with her parents."

I don't want to stay in my room all day, plus I won't run into

Snow because he never attends them, and I don't plan to stay long, so I nod. "I'll go."

"Is it possible you can hook me up with Irvin? I think he's cute."

Irvin is weird from what Snow has told me about him in the past. He's the loner of the group and doesn't hang out with them. I don't know if it has to do with him not getting along with Snow. When we were teenagers, they used to get into fistfights all the time.

"You don't want to get involved with him."

"Can I tell you something that's personal? But you can't repeat it to anyone, not even to Winter."

I nod, twisting my hair around my finger.

Embarrassment colors her face. "A girl in my class told me Irvin has a kink that I want to try."

My eyebrows climb up my forehead. "Which is...?"

"Um... I like to be choked and chased and I like it when a man forces himself on me," she whispers as she looks down at the ground.

She has nothing to be embarrassed about because I have a whole sketchbook filled with something similar to what she's just described, but it's of me and Snow doing primal play. Before the car accident, I was going to ask him to take my virginity, to explore that side I crave together.

I smile at her. "I have the same fantasies too. I-I have a sketchbook of me getting chased by a man. I have dark fantasies about being controlled by a man."

I'm not going to admit to her that I'm speaking about Snow, because I don't want her to pry into my relationship with him.

I told Bailey about the kinks I have, and she looked at me in disgust, so I never mentioned it again—to anyone. I planned to keep my secret buried with me.

"I can speak to him for you. Introduce you two."

We both get up from the bench, heading to our apartment.

Once we make it home, I waltz straight to my bedroom, and I slip out of my clothes, put on my white halter neck dress that says *Bite Me* at the front, along with black boots and the leather jacket Snow bought me for Christmas last year. Usually on the island at night, the temperature drops.

Lilac walks in with her lavender hair down her back, wearing a brown strapless dress with matching cowboy boots.

We loop our arms as we walk across the campus to where the American Gods live. My eyes snag onto the cobblestone mansion with rectangular windows. Gargoyles sit on top of the roof, and the glass mansion sits right in front of the calm ocean. I watch people lingering on the beach with beer bottles in their hands. This place brings back so many memories of me spending the night with Snow, where we played video games and watched movies together. I used to hide out with him when there was a party going on. He's such a loner at times. I miss my best friend so much it hurts. I feel as if I don't know him anymore.

When we stroll up to the archway, Jameson hands out shots to everyone who walks in through the door. His gaze clings to my dress, then he checks out Lilac. He's gorgeous, built like a linebacker, easy on the eyes. His silvery hair is cut close to the scalp and he wears a black T-shirt and denim jeans. My eyes drop to the veins in his arms.

He offers me a shot. "You're brave to show your face around here, Blue."

I shake my head, but Lilac downs her shot and coughs loudly, causing Jameson to laugh.

I walk toward the entrance, but he yanks me by my arm, then he leans down and whispers, "Your fiancé is going to be mad you're here."

We haven't announced our engagement yet, so as far as I'm concerned, he's *not* my fiancé.

"Let me through, Jameson. I'm here to talk to Irvin."

Bewilderment ceases his face and he blocks the entrance. "If Snow catches you speaking to Irvin, he's going to kill him."

I don't believe Snow would kill him, because they have to run the club together and he doesn't like me. Why would he care if I'm speaking to one of his friends?

"Fuck Snow. I can talk to whoever I want."

He sidesteps me. "Go right ahead, princess, I hope you have a grave dug up for him."

Lilac's eyes widen at his words, and she swallows thickly, giving him a timid look. He grins, then whispers something in her ear, and her face blushes as she steps back and says, "I want Irvin."

He winks, then licks his lips. "If you ever change your mind, let me know. You know where I live."

We walk into the crowded living room, and it's hot as fuck. Women wear skimpy clothes, and I spot Keanu getting sucked off by a blonde chick, and another girl is being sandwiched between two men, getting fucked hard. There are so many people packed in the spacious living room. Sex and weed filter in the air, and the music is so loud it rattles the window.

Shaking my head, I peel my eyes away from the scene, then we walk to the kitchen where it's less noisy. "What did he say?"

She blushes. "He wanted that same timid look on my face when he has me on all fours, fucking me."

"Wow."

We search the crowd for Irvin, and fear overrides my senses because I don't want to run into Snow. Even though there's a slim chance he's here, but you never know. My heart hammers in my chest, so I tell Lilac I'm going to step outside for some fresh air.

Once I make it to the patio, I see people stand by a bonfire, the sun sinking below the ocean, glowing orange on the crystal water. I zip up my jacket and rub my hands as the chilly air bites at my skin.

I search the crowd for Irvin but he's nowhere near in sight. I don't want to bump into Snow, so I need to get out of here. I should have told Lilac no, but I'm her only ticket for her to get a dick appointment. Most people can't reach any of the American Gods unless they want to be reached. They mainly keep to their circle of friends.

I walk toward the bonfire, accidentally bumping into someone, and I look up to find brown eyes staring down at me.

"I'm sorry," I say, searching the backyard, then my gaze snaps back to his.

"No problem." He holds out his hand. "I'm June."

I grab it and squeeze lightly. "Lyrical."

He lets my hand go. "Your name is pretty."

June is cute, soft on the eyes, blond hair pulled up into a neat ponytail, and slim build. My eyes venture toward his jersey.

"You want to sit next to me at the bonfire? We're swapping stories."

I turn to look at the lit mansion, then my gaze veers at the people sitting by the fire.

It's safer out here than in the mansion, away from Snow.

I sit on the patio chair as the flames dance, lighting up the faces of the people sitting close to it. I should have worn a pair of jeans, my legs are starting to feel numb.

A guy passes June a joint. He sticks it between his lips, puffing on it, then offers it to me, but I decline. "I remember you. You were in my English class our freshman year." He blows smoke from the corner of his mouth.

My eyebrows rise. "I don't remember you."

"Of course you don't. I was not noticeable. I had acne all over my face and my dress game wasn't on point."

"You play football?"

He nods, puffing on the joint a few times and blowing smoke from his nose. "We're known but not as known as the American Gods."

A blonde-haired girl nods her head. I notice she's wearing a bikini with shorts, and her top barely covers her tits. It's too cold to be wearing that, but who I am to judge people's clothing? "I would love to sit on Snow's lap. I heard he has a big dick and knows how to use it."

Jealous burns in my chest, but it can't be because he's not mine, and he never will be mine even when we marry.

Placing my hand onto the edge of the armrest on my chair, I squeeze tightly, until my knuckles turn white. Then I school my features as much as I possibly can into a tight smile. "His dick is small."

Her gaze shoots up to mine, eyeing me up and down as if she doesn't believe me. "What?"

I lean back in the lawn chair, tucking my hair behind my ears, trying to remain calm. "He has a pencil dick."

She crinkles her nose. "How would you know?"

"Because I know him and his family."

She shakes her head. "Oh, I heard his sister died and the person who was driving was on drugs. Is it true?"

A knot forms in my chest as tears sting my eyes. North Haven's townspeople spread some of the worst gossip about me. Some people said I tried to kill us both, some said I was a junkie, and others said I was mentally unstable like Bailey. It made headlines nationwide, but my parents and Snow's family hid my name in fear it might ruin their almighty names. The only thing they want to be talked about is my marriage to Snow. The question that everyone wants to know is, who will the Gods marry after college? I feel like it should have been me who passed away instead of Bailey. If I could switch places with her, I would have. In a heartbeat.

June twists his body in my direction, and he smiles at me. "You want to go out with m—"

"Lyrical isn't going anywhere with you," Snow snaps, grabbing my arm and yanking me out of the chair.

Everyone around the bonfire grows quiet, as if he's a god appearing out of nowhere, and the blonde girl has stars in her eyes.

June frowns. "Maybe some other time."

"Stay away from my toy," Snow says through gritted teeth.

This motherfucker has the audacity to believe I'm going to be his toy. "I'm no—"

"Can I be your toy?" the blonde girl asks.

"No," Snow answers.

I dig my nails into his hand, and he lets go of me, then I stab my finger into his hard chest. "Are you out of your mind? I'm not your toy, you asshole."

"What the fuck are you doing here?" He ignores what I say.

I square my shoulders because I know my next words are going to piss him off. "I'm here to see Irvin."

He cocks an eyebrow, yanks me from the crowd, and takes me to a more secluded area. "What for?"

"None of your business." I sneer.

"I warned you to stay away from my friends, Lyrical."

"Or what?" I challenge.

He grips my cheeks, dinging his nails into my skin. "I'll kill him if you decide to fuck him."

Would he really kill him? I don't believe that. This is Snow's way of manipulating me to do what he wants.

My cheeks burn in agony, so I push on his chest, but he doesn't flinch. "You're telling me who I can't speak to, but you're fucking Savannah."

He completely ignores my statement as rage fills his pupils. "If I catch you speaking to Irvin, I'll fucking kill him, Blue. I swear I will. I'll send his head to you."

"I hate you."

"The feeling is mutual." He grabs me by the hair, leans forward, and his eyes lock on my lips before he licks his. "Listen to me carefully. Your ass, pussy, and mouth belong to me, and if I catch you even breathing or looking in another man's direction, I'll cut off his body parts and send them to you to remind you who you belong to. You. Are. Mine." He lets me go, and I slap him across the face.

He strokes his cheek, smirking.

The bastard actually smirks at me.

Embarrassment washes over me. "You make me sick."

He doesn't flinch, nor does he show any emotions. "You make my dick hard."

His words turn me on, and I feel my cheeks heating, so I turn around and rush toward the mansion.

"I'm warning you, Lyrical, if you're caught speaking to Irvin, I'll slit his throat."

Ignoring him, I find Irvin and Lilac leaning against the kitchen island as he moves Lilac's hair out of her face, touching her chin.

Welp. My job is done here, so I leave.

CHAPTER FOUR

Lyrical

SIT AT MY DESK, DRAWING A SKETCH OF ME ON MY KNEES IN front of Snow with my hands tied behind my back and his dick in my mouth.

Why do I have this weird obsession?

Better yet, why would I want my first time to be like this?

I've been having these types of fantasies since I was sixteen years old—since I discovered porn—and I can't shake them. I want to speak to Lilac and ask her some questions. Maybe she feels disgusted about it as well. Maybe she doesn't. She was confident enough to hook up with Irvin at the party. I always wanted to explore that side of myself but was too chickenshit to do anything about it. Now I'm going to marry Snow, I probably won't be able to explore it. The way he said I was his toy turned me on, turned me on more than I'd like to admit. When we used to be friends, he never gave me any indication he wanted to fuck me, though he would flirt with me here and there, tell me how beautiful I was, he'd never said such vulgar stuff to me. It turned me on to the point that when I got home, I touched myself thinking of him.

My phone buzzes on my desk, so I grab it to find my mother's name across the screen. We don't talk as much as we used to since the accident. I pushed her away due to the shame I felt of letting her down. The car accident almost ruined the arranged marriage between Snow and me. It's been my father's dream to have a male heir to inherit part of his share of the American Billionaire Club, but since I turned out to be a girl, he adamantly signed my life away to who I was going to marry.

I watch my phone ring, debating if I should answer, but I'm not in the mood to talk to her.

I can't avoid her forever, so I tap the green button and hit Speaker.

"Mother." My tone is low.

She wants me to be a stay-at-home wife like her, thinking owning my own art gallery is a waste of time, so speaking to her about my future feels like it's redundant. In high society, women take care of the household while the men are the providers, but I feel like I can do so much more than be someone's wife, especially to a man who hates me. My mother had this vision of how she wants my wedding to go. She's handling all the details such as the venue, caterers, and flowers, and all I need to do is show up. I hope to God we don't have to go on a honeymoon because I don't want to.

"How is school?" I can hear the disdain in her tone, and I picture her tucking her golden hair behind her ear, tapping her foot against the floor.

She's asking out of respect for me, but my mother has no real interest in my career. When we're around her friends, she only brags about how proud she is that I'm going to be a stay-at-home mother, not mentioning anything about my passion for art. If I tell her I might fail algebra again, she'll nag me to quit school altogether, and I don't need her discouragement.

A tight smile plasters across my face, but she can't see me. "It's okay. How are you?"

"Things are going good. Your father is at the American Billionaire Club and won't be back until next week, so I'm here by myself. You know how things can get with him."

I wonder how my mother feels about him being the vice president of a gentleman's club? After all, they have a section that is a sex club. Does she get jealous or does she turn a blind eye to it all?

Growing up, when my father was home, he loved and doted on my mother. He worshipped the ground she walked on. If someone were to tell me he was cheating on her, I wouldn't believe it.

"Dr. Luna told me you stopped coming to your sessions." Her words are filled with annoyance.

I was going to a psychologist about the loss of Bailey, but I stopped attending the sessions. There isn't anything he can say that will make me believe it wasn't my fault she died. The guilt and rage I feel will never go away. It was getting to the point where I would tell him what he wanted to hear just to shut him up. When I mentioned to him that someone drugged me before the accident, he told me I was looking for ways to escape my mistake. So, I never mentioned it again.

Sighing, I stand from my desk, glance out the rectangular window in my bedroom, and stare out at the crystal-clear sea.

"I don't need it, Mom. As long as I'm not locking myself in my room, then I'm fine. I started painting again and I'm hanging out with my friends."

"I think you shouldn't pursue art. Most people don't make money and end up being nobodies in the industry. They have all the talent but no one respects it."

This is why I don't like to speak to my own mother about my dreams, because she makes me feel so shameful for loving art and being independent. I want to be myself; I want to be *free*. Be free from the demands of being the daughter of a billionaire. Be free to make my own decisions without a husband tied to me.

"I'm marrying a billionaire, Mother. Even if my art career doesn't work out, I'll still be all right. Art is my passion and I want to pursue it. Didn't you have a dream that you wanted to pursue as a kid?"

"Dreaming is for little girls, and you're no longer one. Life is not about passion, it's about being on top. Anyway, how are things between you and Snow?" My mother completely ignores my question.

I wish she would support my dreams. I want her to be excited that I'm doing something I love, not revolving my life around a man. I want to be happy with my life. She has a happy life, so why can't I be happy too? I want to say more but it's going to lead to a big fight, so I keep my mouth shut out for the sake of peace.

"Snow is being Snow," I tell her.

There is no way in hell I'm telling her about how he treats me, not that it will make a difference, because they are still going to make me marry him after graduation. My parents are focused on keeping their generational wealth more than caring about my well-being. They are focused on being one of the most successful couples in North Haven rather than worrying about Snow giving me hell. The only thing my father asked of Snow is to never beat me. Snow is a lot of things—wife-beater is not one of them. He's so high-strung and always wants things his way. I suspect why he was possessive over me before the accident, but I don't understand why he is now as we're no longer friends.

"We're going shopping for your wedding dress right after the engagement party. So many people are going to be there. A-list celebrities, the mayor, and other powerful people."

I don't want to hear any more about my engagement ball and marriage. I feel like an object that's been bought and not a human being with feelings. I hate this lifestyle and what comes with it. I want something more than to pop out babies, and sometimes I wish I wasn't the only child with so much riding on me. I'm supposed to carry on our bloodline. When I have kids, their marriage is supposed to be arranged as well, and we're supposed to continue the age-old traditions. I have never had control over my life and the little control I do have, I use it to do what I love.

"Mom, I have to go. I have my next class, I'll see you later," I lie, pressing the End button.

Tossing the phone onto the bed, I go back to drawing Snow.

CHAPTER FIVE

Snow

I WANT TO KNOW WHY LYRICAL CAME BY HERE THE OTHER night to see Irvin. When I hacked her phone, I couldn't find any conversations between them. I told all my friends to stay the fuck away from her, because they aren't good people. I'm not good either. Irvin is a psychopath who likes to use people as pawns, so he better not have Lyrical on his radar. Hell, he's the worst of the worst out of all of us.

I rush to the backyard and spot him sitting on a lawn chair, a blonde draped over his lap.

The same chick who asked to be my pet the other night. The dipshit motorboats the hell out of her tits, and she squeals. Keanu splashes in the pool playing Marco Polo with Jameson. They both watch me march up to Irvin and his tramp. I yank her by the hair and toss her to the grass.

"What was that for?"

I glance down at her sunburned face and shake my head.

She's not my problem—he is. Irvin has one chance to answer my question or he's going to meet his maker.

Ignoring her, I punch Irvin in the throat, and he places his hand over his neck, trying to breathe in air, wheezing, while I pull out my knife that's strapped to my ankle, holding the blade to his throat. "Why the fuck would Lyrical be looking for you?"

If he has any plans of fucking my girl, I'm going to cut off his dick and make him eat it.

I nick his neck, drawing blood, making it known I'm not fucking around with his ass.

"Put the knife do—"

"Shut up, Jameson," I grit, keeping my eyes glued to Irvin.

Keanu stands in my direct view with his arms folded across his chest, smirking. Standing next to him is Jameson watching me as if I lost my mind.

Irvin has no sense of bro code and sleeps with any damn body, he doesn't care who he hurts. Last year, he fucked Jameson's married mother without so much as a care in the world. I hate Lyrical but she's going to be my wife, so I have to protect her. I definitely don't want his slimy fingers near her pussy. I don't want him breathing the same air as her.

"Let me go, fucker." His voice is hoarse and raspy.

His eyes veer to Jameson and Keanu, but they stay quiet.

God can't save him for what I'm about to do to him.

"If you don't answer my question, I'm going to cut your vocal cords out of your throat." I push the knife harder, watching bright blood slowly drip down his tan throat.

"She wanted to hook her friend up with Irvin," Jameson answers.

I look over to him, and Irvin knocks the blade from my hand, placing his palms around my throat, and I laugh. "Go right ahead and do it," I taunt.

He can't hurt me. He knows it, and I know it. He needs me as much as I need him to run the American Billionaire Club once we graduate. The difference between Irvin and I, I would risk my livelihood to keep Lyrical safe even if I hate her at this moment.

"I should fuck her. Burst her cherry. I wonder, does she have a certain kink like her friend does?" he whispers in my ear, squeezing tight and cutting off my airway.

His words send me over the edge as pure rage courses through my veins.

He's saying it to get a rise out of me, to get under my skin, and it's working. I wish I didn't care if he were to fuck her.

Letting me go, he shoves me to the ground and kicks me in the chin, causing a burning sensation to shoot up my jaw.

When I jump up to my feet, my fist connects with his left eye, and I grab a fistful of his hair and drag his ass against the concrete. Irvin screams at the top of his lungs for me to let him go as he punches me in the gut, but I don't let go despite the excruciating pain burning inside of me. Forcibly, I dump his head underwater in the pool, letting the chlorine burn his nostrils.

Boy do I wish I can blow his brains out.

When I bring his head up for air, he coughs and gags, swallowing for air.

"This will be the last time you will mention ever taking my future wife's virginity," I scream in his ear, dumping his head back underwater.

He continues to fight, and several minutes later, his arms go limp.

"Let him go, Revi."

I glance up, and my father stares down at me with disappointment stretched across his face.

Jameson and Keanu grab Irvin, performing CPR on him, and several seconds later, Irvin coughs up water.

My father ushers me to his Porsche and his driver opens the car door. I slide inside, yanking the seat belt over my body.

Why is he here? I'm not in trouble with school and I'm passing all my classes with flying colors. I already bought my tux for the engagement ball, so the only reason I can conclude he's here is to make an appearance, and he wants to make sure he looks good in the public eye to keep up the image that we get along with each other.

Growing up, my father never showed me love. Bailey and my mother received hugs and affection while I was in the dark, but I see how he acts toward the other men in my family, and he doesn't show them love either, so I stopped taking it personally. I can't think of a time my father ever hugged me and told me he loved me.

I lean my head against the crisp leather seat, taking in the scenery of North Haven town. People walk the streets filled with tall palm trees and skyscrapers made out of glass fiber.

The silence stretches between us until my voice fills the car. "Where are we going?"

"Ocean Front. I'm in town for a week to check on your mom, then I'm off on a business trip in New York City."

We ride to a fancy restaurant on the west side of town. I hate being in his presence because I don't know if he's going to fly off the handle.

Once we make it to the restaurant, we're quickly seated and the waiter collects our orders.

His eyes narrow. "Have you picked out an engagement ring for Lyrical?"

I nod. "Yes, sir."

This is how our relationship has been. He asks me questions and I answer them. He doesn't ask me how school is going. He doesn't ask me about my social life. Hell, I almost ended Irvin's life and he still didn't ask me about it. My father never cared for me and he never will.

The waiter brings our drinks and I sip my beer slowly, drowning out the noise of the restaurant.

My father sips his scotch and sets the crystal glass onto the cloth covering the table. "Your sister would have been excited about your wedding, planning everything right down to the flowers, and if you had been watching her and protecting her, she would still be living right now."

The guilt I feel eats at me every day, and I try not to blame myself. Ever since Bailey passed away, my father has always been on my case, reminding me how much of a fuckup I am. I don't respond, I never do, because sometimes I do believe it's my fault.

"Have you checked on your mother?"

I shake my head and watch the waiter wearing a suit and tie set our food in front of me, but I'm not hungry, though I know if I don't eat, my father will find another way to pick on me about something. I pick up my fork and dig into my sweet peas, but it tastes like dry wood.

"Your mother's depression has gotten worse since Bailey has died, and yet you didn't check on her?"

It's not that I don't love my mother, I do. I can't handle seeing her so sad. I'm the one who made her depressed.

I continue listening to him tell me how I should be a man and stop acting like a boy. It's why I kept to myself because I'd rather be alone than deal with people. My father cares about me as long as I'm making him look good. I killed people for him, just for him to give me a pat on the back, but it's never enough.

By the time lunch is over with, I'm not in the mood to attend my evening class for my master's degree and I don't want to go back to the mansion, so I walk the trail and end up at the back of Lyrical's apartment complex.

Of course I would end up coming here, because whenever I used to have a shitty day, I'd show up at her place and she would comfort me. Lyrical had been my go-to person when I felt like my back was against the wall.

I climb an oak tree that's close by her bedroom and sit on a thick branch, watching her concentrate as she draws something.

She scrunches up her cute button nose and sticks her tongue out.

This is my favorite part about her, how she has a passion for the things she loves. Sometimes, I miss her. Other days, I don't want to have anything to do her, but the one thing that hasn't change is my obsession with her. I miss her stealing all my hoodies, I miss her showing up at my place unannounced with a bag of popcorn and liquor so we can have movie nights. I miss her spending the night at my place even though it took me every ounce of self-control to not fuck her.

I watch her get up from the desk. She removes her shirt, then her bra, both items hitting the floor. Her tits are on display, though I've seen her naked before, accidently walking in on her in the shower, but I only got a glimpse. Her small breasts are the size of apples and her nipples are a dark pink. My dick hardens and aches in my pants.

I don't bother to readjust myself.

She removes her leggings and panties, tossing them to the floor, then she bends over. Her ass is on display, and I want to shove my dick inside of her. I can feel the tip of my dick leaking with pre-cum. I've never wanted to fuck anyone like I want to fuck her.

I watch her as she moves to the bathroom and I take that as my cue to climb inside.

Loud music blasts from the bathroom, but she leaves the door open, so I watch her step into the shower. She has always been an artsy person, while I have always been into reading nonfiction, history, and business. But somehow, we meshed—until the accident, of course. But now I don't want to marry her and I don't want to be tied down to her for the rest of my life. Looking at the girl I hate, whose smile used to light up my day, I want to hurt her.

The room fills up with her apple soap scent, so I sneak into the bathroom cabinet, grab an extra bottle, then slip it into my back pocket while she's unaware. I go back to her room, glance around, noticing nothing has changed. Lyrical still has the comic books I bought her for her birthday last year. She's still a messy person, leaving her clothes everywhere.

I search through her drawers, trying to find something I can use against her to keep her ass in check, to get her to do what the fuck I want her to do. I find a small clit stimulator and I tuck it in my pocket because her pussy is mine, and I don't want her getting herself off either.

Not without my permission.

When I search through her drawer, I find a leather sketchbook which I've never seen before. I know she has another one which she uses for inspiration to paint, but this one looks old, the edges worn and torn a little bit.

I open the book and scan the pages, and I can't believe what I'm seeing.

She has a picture of herself and my hand around her throat as I'm fucking her.

This shit is hot as fuck.

I look at another picture, a sketch of me chasing her in the woods. There are so many graphic sketches of me fucking her in different ways. I thought I would have to force her to crave me, to kneel before me, to force her to like what I like, but it seems I don't have to. She wants me to fuck her against her will, she wants me to have complete control over her, and it makes me want her even more. Making her my toy is going to be so much fun and easy. I can't wait to fuck her until she's crying, begging me for more.

I tear out the picture of my hands around her throat and my dick in her mouth, then I snatch tape from the drawer, stroll into the steamy bathroom, and write a message in her black lipstick.

Once I'm home, I hop in the shower, jack off with her soap and to the pictures she's drawn of us, and I come so hard my dick aches. I watch my cum drip down the tiles.

I've got to have her.

I need to fuck Blue.

After I dry myself off with a towel, I put on a pair of pajama pants and sit at my desk, getting ready to write my term paper for my business class.

My phone dings with a notification, so I swipe up, a message from Lyrical appearing on the screen.

Blue: Where is my goddamn sketchbook?

CHAPTER SIX

Lyrical

I TURN OFF THE FAUCET AS I STEP OUT OF THE SHOWER, snatching the cotton towel from the rack to wipe my body down. Grabbing my phone, I hit the Pause button on Spotify, silencing the music. When I stroll to the mirror, my heart drops and my sketch is taped to the rectangular mirror. My eyes glaze over Snow's handwriting.

My favorite artwork by you. I can't wait until I have you down on your knees.

As adrenaline spikes my blood, I head straight to my night-stand. I don't see my sketchbook, nor my clit stimulator. I don't care about that since I can buy another one.

My heart hammers in my chest as anxiousness travels down my spine.

No one has ever seen my sketchbook, not even Bailey. It's one of the secrets I want to take to my grave, and the fact Snow got his slimy hands on it irks me. I tried to suppress that kink. I even spoke to an online sex therapist, but he told me it was perfectly normal to have those fantasies as long as it was consensual. That's when I knew I was fucked up in the head, because I don't want it to be consensual. I want Snow to take advantage of me. I hope he doesn't use this as another tool against me.

I snatch my phone from my dresser and send him a message.

> Me: Where is my goddamn sketchbook?

> Snow: I didn't know you wanted to be owned by me. You want me to fuck your sweet pussy, Lyrics. Is that it? You want me to come on your tits.

I ignore the sweet ache between my legs.

> Me: Give me back my sketchbook, Snow. Please.

> Snow: You should have told me sooner and I would have taken your virginity a long time ago. How long have you had these fantasies of us?

I've been having these fantasies since I was sixteen years old, but I'm not going to admit that to him.

> Me: I need my sketchbook.

> Snow: Come get it, Blue.

He sends me devil emojis.

My anger boils. He makes me want to punch him in the face.

> Me: I don't have time for your bullshit.

I click on the IG icon and type in his name, trying to figure out his location. He posts everything on his social media. From food to parties to hanging out with his friends. I spot a post from three days ago, a photo of me studying at the library. My face is covered by my hair.

This little shit.

I read the caption.

My new toy. So beautiful, so mine.

The comment section has over eleven thousand responses and the likes are up to five hundred thousand. He knows I don't use social media and I only have a page to show my artwork.

I read some of the comments and a few people ask if I'm going to be the girl he marries.

I scroll through his photos and see pictures of my artwork before the accident, before both our lives were destroyed. I had no idea he was posting pictures of my art. That warms my heart.

I continue to scroll down to another picture of us with his arm around my waist and mine wrapped around his shoulders with the caption, *I beat Blue in a round of pool. My forever girl. My heart.* It's accompanied with a heart emoji.

Tears wet my eyes because there was a time when we used to be so close. I wanted us to be more than best friends. He gave me my first kiss and he took me to prom because my parents only approved of him taking me. The accident destroyed us— or *I* destroyed us because I was feeling dizzy while driving and I didn't think anything about it. Your life can change in a split second, and you can't turn back time. Sometimes, I wish I had a time machine to pause and rewrite history. To not break so many hearts. To bring back Bailey and her mother's smile. To bring back Bailey's smile.

I close out of the app.

Snow's message pops up on the screen.

> **Snow: When you're done lurking on my IG, meet me in 30 mins or I'm going to start posting pictures from your sketchbook on my social media.**

How did he know I was lurking on his page? Did I accidentally like a post?

> **Me: Where?**
>
> **Snow: In front of the woods near the library.**
>
> **Me: Okay.**

I put my damp hair into a high ponytail, throw on an AC/ DC long-sleeve shirt, and a pair of hot pink leggings paired with my Converse, and jog toward the library across campus.

The air in my lungs burns along with my calves. Anticipation and anger eat at me like a disease. The half-crescent moon hangs in the inky sky as I make my way across campus. The wind slaps me across my warm cheeks.

Once I make it behind the library, in front of the woods, I spot Snow wearing the exact same outfit I drew of him where he's chasing me in the woods. My cheeks flush and my skin burns at the sight of him.

He's so fucking hot as he eyes me like a piece of meat, licking his lips.

Is he about to make my fantasy real?

The thought sends a shiver up my spine.

"What the fuck is this shit?" I ask.

He steps toward me, and I step back, hearing a twig snap. My shoes sink into the soft dirt, my nipples harden, and my panties are soaked just at the sight of him.

It finally hits me. He's playing out my dark fantasy, and I'm intrigued and too turned on. This is what I always wanted from him, to turn my fantasies into reality, but I don't want it from him if he's going to use it against me. Right now, I'm on his shit list.

"Whatever game you are playing, I don't want any part of. I don't want you," I snap.

He stomps up to me, grabs my ponytail, and I swallow thickly as he wraps his hand around my throat, feeling my pulse thumping like I downed five Red Bulls.

"You want this as much as I want this. You want me to own you. You want your lips wrapped around my dick as I choke you. You want me to have complete control over you. Using you as my sex doll."

I'm speechless, not able to form words because he's

absolutely right. I do want to be owned and controlled by him. Giving up my power so he can use me. It's been that way since I watched a porn footage of it. I can't help but wonder why he is trying to fuck me when he hates my guts.

"Why are you trying to fuck me if you hate me? You blame me for Bailey's death."

He slips his fingers into my mouth, reaching all the way to my throat, and I gag. Choking, saliva drips down my chin. I shove his hard chest, he yanks my ponytail and my scalp burns.

"You're going to have to give up your ass eventually when we're married. I might hate your guts, but it doesn't mean I won't fuck you. I've been wanting to fuck you since I laid eyes on you when I was seventeen. Heard of hate fucking?"

"Why didn't you make a move on me before?"

"I didn't want to destroy our friendship."

His words make my chest cave and a hollow, empty feeling grows in my chest. I have a hard time accepting that we're not as close as we used to be.

His hand strokes the side of my face, making my skin flush. "I'm giving you to the count of five to run."

My eyes narrow. "What's going to happened if you catch me?"

He smirks. "I'm going to do whatever I want to do to you."

My cheeks flame. What exactly does he want to do to me?

His eyes glint like a star. "I'll even give you a head start—five."

I don't know if I should do this. This is wrong—so wrong.

"Four."

My heart is in my throat and I keep my shoes glued to the ground. I shouldn't play this game.

"What if I don't want to play?"

"You have no choice. Three."

I turn around and sprint into the woods, trying to catch my breath, passing tall willow trees. The woods are dark but not dark enough that I can't see. Crickets sing while the ocean hums in the quiet night. I hear Snow walking toward me, so I take off running deeper into the forest and I duck down behind a log. I breathe in through my nose and exhale out of my mouth, trying to control my breathing. Hoping he does find me and fuck me until I'm screaming his name.

I look over, and he's not in sight.

I'm so fucking horny that I can combust.

"Boo," he says with a wicked smile, so I slap him across the face. He places my hand against his dick print and I feel how rock hard he is. My mouth waters at the thought of me having my mouth around it.

"I love it when you fight."

I love it too, but I refrain from saying that.

He shoves me to the ground, straddling me, and I try to push him, but he's too strong for me. This is what I all ways wanted. My panties are wet from his dominance, from the thrill of him doing this to me. I knew I was messed up in the head, craving things normal people don't. My enemy is about to have his way with me, and I hate how much I love it.

He pins me down, pushing my head to the side, and I taste the wet soil from the grass. I cough hard while he yanks my leggings down, shoving two fingers inside of me. I feel every inch of his digits, my core tightening around him.

Moaning, I kick my legs, thrashing as hard as I can, but it's no use.

"Get off me," I scream at the top of my lungs.

"No."

"Please."

His eyes go down to my shaved pussy, licking his lips as if he wants to taste me.

"I imagined what your pussy would look like. Glistening and wet for me."

I groan as he places his finger on my clit and starts circling them, feeling my orgasm build. He removes his fingers and leans down to lick my clit, and I shudder. It feels weird. I've never had anyone go down on me. He continues to lick me and my muscles tense and my clit becomes sensitive. I don't think I can handle it. The feeling is too intense. My core contracts and my toes curl as my orgasm shoots up my spine.

I try to push him off of me, but he doesn't flinch.

"Pl-please, Snow. Stop."

He ignores me, keeps licking as my eyes roll to the back of my head. I watch his eyes and they are void of emotions. My heart beats faster and my orgasm shatters me again, making my core throb.

I've never experienced an orgasm back-to-back.

He gets off of me. Standing up, I yank my pants up, dusting the wet dirt off my clothes. I enjoyed his touch too much, and I hate myself for wanting more from him. This can't happen again, and it won't. He's the first man to give me an orgasm. He might have popped my cherry on that, but I'm not giving him my virginity.

"This will be the last time you get to touch me."

"I doubt that." He smirks, licking his fingers. "You taste divine."

He stands up and unzips his pants, yanking out his dick. I stare at it, studying the veins and the throbbing head. It's thick and long, the biggest dick I have ever seen. Not that I've seen many.

My core aches with need, and I shake my head.

"Be a good girl and suck my dick."

"I'm not putting my mouth on you."

"It's cute that you think you have a choice, Blue."

His words turn me on. I stare at the tip of his dick, watching pre-cum drip.

"I don't want to."

His eyes darken as he strokes himself. "You want it, though

you keep denying it, because you hate me at the moment. But once you crawl back into your bed tonight, I guarantee that you'll want to touch yourself to this. Page thirty-five." He winks. "On your knees, Blue."

"Ask Savannah to do it."

"Last warning. On. Your. Knees."

He ignores my reply. He said he was going to fuck her while we're married, so I don't know why I should care if he wants her or not.

Slowly, I drop to my knees, and he wastes no time sliding his huge-ass dick between my lips, but I keep my mouth clenched, and he yanks my ponytail hard, causing tears to well in my eyes.

My pulse beats frantically and excitement rushes through my body. He has a devilish smile on his face, like he won a prize.

"I said open."

My panties become so fucking wet from his words. I open my mouth wide, and I use my tongue to lick the head. I've never given head before, so I don't know what to do. I just keep licking.

He slides deeper into my mouth, causing me to gag and choke, but he doesn't let up. He doesn't give me time to breathe, so I breathe through my nose. His dick hits the back of my throat as he shoves forward and tears sting my eyes.

He slips out of my mouth, then shoves back inside, fucking my throat, using it as a fleshlight. My jaw aches and my knees hurt from being on the ground for too long.

I feel the vomit rising in my throat, but hopefully I can keep it down.

"That's it. You like that I fuck your mouth. You like that I use you to come."

Several moments later, I taste a salty flavor. Is that his cum? I feel the head throbbing in my mouth. He throws his head back as he continues to come inside of my mouth, and there's a lot of it. Some of his cum drips down my chin.

"Swallow, Blue."

I stand up and spit his cum onto the ground, and he chuckles. He keeps his hands in my hair with his mouth inches from mine.

"Next time I tell you to swallow and you don't, I'll turn your ass cheeks black and blue."

My throat burns as I swallow thickly. "Fuck you, Snow."

"Don't worry, baby. You're going to get your chance soon."

"Where is my sketchbook? You promised."

He tucks his hands in his pockets. "I didn't promise you anything."

"You asshole! Give it back."

He stares at my mouth, licking his lips. "No." He strokes his knuckles across my cheeks. "Go home, Blue."

CHAPTER SEVEN

Snow

FOR A COUPLE OF HOURS, I WORK ON MY PAPER FOR MY BUSINESS class that's due in a few weeks.

I should be hating Lyrical at the moment for destroying my life.

Yet, all I can think about is her. It feels like how it used to be between us, like I can pick up the phone and call her or text her.

I grab her sketchbook and I glance at it again, trying not to become obsessed with her thoughts. I have always been that way with her, and now I've had a little taste, I don't want to let her go. She's going to make the perfect toy.

Fuck it.

I snatch my phone from my desk and pull the camera up in her bedroom that Jameson installed while we were in the woods.

She's lying on the side of her bed, watching a video on TikTok. Her friend comes into her room, sits beside her on to the bed, and they speak about their plans for the weekend. Once her friend leaves, I send her a message.

> Me: When did you start to have these fantasies about me?

She reads my message, and bubbles appear, then disappear, and my anxiety builds in my chest.

> Blue: Give me my book and I'll tell you.

> Me: Tell me or I'll leak your sketchbook on my IG.

> Blue: I don't like you.

> Me: The feeling is mutual. Now tell me.

> Blue: Fine. I started having sexual thoughts about you the very first time I spent the night over at your house when I slept over with Bailey. You came from a party that Keanu had at his parents' vacation home. It was the 4th of July. I started drawing my first erotic picture of you.

> Me: Why didn't you tell me?

> Blue: Because I'm screwed up in the head. I shouldn't have those types of thoughts. It makes me feel wrong. I thought you would reject me.

The thought that she couldn't come to me makes me feel bad.

> Me: Have I ever kink shamed you? Better yet, have I ever shamed you for anything?

> Blue: No.

> Me: Why would you think I would?

> Blue: I don't know.

> Me: You have nothing to be ashamed of.

For once, it feels like how we were before the car accident. Before both our lives were changed, but I can't go back to being in love with her. Fuck, she's getting back into my head, and my heart. I should keep my distance, but I won't, because I plan to use her as my toy.

My phone dings with a text message from the group chat I'm in with Keanu, Irvin, and Jameson.

> Keanu: Are you joining the hunting party this year? We're hosting it this Saturday. Or are you going to flake like every year?

Usually, I don't attend because it turns into an orgy in the woods. Keanu hosts the party, where the men and women have to wear masks and you hunt down whoever you want, fuck them, then go on about your life. It's not like I've never attended an orgy, but I was waiting on Lyrical to want me to fuck her. I remained a gentleman and kept my hands to myself, but that's changing. I'll force her to go to the party this year.

> Me: Sure.
>
> Keanu: Sweet. Sending out invites now.
>
> Jameson: Is Lyrical coming?
>
> Me: She has no choice.

I shoot Lyrical an invite to the party.

> Me: Pick out a mask for the hunting party. I'll pick you up tomorrow night.
>
> Lyrical: No.
>
> Me: It's cute that you think you have a choice.
>
> Lyrical: No. I'm not attending your stupid orgy, and no, we're not ever going to fuck.

This woman is testing my patience.

> Me: Here is what's going to happen, Blue. I'm to pick you up at 9 at your place. So wear something sexy. Wear a mask. Wear no panties, or else…
>
> Blue: What are you going to do if I'm not home?
>
> Me: Try me and find out.

She leaves me on read for several moments, then sends me another text message.

> Blue: Go to hell. My answer is no.
>
> Me: Your funeral.

CHAPTER EIGHT

Lyrical

TONIGHT IS THE NIGHT OF THE HUNTING PARTY THAT THE American Gods are hosting. Everyone is there, including Lilac and Winter. They wanted to be a part of it. I pleaded with them to stay behind with me to have a girls' night instead, but they turned me down, so now I'm at a hole-in-the-wall restaurant. This is the first time I'm actually trying to enjoy myself since Bailey died. We used to go barhopping, but now that she is gone, some of the things don't seem fun without her.

I eat my wings and fries while doodling on a piece of paper. I can't concentrate, because I'm thinking about Snow. It was stupid for me to not go to the party because I always wanted to go. I want to know how it would feel to be chased down in the woods and fucked until I can't take it anymore, but I don't want to give Snow any more of myself than I already have. Plus, I'm not going to let him order me around. He has always been bossy and possessive over me, but I chalked it up as him being an overprotective friend.

Now, I realize he was acting that way because he wanted to fuck me. Last night when he told me I have nothing to be ashamed of because of my kink, it made me feel a lot better about myself and I quickly forgot we aren't friends. It makes things ten times harder between us because now I know what his dick tastes like. I want more of him. I loved that he forced me to do what he wanted me to do. But I know he's using my fantasies to manipulate me, so I'm going to stay away from him until the wedding.

Someone clears their throat. Glancing up, I see June leaning against the booth. He has the brightest smile on his face.

"Is this seat taken?"

My eyes drop down to his muscles peeking through his dark shirt and my eyes trace the veins under his tan skin. I quickly look away and shake my head no.

"No."

He sits across from me and steals a fry from my plate. "Where have you been lately? I haven't seen you at a party since the one on the first day of school."

"Were you looking for me?"

He nods. "Yeah, I wanted to see if you would like to hang out."

"Partying isn't my thing."

"Neither is it mine."

"Then why were you there?"

He steals a wing off my plate, devouring it. "My ex-girlfriend dragged me there." He rubs his beard. "Anyhow, what are you drawing?"

I cock my eyebrow. "How did you know I was drawing?"

"I was watching you, and you seemed like you're concentrating."

I fold the piece of paper and place it into my pocket. "Sketching nonsense."

The waitress refills my cup with Coke, then she asks June if he wants anything and he tells her no.

He gives me a quizzical look. "What's your relationship with Snow?"

I don't want to speak about my relationship with Snow. I don't want to speak about how he plays into my fantasies and how I want to be touched by him, or that we're on bad terms.

"I don't have a relationship with him," I lie.

He leans back into the booth. "When we were at the party, he told me I needed to stay away from you and that you're his new toy."

My cheeks burn. "Snow can be unhinged."

He crinkles his nose and runs his fingers through his hair. "So, you're not the one he's marrying?"

"I am. Sadly, I'm marrying the devil."

"Shit. I wanted to shoot my shot."

Even if I wasn't supposed to marry Snow, I wouldn't date June; he's not my type.

"I'm sorry."

"I figured you were. The way he looks at you. And the picture he posted on Instagram."

I raise my eyebrows and tilt my head to the side. "What picture?"

"The picture he posted three hours ago. Did you not see? He tagged you in it."

He yanks out his phone from his pocket, taps on the screen, and shoves it in my hand. It's a sketch of me half naked and sitting on his lap. Snow is wearing a suit and I have a collar around my neck. That's the most tame picture I drew of him. In the caption is the word, *Mine*. This is my personal stuff that no one is supposed to see. He's doing this because I didn't go to his stupid orgy party.

I scroll through his comments, and someone asks if I am going to be his wife. The bastard has the nerve to comment "Maybe." With heart emojis.

"The picture is hot as fuck," June murmurs.

This son of a bitch is working my last nerve.

I grab my phone from my purse and type a message to Snow.

> **Me: Take down the fucking picture.**
>
> **Snow: No.**

Me: It's degrading.

Snow: It's art.

Me: When I bash your skull in, would that be considered art?

Snow: My dick is hard. I love it when you talk dirty to me.

Me: *middle finger emoji*

Snow: Let's make something clear, Blue. When I tell you to do something, you do it. If I tell you to jump, you say how high. You're not getting the picture that I own you, and there isn't anything you can do about it.

Without acknowledging June, I get up from the table, strap my purse over my shoulder, and leave the restaurant.

Anger boils in my blood. He wants to make my life a living hell because I won't bow down to him.

He thinks there isn't any consequences of his actions, that I'm some weak bitch who's going to roll over and take his shit. He has another thing coming. I can't believe he actually posted the picture.

I drive to the hardware store and buy a gas can and matches, then I stop by a convenience store and load the can with gas. When I drive back home, I braid my hair, put on my green wig that I wore for Halloween last year, and throw on my black hoodie along with a pair of shades.

With the gas can in my hand, I stride through the woods that leads to his mansion. I'm trying to do my best to keep my cool with him, but he keeps pushing my buttons. He keeps testing my patience. I've seen other people experience his wrath, but I never thought in a million years I'll be on the receiving end of it.

The sky has darkened by the time I make it to his mansion. The garage is closed, so I type in the code to open the door.

Luckily, there isn't anyone outside and no one knows I'm down here. I hear the music faintly coming from the backyard. The thought of Snow joining the orgy party makes jealousy slither down my spine, but I shouldn't be jealous. He has every right to fuck anyone he wants.

Searching the toolbox in the garage, I find a crowbar, then use it to knock down the cameras one by one. I don't want to burn any of his friends' vehicles, just his.

Lifting the can, I douse gasoline all over his black Aston Martin, light the match, and toss it at the car. A small flame glows and before I know it, the whole car is on fire, so I run out of the garage, rush toward the woods, and watch the whole side of the garage engulf in flames.

It's pretty, actually, the way the flame dances to life, lighting up the darkened sky.

Keanu, Jameson, Irvin, and Snow rush to the mansion. People gather around as the fire truck eventually shows up and they put the flames out. Irvin pushes Keanu as they get into an argument.

A victorious smile spreads across my lips as I look at the horror on Snow's face. He barges inside of the smoking garage, then several minutes later, he walks out.

It feels good to get revenge, to see the anguish on his face.

Snow grabs his phone from his pocket and stares at the screen, a frown creasing his brow as he looks at the woods. I swallow thickly and hide behind a tree, but I know he can't see me—it's too dark and the moon is the only source of light here.

He tucks his phone back into his pocket. He looks to the woods again as if he can see me. He tilts his head, his nose toward the sky, rolling his shoulders. He grabs his phone from his pocket once again to type something on the screen.

My phone dings with a message from Snow. With my heart in my throat, I click on the envelope icon and read the text message.

Snow: Run, Blue. Pray I don't catch you.

CHAPTER NINE

Snow

BLUE IS GROWING A PAIR OF BALLS. I DIDN'T EXPECT HER to get back at me by destroying a five-hundred-thousand-dollar car. I'm pushing her buttons because my sweet Blue never had the thirst for revenge.

I'm not going to lie, it makes my dick hard.

If she had shown up to the party and not been at that restaurant, none of us would be in this predicament. I stayed in my room with a huge-ass hard-on because of her. I didn't have any plans of fucking anyone else except her. My plans were to tie her up to my bedpost and fuck her until she begs me to stop, but I'm feeling fucking adventurous right now.

Once I catch her, I'm taking it out on her sweet ass. The thought of catching up to her makes my dick throb in my jeans. I can't wait to see her in tears when I'm done with her. I can't wait to see her beneath me taking my cock into her pussy.

I knew she was pissed that I posted her drawing, but I didn't think she would go to the extent of destroying my stuff. Not only that, but she also put my friends in danger. I don't need to tell them who did it, otherwise they will want to come after her, and I'm not going to allow that shit to happen, especially from Irvin. He's still pissed off that I almost drowned him that day. If they even think about hurting her, I'll kill them off one by one. My loyalty has been to myself and my family—it used to extend to Lyrical too.

I grab my phone from my pocket, watching the dot move on the screen. She's heading east, so I run in that direction. She's never been a fast runner.

Once I reach a tree, I glance over and she tosses dirt in my face. Luckily, it doesn't get into my eyes. I yank her by her hoodie, then remove her green wig and the shades. She tries to kick me in the balls, but she misses, and I grab her by the arm, shoving her down to the ground, pinning her arms above her head.

When I lick the side of her face, she whimpers, trying to school her features.

I use my knee to pull her legs apart, wedging my hard dick between her thighs, resting it on her covered pussy.

"I fucking hate you, Revi," she says through gritted teeth.

I grip her chin, whispering in her ear, "You burned down my car, therefore I'm going to make you pay."

"That's what you get for posting that drawing, asshole. You think I'm going to let you get away with what you did?" She tries to wiggle her way out of my grip, but I hold her wrists so tight I can snap them.

"You destroyed my life, Blue." My tone is harsh.

Tears fall down her cheeks. "Don't you think I don't know that?! Sometimes I hate to look at myself in the mirror because I know what I did to our lives. Bailey shouldn't have died. I should have."

I see the pain in her eyes, and it makes me feel like shit. Even though she made a careless mistake, she shouldn't die either. No one should have died that day.

I glance at the broken girl beneath me.

What if I'm lying to myself? What if she was drugged? I want to believe her, but I can't. I'm going to fuck her. I need to fuck her and punish her for what she did to me. I need to consume every ounce of her until there isn't anything left.

Rage burns beneath my skin like fireworks. Releasing her wrists, I undo her pants, yanking them down, exposing her bare pussy, and the imprint of my hard dick rubs against her clit. She groans.

"S-Snow. We can't. We shouldn't." She places her hand on my chest, keeping her eyes glued to me.

The tension between us is so thick, I can cut it with a knife.

"You like to be own and controlled. You like that I dominate you. You like that I have you at my mercy. Tell me you don't want me to take your pussy."

"Are you going to stop?" she questions.

"No."

She turns her head to the side as tears rush down the sides of her face.

Without a word, I shove my fingers inside of her and she begins to fuck herself on the digits, riding my fingers like a needy woman. The look on her face is one of ecstasy and it makes my balls heavy. The crown of my dick aches, wanting to be sucked. Placing a finger on her clit, I stroke in circles, and she moans my name. Her tears dry up. She digs her nails into my forearms and reaches up, biting the fuck out of my bottom lip as she comes hard. I feel her pussy squeezing my fingers, so I remove them, licking each digit like her taste is my favorite meal.

Leaning down, I whisper in her ear, "My turn."

Her eyes light up with excitement. Sitting up, my knees sink into the soil as I slowly unzip my pants, yanking out my dick.

Her eyes widen. "This is a bad idea."

I don't comment as I shove forward at her entrance, and she takes deep breaths. She's tight as a vise, squeezing the crown of my dick. I expected her to be tight, but I hadn't expected her to be *this* tight. I would tell her some shit like I'll be gentle, that I'll take my time, but both of us know that is not what she wants and I have never been the gentle type. Even if she did want gentle, I wouldn't be. She needs to understand that sex between us will always be rough.

She pushes against my chest, trying to get up, but I hold her still. She wants this—there is a drawing in her book of me raping her, but she was tied to the headboard. She has a rape fantasy? She got it.

She lets out a scream when I slide farther inside of her. I always envisioned how it would feel with me taking her virginity, but not like this—intense. Where I can't control myself. Not when I'm forcing her to do it.

"It stings," she whines.

I wasn't going to stop even if she told me to. I study her pupils like a map. Her eyes tell me she's enjoying this, even though she doesn't want to admit it.

Pulling out, I slam back inside of her. She's warm, wet, and snug. The perfect fit for my dick. The way I like it. Yanking her hair, she moans, and I thrust into her harder. She squeezes around me, milking my dick as she arches her back.

"That's it. Take this dick like a good girl."

I slam into her harder as she calls my name, fucking her as she wraps her legs around my body.

She looks beautiful.

Now that I have taken her virginity, I own her, and no man is getting close to what's mine.

"Say you belong to me."

She snaps her mouth shut, biting her bottom lip to try to keep from screaming.

"Say you belong to me," I repeat again, thrusting hard.

She glares at me. "I'll never belong to you."

I yank up her hoodie, then her shirt, placing my mouth on her nipples, sucking hard.

"S-Snow." My name sounds smooth as whiskey on her lips.

The crown of my dick tingles, and I feel my balls tighten as my orgasm travels up my spine. I come inside of her.

I pull out, light streaks of blood coating my dick. I tuck myself back into my pants as she gets up, yanking up her pants over her hips.

"I'm not on birth control; you shouldn't have come inside of me," she murmurs.

"It's my pussy, I'll come in it if I want to," I snap.

"I'll never be yours, and you'll never get to touch me again."

I grab her by the hair. "You will always be mine, and one day, you're going to say it."

"Fuck you," she spits.

"You did. And you loved it."

She walks in the direction of her apartment with me following behind her. Her face is burning red, but she tries her damnedest to ignore my presence. Crickets hum in the background as the moon peeks between the leafy trees. I feel the tension radiating between us.

"You don't have to walk me home. I can walk myself."

"No, you can't. I'm sick of you roaming the woods out here by yourself."

She stops to look up at the tall trees, shaking her head. "You're the one who has been following me around campus."

I have to keep an eye out on her to keep her safe. No other men are allowed to speak to her, especially now after my dick has had a taste of her. Old feelings I had of her are resurfacing and I don't like it. It pisses me the fuck off that she has this hold on me.

Once we arrive at her apartment, she slams the door in my face, but I open it, walking behind her to her room.

She removes her hoodie, and shirt, the one I gave her to keep, then she removes her pants.

I glance at the faint scars on her arms. How did she get those? Has she been cutting herself again? I thought she broke the habit. If I ask, she'll lie and try to hide it, but once I get a chance, I'll go through her cabinet to look for razors.

She disappears into the bathroom, shutting the door behind her, so I go to her painting area and steal all of her brushes and paint oil, tucking them in my pocket. Little does she know, she's moving in with me after the engagement ball, and if she fights me on it, I'll just kidnap her. Lyrical needs to understand that she doesn't have a say in her life anymore.

I hear the shower running and debate if I should join her, but she needs her space, so I lie in her bed, scrolling through Instagram. Savannah tags me in her post of two love birds sitting on a branch, so I untag myself. I wish she would get the hint that I don't want her. After the night Lyrical sucked my dick, I told Savannah I didn't want to be with her but she keeps trying to push herself onto me.

Once Lyrical is done showering, she walks out of the bathroom, a towel wrapped around her body.

"I hate you," she whispers. "I hate everything about you. You're destroying my life. First, you humiliate me, then you fuck me like you want me."

I stand there, not knowing what to say. Her words hit me in the chest, and I shouldn't care about her. I don't like the pain I caused on her face.

"I hate that I enjoyed it. The way you control me. I hate that you gave me my fantasy, but you do things to keep hurting me!"

She screams at the top of her lungs, fresh tears falling down her face. Without thinking, I remove the cotton towel and stare at her naked body. I shove her to the bed, spreading her wide, getting a good look at her pussy. I place my mouth on her clit, tasting her again. She's addictive, like a drug that I can't quit. Her legs shake after several moments and I lick up her wetness after she comes. I ignore the way my dick throbs in my pants and the urge to release my cum all over her.

What can I say? I'm not giving her what she wants for her benefit. I'm doing it for me. To make myself happy.

Someone knocks on the door as I toss the blanket over Blue's body, and I sit next to her. Her friend with the lavender hair pops her head in. She sees Blue sit up, resting her head on my chest, and her eyebrows climb up her forehead. The one Irvin got his eyes set on. The one I threatened to hurt if he tries to get revenge on me for almost drowning him. My eyes go down to her hand to see she's holding a pocketknife.

Does she believe she can protect Lyrical from me? No one can protect her from me, except me. She takes in Lyrical's tear-stricken face and the way I cling to her.

"Are you okay, Lyrical?"

I whisper in her ear, "Tell her you're okay. Get rid of her."

She nods, wiping her face with the back of her hand. Her apple bodywash lingers in the air, causing my dick to stir in my pants. "Yes, I'm having an emotional breakdown."

Her eyes widen, and she flashes me her pocketknife. "You're not going to hurt Lyrical."

I don't like the urge I have to take care of the woman I used to love.

"Not more than I already have," I say.

The girl, Lilac, looks timid, like she wouldn't hurt a fly, so why would someone like her be interested in Irvin? Irvin did mention that she shares a similar kink to Lyrical. I don't know the depths of their relationship, but I know they are fucking.

Getting up from the bed, I stroll up to Lilac, grab her by the arm, and usher her to the hallway, slamming the door in her face.

I make my way back to the bed and Lyrical rolls to her side, facing me. I glance at her and I miss everything about my best friend before the accident. I feel like I not only lost my sister, but

I lost my best friend. She opens her eyes, pushing me away, and I see the fear lingering in her pupils. She curls up into a ball and cries. I've never seen her drowning in her sorrows like this.

I stand there, shoving my hands in my pockets, staring at her. Those tears are meant for me, and not in the way I like. For the first time, I don't feel right putting them there, so I leave without a word.

CHAPTER TEN

Lyrical

MY MOTHER'S STYLIST COMBS THROUGH MY HAIR AND anticipation fills my chest. The engagement ball starts in thirty minutes and I'm not ready to tell the world that Snow is going to be my ball and chain.

My mind plays the night Snow took my virginity like a broken record. I cried myself to sleep the moment he left. I feel so disgusted for wanting him to do it again. I feel so disgusted for wanting *him*. I shouldn't want those things with him, especially with how he treats me. I want him to treat me like a whore, and deep down, I wanted him to take my virginity the way he did. The worse part, I was hoping he would hit me up to fuck me again, but he didn't.

When I'm on my way to classes, I know he's following me. Though I don't know about his reasonings. He follows me everywhere I go.

I would say I'm disturbed by it, but I'm not. I'm used to him lurking around me. When we were in high school, he followed me everywhere I went. I used to refer to him as my shadow. He cock-blocked any boy I spoke to, and if he got a whiff of a man on my radar, I suspect he threatened to hurt them. I wonder if what Bailey used to tell me was true, that he had a crush on me. She insisted we should hook up already, since we're going to be married.

I get up from the vanity and wiggle my way into the mermaid gown that flares at the end. My face is covered with makeup and my hair is in large curls flowing down my back.

I look at myself in the floor-length mirror and try to keep the tears at bay.

This is me one step closer to signing my life away to a man who hates me.

My mother smiles through the mirror. She's waited for this day. In fact, she planned it before I was even born. For her daughter to be married to a billionaire and follow a tradition that has been passed down from generation to generation. It's a stupid-ass tradition.

"You look so beautiful, Lyrical," she says, tears in her eyes. "You will make a beautiful bride."

I don't respond because this isn't what I want for my life.

I clear my throat, and she loops her arm through mine. Once we stroll to the ballroom, I'm overwhelmed by all the people here. Being at my engagement ball is a once-in-a-lifetime event. Every woman wears a purple gown, and every man is in a tux with a purple tie. My mother planned the engagement ball so, of course, she will pick the color associated with the American Billionaire Club.

I glance up to find an expensive-looking chandelier made out of gold hang from the ceiling. The waitress and waiters wearing all-black suits maneuver through the crowd, passing out champagne flutes and various finger foods. The room fills with chatter, drowning out my thoughts.

I spot Keanu, Irvin, and Jameson, and they look dashing in their suits. They stand in a circle, speaking with Snow. I suck in a breath at the sight of him. He looks striking in his suit. His white hair has been cut short, and his muscles are thick and hard through his suit jacket. He looks bored and uninterested, but when his eyes capture mine, the hint of a glint shines in them. His gives me a once-over, a smirk spreading across his face. He bites his lower lip and winks at me.

My mother ushers me to a golden chair that resembles a throne, and I sit down slowly, trying not to wrinkle my dress. People gasp when they see me, because they are now realizing I'm the one who was chosen to be Snow's wife. This is part of the ritual, where I pretend like I accept the marriage, but it's all for show. People whisper amongst themselves. My heart beats in my chest, blood rushes to my ears.

Snow's face is devoid of emotion, but he leans in and whispers, "You're so beautiful."

My cheeks flame and goosebumps sprout on my arms. Not sure if it's from him or from the cold air. When he gets on one knee, he removes a box from his pants pocket. He opens it, a huge-ass diamond ring glinting from the lights.

"Marry me?" His tone is monotone.

I want to say no so bad. I want to embarrass him like he embarrassed me. I want him to feel the pain he caused me, but I can't embarrass my parents nor his. Snow wouldn't take no for an answer anyway, so why bother? Even if my parents give me a way out, he'll force me to accept the engagement. I take my time before answering, enjoying the view of him on his knee before me.

My heart leaps in my chest as I feel the eyes on me. "Yes."

He slides the ring onto my finger, and everyone cheers as he pulls me into a hug, placing his hand on my lower back. He presses his lips to mine, and a shiver snakes up my spine. Butterflies flutter in my stomach, and I melt like butter.

He slips his tongue into my mouth, and I slide my own into his. We stand there a second or two longer as we continue to kiss. He nips my bottom lip before pulling away. My gaze snags onto

Snow as he steps back, the look of complete shock over our kiss on his face. A pool of emotions flashes through his eyes, then he clears his throat. His demeanor is weird.

He leans forward, bending down, whispering in my ear, "You're mine. Now the whole world knows it."

I don't have time to respond because his mother comes up to me, hugs me tight, along with his father. She has bags under her eyes and a few tears slide down her face. She's lost a lot of weight, because the last time I saw her, she was plump, but now she's tiny. His father looks the same. Powerful, elegant, and dominant.

They say their congratulations and welcome me into the family.

The band plays a slow love song and nervousness hits me like a tidal wave. Snow grabs me by the waist, and we slow dance, everyone's eyes on us. Cameras flash, and there is no doubt this will be all over social media tomorrow.

"You look beautiful wearing my ring, Blue," he murmurs. "I can't wait to shove my dick inside of you, owning your pussy again."

I hate that he knows what I want and what I love, but I hate even more that he's the only man who knows how to give me what I want. I'm still sore from the other night when he took my virginity. "I'm only wearing your ring for tonight. I'm not wearing your ring nor am I referring to you as my fiancé after this party." I shake my head. "I don't want to have anything to do with you."

"You weren't saying that when you were taking my dick like a good girl. Tell me, is my Blue sore?"

His words annoy me. "No, actually, I couldn't feel anything with your pencil dick," I lie.

The bastard laughs at me.

I storm off to the balcony overlooking the city. I watch as people stroll along the sidewalk and cars litter the busy street. I don't think I'm ready for the city life once I'm married. The moon is high in the sky. I need fresh air and I need to get away from him to put some distance between us.

"I'm glad I'm not the only one who's not enjoying the ball."

I glance to my left at Professor Carter who looks good in his tux. I don't respond as I look back at the well-lit skyscrapers. He's been my art professor since freshman year, and Bailey had a huge crush on him. He wouldn't give her the time of the day because there is a rule that professors aren't allowed to fraternize with their students.

He stands next to me, but not in a weird way, and his cologne filters through my nostrils. We're in complete silence, listening to the muffled noises coming from the ballroom.

I don't have anything to say to him. I notice a wedding ring on his finger; I had no idea he was married.

"Are you're going to make sure you have your painting ready in the next few weeks?"

He handpicked me and a few other students to display our best work in a museum, and this can make or break my career.

"Yes."

"Good. I can't wait to see it, you have so much potential to be an artist." His smile is cheery.

I wish I had the confidence in myself that I fake. My work is far from perfect, I'm constantly learning.

Someone clears their throat, a woman who has streaks of gray in her hair and is wearing a floral dress. She comes up to Professor Carter, offering me a fake smile.

"It's time for us to leave."

"I'm Lyrical, it's nice to meet you." I hold out my hand, but she just stares at it.

"I know who you are." Her eyes move to her husband. "Let's go."

"Congratulations on the engagement," Carter says.

What was that about? She comes to my event and is rude to me.

Shaking my head, I continue to gaze up at the sky.

Someone intertwines their fingers with mine, and my gaze

shifts to Snow, so I try to pull away, but he keeps his fingers interlocked with mine. Usually, I'd want him to take me to the back room somewhere and own every inch of my body. I'd want him to hurt me in the most primal way, but not right now. I want to beat the fuck out of him. He grabs my forearm, dragging me to the double doors leading back to the ball.

"Where are we going?" I ask.

I want to snatch my hand away from him, but we have prying eyes on us, and if anyone gets a hint we're not a happy couple, the media will eat it up like candy. His family doesn't need another scandal like the car accident on their hands.

He yanks me into a storage room, and I push on his chest hard, but he doesn't flinch. He places my wrists above my head, sliding his hand under the top of my dress, yanking my nipple, pulling hard. It stings but feels good at the same time, causing my core to tingle. He pulls away, searching the shelves for something, and he finally grabs some duct tape, tears a piece with his teeth, wrapping it around my wrists tight.

"What are you doing?" I say in a panicked tone.

"Showing you who you belong to. You want to be treated like my slut, so be it. You don't want to call me your fiancé and not wear my ring, that's fine, but you will have to deal with the consequences. Try not to cry too hard, I'm not going to be gentle."

With that, he tapes my mouth shut.

I feel my panties dampen and my nipples are so hard they can cut glass.

This is what I wanted, but not from him. Not the man that haunts my nightmares.

He unzips my dress, yanking it down. He eyes my lacy white panties and circles his fingers around my nipples. Then he grabs a fistful of my ass before slapping it hard. Pain shoots up my spine.

"When will you learn that you belong to me and you will be mine forever?"

I don't respond.

"When should I fuck your ass? On our wedding night?"

I shake my head and make muffled sounds. I'm not ready for anal; I heard it hurts like hell.

He unzips his pants and pulls out his hard dick.

My mouth waters at the sight of him. I want to drop to my knees and suck him hard. He shoves my panties to the side, brushing my clit, and I whimper.

I want to be taken without permission, and he knows it. He knows how much I crave this. He knows I don't want to have any power.

"This is page eighty-five. Where I have you duct-taped and you want me to fuck the shit out of you."

I shake my head.

Those are fantasies, ones I didn't intend for him to see. He needs to stop using my sex fantasies as a way to control me.

He shoves two fingers inside of me. "You're so wet, Lyrical. So fucking soaked. You're about to enjoy what I'm going to do to your body."

No one will ever hear us because I can't even scream. He has complete control over me and there isn't anything I can do about it. Adrenaline spikes my blood from the thrill of him using me as his sex toy.

He pushes me against the wall, and he faces me against the shelf, and I'm struggling to hold myself up because of the duct tape around my wrists. He shoves his fat dick inside of me and I sigh.

"You love this shit. You love me fucking your pussy hard. You want to be my slut. But I need you to nod your head and agree that you're mine."

I wish I could say I'll never belong to him, but instead I shake my head.

He grabs my hips and pulls out before slamming into me hard, his finger on my clit. My core clenches and I'm snug around him. I feel my wetness leaking around his dick.

"That's it, milk my dick, baby." His tone is husky. "God, your pussy feels amazing. So tight. Meant for me. Do you know how many nights I dreamed of coming inside of you?"

I arch my back as my orgasm shatters through me and my body sags against the shelf, but he holds me up, keeping me in place as he fucks me hard. My moans are quiet, and sweat builds on my forehead. He thrusts so hard inside of me that the things on the shelves rattle.

"You're going to wear my ring whether you like it or not. Once we're married, you're mine permanently and I'll do to you whatever I want."

Marriage is a piece of paper. You don't own me.

He bites my shoulders, and I moan. I can't get enough of him. Of this.

"Down on your knees, Blue."

He spins me around, removes the duct tape from my mouth, and I scream at the pain. Once I drop to my knees, he slides the crown of his dick between my lips.

Tears gather in my eyes as he fucks my mouth, and I feel his dick in the back of my throat. I choke and gag, my jaw aching.

This is too much. I can barely breathe.

"That's it. Taste yourself on my dick. Lick it clean."

Several moments later, I feel him throbbing inside of my mouth, his salty cum on my tongue. He keeps his dick in my mouth until I swallow every drop.

He strokes my cheek. "Good girl."

Next, he tears the duct tape from my wrists, and he stuffs himself back in his pants. Without another word, he leaves me in the closet in a mess.

CHAPTER ELEVEN

Lyrical

I WAKE UP TO DROOL SLIDING DOWN MY CHIN AS THE SUN PEEKS between the blinds, shining light on my face. I sit up, then rub my eyes and my head feels like I've been hit by a sledgehammer. Tossing the blanket off me, I force myself out of bed and walk sluggishly to the bathroom. I grab a bottle of aspirin, unscrew the lid, and toss back two pills, chasing it down with a glass of water.

Last night after my engagement party, I went barhopping with Winter and Lilac and consumed so much alcohol, to the point I blacked out.

The only thing I remember is Snow fucking me in the storage room, wanting me to admit that I belong to him. I glance at my engagement ring now sitting on the side of the sink, and I can't believe I'm going to be stuck with him for the rest of my life as his sex toy. He wants me addicted to his dick and crave him, but I refuse to be treated like shit. I refuse to allow him to use my dark sex fantasies against me.

I rush back to my bedroom and grab my phone from the nightstand to look at the time. It's eleven in the morning and I've missed my first class. I have time to make it to my second class, which is art.

I return to the bathroom, brush my teeth, and put my hair up in a messy bun, then I throw on a light sweater and a pair of leggings and I toss my book bag over my shoulders.

I head to the living room and find Lilac and Winter passed out on the couch.

As I make my way to the spacious kitchen, the doorbell rings.

Who would be here so late this morning? I wasn't expecting any guests, and I doubt Lilac is either.

I open the door, and a guy with brown hair and matching eyes, wearing an all-white uniform with a clipboard tucked under his armpit, stares down at me.

The aspirin finally kicks in and my head doesn't pound as much.

"Can I help you?"

"Lyrical Haynes."

"Yes?"

"Your fiancé sent me here. He wants my company to start packing your stuff and he's moving your furniture to storage."

"Excuse you?"

The guy looks just as confused as I do. "You didn't know?"

"You're not moving shit."

"It says, right here, that we have to move your stuff into storage."

A few men with boxes in their hands push me out of the way and head straight to my room, and I follow them as they gather random stuff, tossing it all in boxes.

Hell no, I'm putting my foot down with Snow. He thinks after our engagement he's going to control every aspect of my life? It's the only reason why he wants me to move in with him.

Fuck that.

I need time away from him to think. He can control me in the bedroom, but he can't control me outside of it.

"Hey, don't touch my shit," I snap.

The guy I spoke to stands in the archway of the door. "We're here to do our jobs."

I grit my teeth, snatching a box from one of the workers. "I said, don't touch my shit. I don't care what Snow told you. We agreed to live together *after* the wedding."

"Ma'am. Please let us do our job," the same guy says.

I grab a shoe and toss it at the guy, and he ducks his head. I rush to my closet, continue to throw shoes at the workers, screaming at the top of my lungs for them to get the fuck out.

Snow has crossed the line and I'm not going to take his fucking bullying. I'm not moving in with him, and I meant it when I told him that.

"Fuck that, I didn't sign up for this. Let's get the hell out of here," one of the workers says.

They leave my apartment, and a smile of victory spreads across my face. I feel proud to finally stand up to my future husband. Now, he will know he can't control me.

CHAPTER TWELVE

Snow

I SIT IN MY BUSINESS CLASS, GLANCING OUT THE WINDOW, watching the calm sea. I completely tune out the professor, lost in my own thoughts of Lyrical.

What am I going to do with her?

I tend to forget all about how she destroyed my family, and the urge to exact revenge is becoming less desirable by the day. It doesn't help that I wonder if I'm being too hard on her, and that maybe she was, in fact, drugged. I want to believe her, but I don't know if I can. Lyrical has always been the type of person where she's not honest with herself. She'll lie to get herself out of trouble and she doesn't want to face her issues. Being in close proximity to her, I lose my common sense and quickly forget I'm meant to hate her.

Sometimes, I wish we could go back to how things were before the car accident. Me, Bailey, and her. Hanging out, or them doing shit that they don't have any business doing, where I have to clean up their messes. I miss Lyrical spending the night at my place when she wasn't hanging out with my sister. We would spend time at our hangout spot on the cliff overlooking the ocean.

I receive a text message from Miles, the owner of the moving company I hired.

> **Miles: Your fiancée threw shoes at my workers and told us to leave and that she wasn't moving in with you.**

I look at the time. She's supposed to be on her way to her art class. When I tap the GPS app, the red dot shows her moving toward Gogh Hall.

> **Me: I'll handle her. Go back to her place and pack her stuff.**

We are supposed to move in after our marriage, but I'm not waiting. I need her in my space, I need her available for me to use as a toy when it's convenient for me, plus it's for appearance's sake. My father has been on my ass about going out in public with Lyrical, since our engagement ball, in fact. We have to paint this picture to the media that we're a happy couple. Show the world we are still on top, and we're as powerful as the rumors say we are.

The professor dismisses the class, and I grab my backpack, sling it over my shoulders, and leave the room along with the rest of the students.

When I step outside, I see Savannah leaning against the cobblestone wall, watching me like a hawk, and I shake my head because clearly, she isn't getting the hint that I don't want her.

She's been sending me messages, asking me why I ghosted her, and when the news broke free that I'm engaged to Lyrical, she sent me messages asking me to meet her and talk. There isn't a reason for us to talk; Savannah was a tool I used to get back at Lyrical, a warm hole—a warm, *loose* hole—I used from time to time. She doesn't satisfy the dark side I share with Lyrical. She always complained I hurt her, and she doesn't like choking. She wants to lie on her back and allow me to fuck her. She doesn't even suck dick right. A total fucking bore.

Savannah stomps up to me, her hands on her hips. "Why didn't you tell me you were going to marry Lyrical?"

"It's none of your business. That's why. Move the fuck out of my way, Savannah, so I won't be late for my next class."

"Why didn't you convince your father to choose me? I can give you what you want. You want to choke me? I'm okay with it."

No, she's not. She's okay with my bank account balance and my endless connections. I heard her having a conversation with her best friend Tanya about how she wanted to snag me because I can provide for her. I never wanted her, but I definitely don't want her after she told her friend that.

"I never wanted you, Savannah. You're a slut who can't keep your pussy to yourself."

She cocks her eyebrow. "You want the virgin who isn't experienced?"

"My fiancée isn't a virgin anymore, thanks to me, and she takes my dick a lot better than you. She isn't fucking me because she wants a rich husband, and she isn't fucking me to get paid. You're a dried up whore." I chuckle. "You fucked my friend, that's how desperate you are for a payday."

Tears form in her eyes, but I don't care about her feelings. I have had enough of her needy ass. Her palm connects with my face, slapping me across the cheek. I instantly see red, so I grab her by the throat, squeezing tight, cutting off her airway. Savannah digs her nails into my skin, her eyes bulge, but I don't let go.

God, I want to kill this bitch.

I lean in, my mouth so close to her ear. "If you put your hands on me again, I promise you, I'll slit your throat and toss you in the Atlantic Ocean and let the fish feast on your body. Stay the fuck away from me." I let her go, and she slides down to the concrete floor, sobbing.

"You will pay for how you treated me, Revi Williams. Mark

my words. You've just fucked with the wrong bitch," she screams at the top of her lungs.

Lyrical

I take an Uber to Snow's parents' mansion that sits on the top of a hill, surrounded by trees. The city is alive tonight but you don't have to worry about paparazzi following you around. The small buildings made out of cobblestones light up the dark sky.

I need to figure out who Bailey's boyfriend was and if he was the one who drugged us the night of the accident. Before we went to Snow's party, we went to a football party. A memory pops up in my head about Bailey. I remember a cop pulling me over, tapping on my window, then I blacked out and woke up in the hospital. I believe someone roofied me, because I didn't take any drugs at the football party. Someone offered it to everyone, but I didn't think anything of it at the time. Professor Carter and Professor Neil busted the party, so we left. I remember Bailey telling me she had to use the bathroom, but maybe she spoke to her boyfriend because she came back to me looking pissed off.

After the funeral, I couldn't show my face here because I caused her mother to go into a bout of depression. I'm the reason why their baby girl is six feet under.

I swallow the pain in my throat, trying to work as much courage as I can, then I knock on the door. Several moments later, the maid answers.

"What brings you here, Lyrical?"

"Is Mrs. Williams around?"

She nods. "She's in the living room."

"I need to speak to her. It's about Bailey."

She opens the door wide, letting me through. When I step

inside, the smell of lavender air freshener hits my nostrils, and memories flood my mind. It's like stepping into a time capsule and for a second, I imagine Bailey rushing down the stairs, throwing her arms around me as if she hasn't seen me in a long time. She was always an affectionate person, and I wish I had more time with her.

I walk into the living room, and Mrs. Williams stands near the window, looking outside at the trees in her backyard. We only exchanged a few words at the engagement party, nothing more. When I clear my throat, she turns around.

Surprise flickers on her face and a sad smile stretches across her lips. "Lyrical, what brings you here?"

From what my mother tells me, she's supposed to be taking antidepressant pills and her depression is driving a wedge in her marriage. But that's the thing about grief, it changes you in so many ways, so I have no business passing judgment on her. I hope to God I never lose a child.

My anxiety is getting the best of me. "How are you holding up?" I ask, biting the inside of my cheek.

"Barely hanging on. Sometimes, I can hear her coming down the hallway, asking me to eat some delicious chicken sandwich she made."

She's stuck. Everyone else seems to have moved on with their lives, but not her. She's stuck with the memories of Bailey, and so am I. I often find myself sketching old memories. That's another thing I hate about grief. Everyone moves on with their lives while you are stuck on the person you're missing. She's right; Bailey did make some fire-ass chicken sandwiches.

"I miss her too. I'm here to grab something from Bailey's room, if you don't mind?"

"I don't mind at all."

She turns her back to me, and I take that as my cue to head upstairs. Once I arrive to her room, I suck in a breath as I turn the knob of her door, exhaling when I step inside and shut the door behind me.

Tears gather in my eyes as I take in her room. Pictures of us and her family and sketches are all over one wall. Her faint cherry scent lingers in the air. Her mother hadn't changed anything about this room, and I'm grateful for it, though she's kept her room clean because not a dust mite is in sight.

I exhale, trying to not get caught up in my memories of my best friend, and I go to her drawer. I open it, finding our journal that we used to draw in. I scan through the pages.

The tears finally fall down my cheeks as I study a picture of me sitting on her lap, kissing her cheek, with Snow in the far corner with tears in his eyes. The caption reads, *Crybaby*. I remember this picture. Bailey told me Snow was pissed that I blew him off to go to the movies with her. She often said her brother had a crush on me and how I didn't want to see it. I don't think he ever loved me in the same way I loved him before all of this.

I flip through to the last page, which was completed by us a few days before the party. Bailey drew a picture of herself in a hospital bed, and she pictured this one, *Bad tummy aches*. I drew a picture at the bottom of it with a red rose—my caption, *Get better soon*. I hold the sketch journal to my chest and sob like a newborn baby. I miss her so much, I don't know how to process her death. I usually deal with it by cutting myself, but sometimes that doesn't work.

Wiping the tears from my eyes, I tuck the sketchbook under my arm, then search through her drawer. Here I find a photo, so I pick it up, studying the person who has his arms wrapped around her waist. He has a tattoo on his chest—a snake with an *X* over it, but the face of the person is cut out. They both seem to be on a beach.

I don't know anyone who has a tattoo on their chest. I flip the picture over and it reads, *Me and my forever person. The love of my life. Him and Bailey for life.*

Tears fall down my cheeks because I'm the only who believed she was dating anyone. And I was the only one who didn't think she was crazy and accepted her for who she was.

"I'm so sorry, Bailey." My tone echoes in the room. "I'm so sorry."

CHAPTER THIRTEEN

Lyrical

After I leave Snow's parents' mansion, I take an Uber back to my apartment. After a long and emotional day, I can use a hot, steamy shower. I glance in the direction of Lilac's room. When I glance at the bottom of the door, I notice there aren't any lights on, so it means she's either sleeping or she's not home. Which sucks because I could use some girl time.

Shaking my head, I turn the knob to my own bedroom door and flick the light switch. My eyes widen in horror and fear wraps around me like a cozy blanket. My stuff is gone. My desk, my bed, even my bookshelf. It's like I never lived here. I rush to the bathroom, and all of my towels and facial products are gone too.

"What the fuck?"

"What the fuck is right," Snow says, climbing into my window with a smirk on his face.

He is wearing a polo shirt with beige shorts, and my eyes

venture up to his white spiked hair. My cheeks flush at the near-ness of him. He stands in front of me with his arms crossed.

I tilt my head back to look him in his eye. "Where the fuck is my shit?"

"In storage. Where it belongs. I told you we're moving in together."

Rage fills my blood. Removing my shoe, I toss it at his head, but he catches it before it makes contact.

How fucking dare he try to control my life. He's treating me as if I don't have a say in my own life.

This is about power.

I want to slap that stupid-ass smug look off his beautiful face.

I'll buy more stuff with my trust fund money, I don't need the things he's taken. And I don't care, I'm not living with this bastard.

Fuck him.

"No."

"Suit yourself, Blue."

When he leans down, he picks me up and throws me over his shoulder like I'm a sack of potatoes.

I beat my palm on his back. "Put me down, you bastard!"

He doesn't respond, just proceeds to climb out of the win-dow and down an oak tree.

Snow has lost his fucking mind if he thinks I'm actually going to live with him.

Once he carries me to his car, he opens the passenger door, tosses me onto the leather seat, and slams the door shut. I yank on the handle but it's no use; he has me locked from the inside. Once he enters the car, he taps the Start button and the engine hums to life.

"Why do you have to force me to move in with you now?"

He doesn't respond as he turns up the radio and "Bad and Boujee" by Migos blasts through the speakers. Sighing, I lean against the seat, my arms folded across my chest.

I'm trying to think of ways to get out of this situation and from under him, but my mind is foggy. Snow drives for a while, away from North Haven.

Are we in the middle of nowhere?

He stops at a black iron gate, then hits a button on his phone. The gate slowly opens and we drive down a long path and pull up in front of a farmhouse. A farmhouse I wanted so badly to build one time. Though I don't remember telling Snow about my dream home.

I stare at the white wraparound porch with two rocking chairs by the red front door. In the back, I can make out the barn and stables. The house is made out of painted white wood. Flowers and trees surround the property.

My breath hitches and I look at Snow. "When did you have this built?"

"Last year. It was supposed to be a wedding gift." He kills the engine and turns toward me. "This is your new home now."

"You can't do this. You can't keep me locked up here."

"Do you want to test that theory?"

"Snow."

"Lyrical."

He gets out of the car, opens my door, and I sit there for several seconds before he gets impatient and yanks me by the arm, ushering me to the porch. He pushes me into the front door, and I stand in the foyer, trying not to gawk but I can't help myself. There is a staircase to the right side and in the middle sits a dark round table with a fresh boutique of white lilies. The house is everything I wanted in my dream home. Pictures from our childhood hang on the wall throughout the hallway, and I walk into the living room to find it is filled with furniture that I pinned on my Pinterest boards. My heart flutters in my chest, and I can't believe he did all of this for me. Snow can be so thoughtful when he wants to be. I don't know if I should jump in joy or beat his ass.

He kidnapped me, brought me to my dream home, and it makes me wonder if he had feelings for me at some point. I'm torn between whether I should be pissed off that he forced me against my will, but at the same time I'm smiling on the inside. Though I'm not letting it show.

So many emotions stir inside of me, but I mostly feel overwhelmed.

"You never answered my question in the car," I state. When he doesn't respond, I ask, "Why are we moving in together so soon?"

"We're engaged, Lyrical. Why wouldn't we? Besides, it's for appearance's sake, to make it seem like we're a happy couple, and this way I'll have more access to you. To use you in any way I want to."

I snort at his response. He grabs me by the hand, leads me upstairs, and opens the door to the master suite. There is a bed that sits in the middle of the room like a throne. The two walls on either side are red and black.

Snow leans down and kisses me on the shoulder, causing me to shiver.

"You need to be punished for defying me." He grabs my hand again and pushes me over to the bed. "Bend over."

I shake my head. "No."

"You make my dick hard when you fight me, Blue."

He goes into what I assume is a walk-in closet, then comes out with a rope. My eyes light up in horror.

My heart thunders in my chest.

"What are you about to do with that?"

Without a word, he grabs my arms, places them behind my back, and wraps the rope around my wrists, tying a tight knot that digs into my flesh.

My heart beats with anticipation while arousal swims in my lower belly.

"Snow, please don't do this."

I've been wanting this forever. For him to take me like I'm his.

He grabs a ball, a small belt attached to it.

I tilt my head to the side. "What is that?"

"A gag."

My eyes widen. "W-why are you using that on me?"

"You can't tell me no if you can't speak."

I shake my head, attempting to sidestep him, but he blocks my path and strokes my cheek with his thumb.

"Please... don't. I'll obey you."

"You will after I'm done with you."

When he tries to place the gag in my mouth, I move my head to the side.

"You either allow me to do it willingly or I'll force you to do it, and trust me, you don't want me to force you."

Nodding, I open my mouth wide and he places the ball in my mouth. I can't help but lick it, noting it has a rubbery taste. He ties the small belt around my head—tight.

My panties are soaking from the sweet ache between my legs. This scene was not in my sketchbook, so this must be what Snow wants to do—his fantasy.

"This is what happens when you disobey me. I show you who controls who."

He lifts up the hem of my dress and yanks down my lace thong. I feel the cool breeze against my ass. My nipples pucker and desire blossoms in the lower pit of my stomach.

Fear wraps around me and my pulse thunders through my veins.

He slides his finger inside of me, and I whimper, needing his touch all over my body.

"You're so wet for me."

I want him to continue to touch me, I want his mouth on my clit, and his dick inside of me. I crave him like a needy slut.

He places me on my stomach, positioning me with my ass in the air.

I shake my head, trying to get away from him, but he holds me in place.

My face is buried in the silk sheets, and I suck in a breath as I feel his tongue on my clit. I grind my core into his face, my juices on his tongue. I feel my orgasm building, wanting the release.

Anticipation slithers through my veins.

He kisses my inner thigh before I hear him walk into the closet. Snow comes back out, then I feel a cold object inside of me. I feel something simulating my clit, and I scream even though any sound I make is muffled. Snow moves the object inside of me, and I groan, sliding myself up and down on what I assume is a dildo as he fucks me with it. He pulls out, replacing it with his tongue on my clit, licking me like he's dying of thirst. I feel as if I'm about to explode. Several moments later, I come all over his tongue while he keeps licking me, and I shake my head as my toes curl. He slides the dildo inside of me again, this time keeping the stimulator setting on low.

"Your punishment is I take your sweet ass."

I shake my head as he kisses the side of my neck. "You will look so beautiful with tears in your eyes. Such a beautiful masterpiece."

I hear him unzip his shorts, then I feel lube in the crack of my ass, and I try to move away from him once more, but he holds me in place.

His lips brush across my ass, but I'm not ready for this, for him to fuck me there. My heart thunders in my chest when I feel the crown of his dick there, and I breathe in quickly.

He glides in me slowly and I scream at the top of my lungs. It's painful and his cock stretches my ass—Snow isn't allowing me to adjust to his length.

He turns up the intensity of the clit stimulator, and it feels so good, I don't think I can take any more. I can't take the pain and pleasure at the same time. He fucks me hard—and fast.

"Fuck," he says. "You're taking my dick so well. Such a good little slut."

My heart warms at the praise, and I turn my head to the side to look at him. I'm going to come soon. He keeps his eyes on his dick, watching himself as he fucks me.

"This is your new life now. I'm going to fuck you how I want to fuck you, whenever I want to, and there isn't anything you can do about it."

I sigh at those words because that's what I want from him. To be used like a toy.

My muscles tense, and my heart races like a horse as my orgasm rips me in half, and I sag onto the bed.

Several moments later, I feel hot ropes of cum against my ass, then Snow leans down and whispers in my ear, "I'm not done with you."

CHAPTER FOURTEEN

Snow

I REST MY ARM ON THE TABLE, WATCHING HER LIKE A HAWK. Anger grows in her eyes as she sits across from me. The smell of her apple scent lingers in the air, making my dick hard.

God, I want to punish her all over again for disobeying me. I want to fuck her. After I fucked her in the ass, we showered, and I fucked her against the shower wall.

She avoids eye contact with me, but I keep my eyes glued to hers. Our maid sets her food down. It's one of her favorites, rib-eye covered in sauteed mushroom with a side of sweet potatoes. She picks up her napkin, places it on her lap, and begins to cut her steak. A few strands of her hair fall across her forehead.

As she stuffs her face, she glances around the dining room in awe.

"You built everything to the T the way I wanted it."

I started this project a year ago, and it only finished a few months ago.

I pick up the neck of my beer, place my mouth to the rim, and gulp down the foaming liquid, choosing not to respond.

"I never told you my dream about owning a farmhouse."

"Bailey showed me a sketch of your dream home that you gave her."

She nods, continuing to dig into her meal.

"I noticed my razor blades are gone. Did you forget to pack them?"

I noticed every little thing about Lyrical, and I paid attention to the faint scars that are on her arms and inner thighs that she uses makeup to cover up.

"You're going to stop cutting yourself, so I threw them out. When did you start cutting yourself again?"

She pokes at her sweet potato and the maid pours her a glass of wine. "After Bailey's death. You have no right to throw them away."

"You're not allowed to do it again. If you do it, then I'll do it." I take a swig of my beer.

She finally looks at me, her eyes flickering with surprise. "If I jump off a bridge, would you jump off one to?"

I might be pissed off at her, but I don't want her to harm herself in any way.

"If it means keeping you safe and protecting you."

"Why would you help me?"

"Because it's my job as your future husband to take care of you."

She grunts as she polishes her meal, then uses a napkin to wipe her mouth.

"Why do you have Bailey's sketch journals?"

I went through her book bag right before I came in the dining room, and I saw on the GPS app she was at my parents' house earlier.

"She had a boyfriend. I don't know if she told you."

No, she didn't tell me because she knows how Dad and I

would respond. She wasn't allowed to have boyfriends because she was engaged to Tim. If she was caught dating another man, she would ruin our family image. Last year, she and Tim had their engagement ball.

"I never met him, but I think he was the one who drugged us."

"You weren't at the par—"

"We went to another party before we went to yours. It was a football party at a frat house."

"Why the fuck were you two at a football party?"

"Bailey wanted to get out of the house. She was depressed about something."

What was she depressed about?

I glance into her eyes, and I don't think she's lying. She really believes she was drugged.

"You think he drugged you two, but why would he drug you?"

"So he can make it look like the car accident was my fault. I want to show you something." I get up from the stool and follow her, watching her ass sway in her pants. It makes me want to fuck it all over again. My dick hardens at the thought.

Once we walk into the bedroom, she goes to the walk-in closet and grabs a book from her book bag. She flips through it and shows me sketches of a man with his face blurred out. I realize it's drawings of Bailey's day-to-day events in her life. The pictures get more disturbing as she flips the pages. I stare at the sketch of a man slapping her, tying her up in some sort of basement.

Rage flows through me like a volcano.

"Bailey has schizophrenia. She hallucinated and saw things that weren't there."

She crinkles her nose and sets the book on the nightstand. "Yes, I know. But I can tell when she was hallucinating, plus she was taking her medication religiously. She would blow off friend dates with me to hang out with him."

What if I was wrong about Lyrical taking the pills? What if this whole time I was taking my anger out on the wrong person?

I don't think I could forgive myself for the way I treated Lyrical. I stroke the back of my neck.

"You've lied before. About not popping a Molly back around your freshmen year, and I had to bail you out and pay off the cops so they wouldn't charge you."

Frustration colors her face and her shoulders sag. "I know. And I understand what you're saying, but I'm serious about Bailey. She wasn't imagining it. Like I said, he was real. She felt like I was the only one who got her, you know. She felt like you and your parents judged her."

"We loved her, and I still love my baby sister."

She strokes my back. "I know, Snow. I know," she says. "This picture fell out of her journal."

She hands it to me, and I study the tattoo of a snake with a *X* on it. Whoever this is. The motherfucker is going to die a slow death.

"Flip it over," Lyrical says.

I do what she says. *Me and my forever person. The love of my life. Him and Bailey for life.*

I don't see how a car accident is linked to her dating someone, but I don't think Lyrical would make up this story either. Her story sounds far-fetched. She mentioned she was pulled over by a cop but when I had Jameson hack into the traffic light cameras, I didn't see anything.

"She told me her boyfriend was stalking her. I believed her, and I'm going to figure out who he is."

I fold my arms and lean against the wall. "If you believe what happened was true, I'll help you find him, and when I catch him, I'm going to chop his body up into pieces and toss him into the ocean."

She searches my eyes for something I can't figure out. She stands on her tippy-toes and rubs my cheek. "Have you killed someone before?"

I never wanted to reveal to Lyrical that side of me, because I was afraid she would look at me in disgust. Now, she's stuck with me forever, so she has no choice to but accept me.

"Yes." This is too intimate for me, so I remove her hand from my face. "I took care of the guy who tried to drug you at the party."

Her eyebrows climb to the top of her forehead. "What guy? What party?"

"The one you were talking to at the party the night of the accident. I beat him to death with a bat."

Her cheeks turn pale pink, and she bites her bottom lip.

I want her to say something, anything. Not just stare at me.

She finally breaks her silence and asks, "When did you start killing?"

"When I was fifteen. My father took me to the basement of the club and told me I had to prove to him I have what it takes to run it. I killed a sex predator. He raped a seven-year-old. He was a member of the club, and we don't tolerate anyone fucking kids."

Her face pales. "My father never talked about what he did at the club."

"Because we aren't allowed to. We take care of matters ourselves; we don't get the cops involved unless we have to. But then there are politicians and high-status people that are members of the Billionaire Club. Whoever joins is protected." I run my hands through my hair. "You have no choice but to accept me for what I do. If you don't, then tough tits, you aren't going anywhere. You try to leave me, I'll keep you locked up in this house."

"I already suspected you did, but I don't care. I accept you for who you are, Snow. I always have. I feel honored you would kill anyone who wishes to harm me."

Her words do something to me, but I quickly shake the feeling away. I didn't expect that response from her.

"How does it feel to take someone's life?" she asks, sitting on the bed I fucked her in only an hour ago. She winces, and I'm assuming her pussy and ass are sore. She needs a reminder that I was there.

"Power. It gives me power. Makes me feel like I'm a god," I answer honestly.

She smiles. "I want Bailey's boyfriend's head on a silver platter."

I nod my head. "Gladly."

Memories of her in my bedroom slam into my skull and I miss her—us. I miss being so close to Lyrical. Having her near me without any animosity. I miss her laugh, her smile. I miss the happy Lyrical, the one who brightens the room. The accident destroyed both of our lives. Speaking of which, I remember her wanting to meet me after the party to ask me something that night.

"What was it you wanted to talk to me about on the night of the accident?"

She glances down at the marble floor and shakes her head, rubbing her nose. "Nothing important. I wanted to ask you what you wanted to eat that night." She rubs her nose when she's lying.

I'm going to find out what she really wanted to say to me.

CHAPTER FIFTEEN

Lyrical

FOR THE LAST TWO WEEKS, SNOW MADE SURE TO DRIVE ME to and from campus. In the evenings, he'll force me to do my homework and eat dinner with him, then he'll proceed to fuck me. We'll talk like we used to when we were friends and I try so hard to keep my distance, but it's hard. He makes me horny beyond mental reasoning and punishes me if I "don't act right."

Snow has complete control over my life and most days, I don't like it. I see him in a new light now. When I stayed home on the days I didn't have class, I tore the fucking house up looking for the sketchbook he stole from me. I even checked his safe, and it wasn't there. He opened up to me about the murderous side of him and how many people he's killed. Apparently, the guy at the party wasn't the only person he killed who tried to harm me. A guy from my freshman year had groped me and tried to force himself on me, and Snow slit his throat, then Keanu got rid of the body. I should feel grossed out that he's a murderer, but I'm not. No one is perfect. In fact, I feel honored he would go to such lengths to protect me.

I tuck my legs under my butt on the couch, look out the floor-to-ceiling window, noting our farmhouse is on a cliff overlooking the ocean. The sky is inky black, and the leafy trees sway while raindrops leave streaks against the glass ceiling. Snow really made this farmhouse the way I wanted it. He doesn't realize he's giving me a slice of heaven on earth.

My eyes go back to my college algebra book, and I stare at it. I tried to bribe the professor into letting me receive extra time on quizzes and tests, but he told me I have to take it up with the disability department, but he's one of the directors. Some teachers on campus resent us rich people because we have so much power, and I suspect he's one of them.

I close the book and set it on my lap.

Snow walks into the room. He's been up all night, trying to piece together who drugged Bailey, and I'm glad we're not at each other's throats right now because I don't think I can take his wrath any longer.

He eyes the college algebra book and I quickly tuck it under a decorative pillow, but he walks over to the pillow and yanks the offending book out. I try to snatch the book from him, but he holds it over his head.

"I thought you already passed college algebra."

No one knows about my inability to solve math problems, and right now I feel stupid as fuck. This is my fourth time repeating the course—I need this class to pass in order to graduate. It's been one of my dreams—I would be the very first woman in my family to have a college degree.

"I did take it, but I failed it," I finally admit.

He sits next to me. "Since when did you have a problem with doing math?"

I feel even more embarrassed at his words. I know he didn't

mean to make feel embarrassed, I'm sure he didn't. I rub my nose, glancing at the marble floors.

Lightning splits the sky in half and the sound of the thunder makes me flinch.

"Since I was a little kid. I can't do simple math. I can barely do three-digit addition and subtraction."

"Why didn't you let me know, Lyrical? How were you able to pass your math classes in high school?"

I hope I don't regret telling him this.

I swallow thickly. "My parents. They made fat donations to the private school so they can pass me."

I eye his tattoo on his chest, the one I drew for him. A skull with a snake slithering around it.

"How it's going to help you if your parents paid teachers to pass you?"

I hate that he has a point.

I tuck a strand of hair behind my ear. "I suffer from dyscalculia. I know I'm stupid, so let's drop the subject."

He lifts my chin so I meet his gaze. "Who said you were stupid?"

"No one… But you must think I am because I can't move past third-grade math."

"I'll talk to the professors about giving you extra time to do your schoolwork, and I'll make you a study guide. I won in the math league and I've always been at the t—"

"No, I don't need your help. Why *are* you helping me? Are you afraid you are going to be married to a dumb woman?"

"First of all, you don't tell me what to do. I'm going to help you because I want to. And second, don't ever refer to yourself as dumb or stupid. You're one of the smartest people I know."

His words make my chest warm and my cheeks flame.

He flips through the book to a section I bookmarked, crinkling his nose. "Hmmm," is all he says, then he grabs my notebook from my backpack and begins to write out the problem step by step.

I close my eyes and open them, not knowing what to say to

him. Normally, when we used to hang out, I used to be able to talk his ear off, but all the tension between us is too much for me to form words.

"I miss this," he says out of the blue.

I tilt my head to the side. "Miss what?"

"Us. When we used to hang out. When you spent the night at my place and we would watch a good movie, how you would draw and sketch. Remember the time when we went swimming in the ocean for your birthday?"

"I do," I answer.

My cheeks flush thinking about that night. His dick was hard, and I couldn't help but think about how it would feel inside of me. We stayed on the shore all night talking until eventually, we fell asleep and our parents got worried sick because they couldn't find us.

I miss my ex-best friend more than he knows, but I won't admit it to him. "You always looked out for me, Snow. Even when I was being crazy and annoying. Even though we're not friends anymore, I want to say thank you."

He doesn't say anything else as he continues to write out math problems, but I see a smile tug at the corners of his mouth. "Put on *Coraline*."

"It always been my favorite."

I grab the remote from the table, turn on Netflix, and find the movie. We sit in silence, but I can feel the tension building between us despite the silence. As the movie plays, I wrap a blanket around my body. Mindlessly, he snatches a pillow from the couch and places it on the floor between his legs.

"Sit here."

Without a word, I sit between his legs, dragging the blanket with me.

For a moment, it feels like I have my best friend back. For a moment, I remember he was my first love and will always be my first love. I wouldn't dare tell him that, because some secrets are meant to be taken to the grave.

CHAPTER SIXTEEN

Snow

GRIP THE STRAP OF MY BOOK BAG WHILE I HEAD OUT AS MY father's Porsche pulls up to the driveway of the mansion that's on campus, and he steps out.

Great.

Fucking great.

I don't want to see his ass.

What the hell does he want?

With his hands in his pockets, he walks up the driveway and stares me down. This shit is getting old. I wish like hell he would call before he shows up. I told Lyrical I would meet her at the library.

"Where are you heading, boy?" he asks.

Where does it look like I'm heading to? I want to say, but I don't. Some battles aren't worth fighting, and it's not worth my time right now.

I sigh. "I'm on my way to meet Lyrical at the library."

"I'll walk with you, then we have to leave. Duty calls."

"What duty?"

"You and Keanu need to take James Hendrix out because he stole money from the club."

We walk the trail which leads to the campus, the silence between us thick and heavy. I don't want to say the wrong thing to upset him. My father makes me feel as if I'm walking on eggshells—anything will set him off, and he's been worse since Bailey's death.

The birds chirp and the sky is cloudy. I spot people throwing Frisbees along the shore.

I need to tell him about what Lyrical discovered about Bailey, that she had a boyfriend.

"Did Bailey ever mention to Mother that she had a boyfriend?"

My father stops in his tracks to cast me a bewildered look. "Not that I know of. I thought she was dating Tim."

I shake my head. "Lyrical believes her boyfriend—whoever he was—had something to do with the accident."

He slides his hands back into his pockets. "What evidence do you have of this?"

He doesn't believe me, just as I suspected he wouldn't.

I run my fingers through my hair. "Bailey's sketch journals. She had a picture of her and a man, but his face was hidden."

He crinkles his nose. "Your sister was delusional about a lot of things and made up shit in her head. Bailey often lied about a lot of things. The picture was probably someone she met randomly."

Now I see what Lyrical was talking about. We, as a family, wrote her off as some kind of cuckoo and my parents went to great lengths to hide her illness. Even when she had to stay in the mental hospital, they lied to their friends and family members about her whereabouts. I understand how she felt like no one took her seriously. That's why Bailey always did wild shit to get my parents' attention, and when they didn't show her the attention she wanted, it got worse until my father threatened to put her back into the hospital. My father didn't treat her right.

Guilt eats at me like a disease. "What if someone was after Bailey, Father?"

He shakes his head. "I don't know what's gotten into you, but you need to deal with it. Stop trying to not take fault for what happened at your party. Bailey and Lyrical consumed a substance that destroyed both of their lives, not to mention you allowed them to get in a car in that state. If it wasn't for you, Bailey would still be here. You need to learn how to control Lyrical."

Anger burns in my chest like lava, but I don't say anything. I couldn't, and maybe he's right. Maybe it was my fault that Bailey died. I want the rage to go away. I want to make Lyrical pay; she got behind the wheel—not me. It was her fault, but I don't want to take my anger out on her. Not until I figure out what is really going on. If she's right, then I don't know if I can forgive myself for how I treated her since the accident. I'm so confused about everything.

Lyrical is convinced they were both drugged. What are the odds of her not remembering that she took a Molly before getting behind the wheel?

We arrive at the library, where Lyrical sits at her usual spot. She doesn't look up at me, too focused on her drawing.

"Three weeks from now, Lyrical and you have a photo shoot with *Vogue* magazine and an interview. If they ask about Bailey, avoid the questions. Just focus on your love story with Lyrical. When you see your mother, don't speak to her about Bailey's death. Don't mention your ludicrous idea that she was drugged. She's already depressed as it is, so you don't need to make it worse for her."

Sometimes, I want to punch my father in the face, gut him like a fish.

Lyrical looks up, then she waves at my father and he waves back. I toss the study guide onto the table.

I need Lyrical; she was always my go-to person when I felt like my back was against the proverbial wall.

"I'm going out of town."

"To where?" she asks, grabbing the study guide and placing it in her folder.

I'm not allowed to tell her what I'm up to. If my father knows I told her about the people we killed in the club, he'll be pissed.

"Don't worry about it. I'll be home when I'm ready to come home."

Her eyes venture to my father. She knows our relationship is rocky, but she doesn't know the extent of it.

"Um. Okay."

She goes to say something, but I turn my back to her, leaving her alone in the library.

This past week has been a shit show. My father had me in meetings, listening to every complaint about American Billionaire Club. Someone shoved a huge-ass dildo in their ass and couldn't remove it, so we had to call the ambulance. My father had Keanu and I kill a few more people. Lucky for Keanu, he got to leave a few days ago, while I'm still stuck in a meeting with my father. His secretary is sitting on his lap as he goes over the stock for the business. My mother is depressed, meanwhile he cheats on her. Yet, he is mad at me because I don't visit her often. I have flowers sent to her every week, and I often check on her through Zella, our maid.

I shake my head and my gaze drifts off to New York City's skyscrapers. Seven months from now, I'm going to step into the position as a CEO of this company and be married to Lyrical, and I don't know how I feel about it all. Before the car accident, I was looking forward it, but I don't know anymore. My future wife suspects she was drugged but listening to my dad, her story does sound silly. Speaking of Lyrical, she has sent me a message every day asking me if I am okay, but I never respond. Though I could have responded, I choose not to because I need the space. Plus, my father has this stupid-ass rule about us texting during meetings.

My phone lights up with a message from Savannah. It's a picture of Lyrical sitting on a man's lap, the caption reading, *I know you told me to stay away from you, but this is what your fiancée is up to*.

Rage burns through my veins as I ball my fists, digging my nails into my palms. Seeing red, I get up from the table, slide my jacket on, and head to the door. Whoever he is, it's going to be the last time he touches my fiancée.

"Where are you going?" my father asks.

"Something happened with Lyrical, I have to go."

My father frowns, folding his arms across his chest. He doesn't want to cause a scene in front of his coworkers, so he nods, but I know I'm going to hear from him about this soon.

I text my pilot and tell him to have my jet ready.

What the fuck?

Is she doing this to get back at me? Because I wouldn't return any of her calls and texts? I call her a few times and she ignores them, then I send her a few text messages and she leaves me on read. I look forward to punishing her.

Once I make it to the jet, I check her location, noting she's at a bar.

Twenty minutes later, I arrive there and my eyes land on her, finding her on the lap of a politician. He's looking at my woman like she's a piece of meat. Lyrical's eyes connect with mine, then she kisses him on the lips, before she rushes toward the back doors.

CHAPTER SEVENTEEN

Lyrical

I'M ANNOYED BECAUSE I HAVEN'T HAD SEX IN A WEEK, THANKS to Snow. I'm annoyed because he won't return any of my calls or text messages, and I know he read my messages because it says *Seen* at the bottom of the screen. I hate this cold and hot behavior.

Is our marriage going to be like this? I hope not. Well, I want the sex to be like how we have sex, but not his behavior. I told Lilac and Winter to meet me at a bar, because I need a girls' night out and I don't want to be sitting at home waiting for him. He's not my real fiancé and I'm not in love with him like I used to be.

We sit at the table, and I allow myself to have a few drinks as I laugh so hard my belly aches.

Honestly, I needed this.

I need to let my hair down and enjoy life while I can because I don't know how my marriage life is going to be.

"I have something to ask you," Winter says, before taking a

long sip of her beer. "Can I be your maid of honor or a bridesmaid?" She looks at me sheepishly.

I have been putting off planning my wedding with my mother because I'm dreading it. I don't want to be married just because our family forced it upon us.

"Of course you can be my bridesmaid, and you too, Lilac."

They both grin from ear to ear.

"So, what colors are we supposed to wear?" Winter asks, finishing the last bit of her beer.

"I don't know but once my mother lets me know, I'll shoot you both a text."

She's more excited about my wedding than I am.

"How are things with you and Irvin?" I ask Lilac, changing the subject and taking the spotlight off me.

She shrugs her shoulders. "I slept with him a few times, and that was it. He's in an arranged marriage, so I ended things between us. I'm not going to keep giving myself to a guy who belongs to someone else."

Pain etches on her face, and her smile deflates.

Whistling comes from the front entrance, and I glance at Savannah. She strides in, wearing a tight polka-dot dress along with matching Vans. Her best friend, Tanya, is right behind her, wearing a snarl on her face. I never liked her. She always had an issue with me for no damn reason. One time we almost got into a fistfight because she thought I was sleeping with Snow, though now I am.

She spots me, before making her way to our table. "Well, well, well. What do we have here? The girl who begged my ex-boyfriend to be his slut. You know the only reason why he's marrying you is because he had no choice. If he could, he would have chosen me to marry him."

I roll my eyes, because both of us know that's not true, though her father is a member of the American Billionaire Club and owns a tech company similar to Apple and Samsung. "I don't want Snow. If you want him, he's all yours."

I want to believe my own lies, but I do care if he's fucking her. Is that why he's been ignoring my text messages? Is that why he went ghost on me? I try to wrap my head around why he hasn't contacted me. I even stalked his social media, but he hasn't posted any updates since he left.

"No. It'll be more fun for me to be his side piece and fuck him so when he comes home to you, you would wonder if he has been with me." She smirks.

I get up from the table, trying to move around her, but she blocks my path. She's a few inches shorter than me.

"Savannah. I'm warning you. Step back."

Anger clouds her eyes. "Honestly, I don't understand what he sees in you, you're not all that pretty."

Her insult doesn't bother me. I want to get away from her before I do something like smash a bottle at her head. Savannah thinks because I avoid her, I'm scared of her. But I'm not. I try to avoid conflict as much as possible because I know how my anger can get.

"No wonder Snow stopped fucking you. Your personality is boring, and you stink of desperation," I snap.

"I fucked him the last few days, that's why you haven't heard from him."

The hell? How does she know I haven't heard from him? She reads my face like a map, giggling at me.

"You didn't know he's in New York City, working with his father? My father and I were there. Snow rented a hotel for us, and he fucked me so good, I'm still sore."

"Whatever, Savannah." I finally move away from her and head over to the bar. Lilac and Winter follow me and sit on either side of me.

"I think Savannah is lying and jealous because you're marrying Snow," Lilac says, then she orders herself another beer.

"What a bitch. If you need help kicking her ass, let me know. I'll help you," Winter murmurs, resting her elbow on the bartop.

They continue to speak, but I tune them out.

Why would she lie?

I grab my phone from my pocket and swipe across.

I don't have any of Snow's friends' numbers.

I tap the IG icon, and my newsfeed pops up. I need answers, and the only person who will give them to me is Keanu. Jameson seems like the type who would snitch on me to Snow, and Irvin and Snow hate each other. I type in Keanu's name, and it pops up. There is a blue button that says *Follow Back*. I had no idea he was following me. He has over a million followers and he's only following fifty-three people. I shoot him a message. Hopefully, he'll respond.

> **Me: Was Savannah with Snow in New York City?**
>
> **KeanutheMG: Yes, her family had dinner with him and his father.**

I glance at Savannah, and she gives me a mischievous look back. Why would she make this up? She knows I can ask Snow and he will be honest.

So why lie?

I shake my head. She's not lying, she has to be telling the truth. I don't like the fact that she's gloating in my face about sleeping with my fiancé, and I shouldn't be mad because Snow isn't mine. He's forcing me to have sex with him, and I enjoy it, and that's all I am to him—a sex toy for him to sleep with anytime. He's using my sex journal against me.

I don't mean shit to Snow. So why the fuck do I care if he was with her?

If Savannah is going to be the side piece in our marriage, then I'm not going to be a wife waiting for him by the door. I'm better than that; I deserve better. So, I'm going to find a guy to fuck.

I search the bar and I spot a group of men sitting a few feet away. I spot a blond-haired man with gorgeous blue eyes, wearing an expensive suit. He looks at least ten years older than me.

"Oh, he's yummy," Winter says, following my line of sight.

I get up from the bar, dust off my blouse, and put on a fake smile.

Lilac cocks her eyebrow. "Where are you going?"

I shrug. "To get laid."

"I don't think that's a go—"

I wave my hand, cutting Lilac off. "I'm not in a relationship with Snow. Our marriage is strictly business."

Without another word, I leave my friends and squeeze between two guys, keeping my eyes glued to the blond man.

He looks me up and down, licking his lips. "What are you looking for, sweetheart?"

He's older than I thought, pushing late thirties or early forties. He's old enough to be my father. It's one night, though, and I need the escape. I've never done a one-night stand, so I don't know what to expect.

Once Snow and I are married, I'm going to find me someone to fuck on a regular basis. Since he wants to play games with me, I can play them right back. He can have Savannah's trashy ass, and speaking of the dumb bitch, I glance at her, finding her watching me as she speaks to Tanya.

"Let me buy you a drink," he says.

I shake my head. "I'm not here for the drink, I'm here for you."

His eyes brighten and he grins from ear to ear. "You want to go back to my hotel?"

The guy puts me on his lap, tilting my chin to look up at him, and I can feel his erection wedged between my ass cheeks. The way he asks me to go back to his hotel turns me off. I like to be owned and controlled, the way Snow does it. I'd like him to force me to do things. I don't want a gentleman; I want a man to take from me, like Snow does. Now, I'm all of a sudden losing interest in the blond guy. He seems like a boring lay, someone who only likes missionary.

My phone rings and it's Snow, but I hit the Decline button since he hasn't been answering any of my phone calls the past week. I'm not going to answer his either. It's not fair that he gets to treat me like shit, and I'm supposed to just take it. He did say he was going to make Savannah his side piece and I'm going to have to watch, but let's see how he feels when those tables are turned.

He sends me a message.

> Snow: Answer your phone.
>
> Snow: Answer the fucking phone, Lyrical!
>
> Snow: I'm going to have fun punishing you.

I can't believe he's fucking her behind my back. He calls my phone again, so I turn my phone completely off.

The blond man grips my hips, trying to dry hump me. I ease my way off his lap and sit in the empty chair next to him.

"Easy, boy, I'm trying to get to know you better." I sigh. "What is your name?"

"Melvin, and yours?"

"Lyrical. I go to college."

"What for?"

"Art?"

Thirty minutes later, I watch Snow storm toward me, and my heart freezes in my chest.

I'm assuming Savannah told him.

Of course she did.

I hope Snow kills her one day.

Stupid bitch.

I press my lips against the blond guy's. They're dry and chapped, but I don't care. I'm using him to get back at Snow.

"I've got to go," I say, then I head out of the back doors. I see Snow marching after me from the corner of my eye, so I head down the street, and he picks up his pace.

My panties are wet from him chasing me, stalking me like I'm his prey.

I rush back to the campus iron gates, since it's walking distance from the bar. The wind cools my face, and the lit apartments brighten up the dark sky. I head straight to the green forest, my heels sinking into the muddy ground, slowing me down. Adrenaline spreads in my veins and my heart damn near jumps in my chest.

He catches up to me and yanks me by my hair, pure rage darkening his pupils, but I don't care.

I try to fight him off, but he grips my hair harder, wrapping it around his wrist and causing my scalp to burn like fire, yet the act turns me on. I let out a squeal, then a moan.

"What was that shit back there? You sat down on that motherfucker's lap. Letting him touch what's mine. Are you out of your rabid-ass mind?!"

I've never seen him filled with so much rage. I've never seen him so pissed. His anger makes me crave him. Makes me want him more.

"I saw Savannah, and she told me about how you fucked her in New York City. That's why you didn't show your face. You asshole! You left without a word and kept ignoring me for days, and now you want to pop up out of nowhere and mark some claim over me? Motherfucker. Go to hell!"

He leans down, grips my chin, digging his black-painted nails into my skin. "I wasn't with Savannah. I had to help my father at the Billionaire Club. Savannah was there along with her father, and they were trying to convince me to marry her instead, and I told them no. Because I told them I wanted you."

"Bullshit, and you know it. Why were you ignoring my calls then?"

"I don't have to give you an excuse about what I fucking do. You're nothing but a toy to me."

I don't know why his words sting. I don't know why I believed I could be more to him than a piece of ass.

"Fuck you, Revi. Fuck you."

He pushes me down to the ground, pulls up my leather skirt, and I try to get up from the ground, but it's no use. He hovers over me, pressing his body against mine, and I feel his hard muscles under his dress shirt.

No point in fighting, he's too strong for me. This is what I wanted, right? To get him upset. To hurt him. But I realize I don't mean anything to him, and I've been playing myself. I was beginning to have a little hope that he sees me as more than a blow-up sex doll.

He keeps his palm on my lower back so I can't run, then I hear him unzip his pants.

"You dare kiss another man. You need to be shown who you belong to."

"Sto—"

"Shut the fuck up," he says, sliding my panties to the side before shoving his length inside of me, stretching me good. I'm snug around him as he thrusts inside of me.

Fucking me like a madman.

I taste dirt in my mouth as the side of my face is mashed to the ground, getting mud in my dark hair. My eyes roll to the back of my head. This is what I wanted, the adrenaline, the rush of blood going to my core, my nipples hardening. I'm leaking around him and the sound of him fucking me hard fills the night air. I try to look around to see if someone is watching us, but then again, no one comes back this way to campus.

"You wanted my attention? Well, you got it, Lyrical."

He grips my hips harder, fucking me senseless, then he pulls out and I feel warm cum on my back. He flips me over, slides back inside of me, then wraps his hand around my neck, squeezing tight, but not enough to cut off my airway. I feel the cold dirt on my back and my ass throbs.

"Someone might see us."

"I don't give a shit."

He pounds into me more, and I scream at the top of my lungs.

"I was going insane thinking about you. I missed you while I was gone." His words melt my heart. He fucks me like he misses me. He fucks me like he wants me. And I don't know why I care about him. He has been treating me like shit, taking his anger out on me, and yet, I care.

I hate that I fucking caring.

Once he empties his seed inside of me, he sits up on his knees, tucking himself in his pants.

"What about me? Aren't you going to make me come?"

He pulls me up to my feet, and I yank down my skirt.

"No. You don't deserve to. That's your punishment." He sighs. "Now, I've got to clean up the mess you made. The guy whose lap you were sitting on is known to prey on younger women. He's got his eyes set on you."

"What are you going to do?"

"Don't worry about it."

I dust myself off and I head toward my old apartment. I told Lilac I was spending the night at her place.

He grabs me by the wrist. "Where are you going?"

"I'm spending the night with Lilac."

"No, you're going home with me."

"No. I need space."

"Hi, my name is Space," Snow mocks.

"Snow, please let me go."

"I said *no*. Take a rain check, or I'll punish you again."

"You can control me in the bedroom, Snow. But outside of our sexual relationship, you don't control my life."

He cups both of my cheeks, stroking my lips with his thumbs. "That's where you're wrong. The seven-point-five-million-dollar engagement ring I bought you shows I do control you. You're mine." He looks down at my finger, frowning. "You're going to wear your ring. People need to know you're taken."

"I'll never wear your ring, Revi."

He might control most of my life, but he won't control what I wear. I will never be his, and I'll never admit to anyone that I'm his. He can fuck me however he wants, do anything he wants to me and my body, but I have some power here.

He strokes the side of my face and I suck in a breath. "You'll learn that I own every inch of you."

He does—my body—but never my heart.

I'll never give him my heart.

The next morning, I wake up and look to my left to find Snow is not in bed. He must have gone to class, thank God, because last night he fucked the shit out me until we were both out of breath. I stretch my legs out and glance out the window. The sun reflects off the crystal-clear water. Yawning, I roll out of bed and head to my vanity.

There is a small box sitting on the table.

Crinkling my nose, I remove the lid and scream at the top of my lungs. There is a pair of bloody lips sitting on a small pillow with a note written in blood. No doubt, it's Snow's handwriting.

This is what happens when you allow a man to touch you. If you don't want me to leave a trail of dead bodies, then I suggest you don't let another man touch you ever again.

CHAPTER EIGHTEEN

Snow

S TRAPPING MY BACKPACK OVER MY SHOULDERS, I LEAVE THE classroom and head to her professor's office, which is on the other side of campus. I need to make sure Lyrical is graduating on time.

My phone buzzes in my pocket, so I grab it and read the text message from her.

> **Blue:** What am I supposed to do with your "gift"?
>
> **Me:** Keep it as a reminder of what I would do to a person if they were to touch you.
>
> **Blue:** You're insane. I'm the one who came on to him and I'm the one who had intentions of sleeping with him.
>
> **Me:** Don't piss me off, Lyrical.
>
> **Blue:** It's true. I feel responsible.

As she should, because no one should be touching her and

I'll kill every guy she flirts with just to prove a point. She sends me another text.

> **Blue: Did you… you know?**
>
> **Me: Yes.**

I chopped off his hands and lips and told Keanu to do whatever he wanted to do to him. Keanu tied him to cinder blocks, then used his father's yacht to dump the body in the middle of the ocean. I didn't have time to do what I wanted to do with Melvin. I wanted to keep him around in my basement, torture him a little bit more, but I was too consumed with rage, so I made his death quick and easy.

I tuck my phone back into my pocket and head straight to her professor's office, because he didn't respond to my email about Lyrical's diagnosis. I had Jameson hack into her medical records to retrieve them. She has every right to graduate on time and make her dreams come true. I also realize I'm going soft and reverting back to my old ways before I stopped being friends with her, cleaning up her messes.

She has no idea what she does to me.

If the car accident never happened, would I be fucking her? Would we even be where we are now?

If I had known what I know now, I wouldn't have fucked her. I would have forced her to be my girlfriend, because she's the only woman I saw myself with. Though the love I had for her was unrequited.

Once I make it to Professor Jesse's office, I knock three times. He opens the door wide, inviting me in, and I lean against his oak desk.

"What brings you to my office, Mr. Williams?" he asks.

"I sent you an email about Lyrical, my fiancée. She has a learning disability, and I haven't received a response. She needs to graduate because she wants to open up her own gallery. You wouldn't want to stop a gorgeous girl from pursuing her dreams now, would you?"

"Like I told Ms. Haynes. It will be a while to get her documents approved, and if she can't pass my class, then that's on her."

The devilish smile I give him makes him wipe the smirk from his face. Sighing, I reach into my bag, pull out a folder, and set it down on the desk. The one thing I love about North Haven? It's so easy to find dirt on people.

"This is what's going to happen. If you don't give Lyrical enough time to complete her work, and if you fail her, I'm going to show the mayor pictures of you fucking his wife. You don't want that. If you tell Lyrical I helped her pass her class, or anyone else, I'll leak these photos online. And no one will ever work with you again."

He swallows thickly, then proceeds to open the folder, searching through the photographs. "You wouldn't do that."

"Oh yes, I would. I have an email on standby."

"Fine, Mr. Williams. I will do it. I'll make sure Lyrical passes my class."

I tuck the photos in my backpack and head out the door.

Once I make it outside the building, my phone dings with a text message from Lyrical.

Blue: Are you following me?

CHAPTER NINETEEN

Lyrical

I'M AT BAILEY'S STORAGE, TRYING TO FIND MORE EVIDENCE that her boyfriend exists and maybe get an address or a name. Something to prove his existence besides a faceless picture and the journal full of sketches.

This week has been a shit show. I'm going to get back at Savannah for trying to sabotage what little relationship I have with Snow. I have a plan, but I have to do this alone and not involve Snow. The bitch is going to pay for what she did.

I now know that Snow doesn't care about her—that he chose me.

Me.

To be his wife.

He could have gotten out of this arrangement and chose her. I'm not going to read into it too much, and I'm not going to get my hopes up about our relationship because, after all, our marriage is still arranged. I'm realizing now that my feelings for Snow are slowly returning. I don't think I can ever look past the way he treated me since the start of the semester, nor the fact he doesn't believe I'm telling the truth about me and Bailey being drugged, but I do know I can't help how I feel about him.

I'm conflicted.

Confused about what our relationship is. Our marriage is less than seven months away and I don't know if I'm ready for it.

After searching through Bailey's things for thirty minutes, I don't find shit, and it annoys the hell out of me.

I drop to my knees on the hard concrete, sighing, wiping sweat from my forehead.

There isn't much to be found in the boxes, just her clothing, old school textbooks, a few folders with sketches.

Opening up a folder, my eyes stay glued to a sketch Bailey had drawn of herself with a baby dangling from her stomach. She went into great details drawing this picture. At the bottom, there is a picture of hands folded, a photo of the guy with his hands wrapped around her. I read the handwritten text in the corner.

I shouldn't have aborted our baby, even though it was for our relationship. You said it was my choice, but have I been manipulated? I did this for you. I hope you know that.

She was pregnant. I don't want to believe it. Why would she keep it a secret from me? I picture her being alone and scared while going through that awful experience.

I search through more stuff, find some old photos of us, so I grab those along with the sketch, lock the storage back up, and make my way to the parking lot.

It's been raining on and off, and the smell of mist and wet asphalt hits my nostrils.

A guy is walking slowly behind me, wearing a black hoodie, his hands tucked in his pants pockets. Is that Snow following me? I told him where I was going and I gave him my location.

I take out my phone to shoot him a text.

Me: Are you following me?

I watch the guy behind me from the corner of my eye. I note that he doesn't bother looking at his phone, so my spidey sense is telling me it's not Snow; he wouldn't hide behind a hoodie either. With my heart beating loud in my ears, I have to remain calm. I can't let the guy know I know he's following me. I pretend to be looking around the empty parking lot, trying to calm my nerves, but my stomach turns, and fear overrides my senses. I glance back at the guy to see a knife is tucked between his fingers, so I run to my car, get inside, and slam the door shut in his face. The guy beats on my door, screaming at me to get out, banging the handle of the knife against the window to try to break it. Fortunately, my windows are both shatterproof and bulletproof. I watch the guy leave, get on a motorcycle, and with shaking hands, I put my car into gear and rush out of the parking lot.

The guy is right behind me. We're bobbing and weaving through traffic as anxiety tightens in my chest.

He's fast on my tail and my car isn't a sports car, it's a Lexus I got after the accident.

My dashboard shows Snow's name, so I answer on the first ring. "Someone is following me, Snow. I'm so scared."

"Calm down, take deep breaths. Go straight to the mansion, the one where Jameson, Keanu, and Irvin live. I'll be waiting for you."

I switch lanes, even run a red light, but he's still on my ass, like white on rice. "Are you sure it's safe?"

"Yeah. Trust me, it is."

I do eighty through the town and the guy on the motorcycle pulls up beside me, trying to run me off the road, but I floor the gas pedal, speeding up, and now he's right behind me.

Once I make it on campus, I take the path which leads up to the mansion. Snow and Jameson are waiting in the driveway, guns in their hands. I park just as Snow shoots the guy in the arm, but he takes off at full speed. Keanu then speeds off on his motorcycle, following the guy in the hoodie.

Snow rushes to my car, opens my door, and I hug him tight. Tears fall down my cheeks, and I feel safe and protected in his arms. He squeezes me back, stroking the back of my head, soothing me, whispering in my ears that I'm safe. All the while my tears wet his cotton shirt.

"Come inside," he says, wrapping his arm around my waist.

When we're in the living room, I exhale, slouching on the couch, relaying everything I learned at the storage. I even show Snow the sketch and my theory that Bailey was pregnant at one time, about the way she was acting strange before her death and how she was paranoid. He punches the wall, screaming.

Guilt flashes in his pupils. "I failed my sister," he says to himself. "She was suffering, and I wasn't there to protect her." He hangs his head as he runs his fingers through his hair.

No one says a word for several moments. I place my hands on his cheeks, and to my surprise, he leans into my touch, causing me to blush.

"Snow, look at me."

He shakes his head, and I'm assuming he feels too shameful to look at me.

"Please. I need you to look at me."

"It's not your fault. Bailey kept a lot of secrets from us. It's no one's fault," I say, genuinely.

He nods, but I don't think he believes me.

"I mean what I say, Snow. I'm serious. I don't know what to believe, what was real and what wasn't. She lived a double life, and who knows what she was into."

My best friend hid so much of her life from me the last few years of her life. At first, I thought I was being crazy, that I'm the one who should feel guilty and not him. I was the one who was spending a lot of time with her. I should have seen the signs that something was off. Tears wet my eyes because I truly don't know who she was during the last few years of her life. If I had been more forceful, maybe follow her to places when she used to disappear, then maybe I could have saved us both. When she said she felt like someone was following her, I should have taken her seriously. I failed her more than anyone else in her life.

I've never felt as much guilt as I do now.

"Did Keanu track him down?" Snow asks, squeezing my shoulders tight.

"Yeah. He sent me a text, he's on his tail," Jameson replies, kicking up his shoes on the coffee table, typing on his phone. "He's going to beat him and bring him to the basement."

"Go lie down in my old bedroom. You need to rest, Lyrical."

Usually, I would fight him, but not tonight. So, I head upstairs, go directly to Snow's bedroom, kick off my shoes, and slide under the covers. And I fall asleep.

Snow

I watch Blue sleep. She has her arm draped over her face, letting out a loud snore. I move her hand, swiping her dark hair from her forehead, and I stroke her chin, studying every inch of her face. I used to do this a lot when she spent the night at my place. I used to wonder what her lips would taste like, what she would do if she woke up with me buried between her legs, eating her pussy like I'm starving.

When I slide off the bed, I open the window, letting the breeze touch my face as I stare out at the crescent moon. The sky is cloudy tonight and the salty air wafts into my nostrils. I need to clear the thoughts and emotions I have for Lyrical. Her almost being attacked by the guy in the hoodie made me realize how much I still want her, that I care about her. I should hate her for destroying my family. I should take a knife and stab her with it, but it wouldn't benefit me in any way. I thought I was going to lose her, and I don't want to feel as if my chest is sinking and I'm gasping for air.

The idea of seeking revenge on her doesn't sound appealing anymore. But I feel as if I'm not getting justice for Bailey by not getting back at Lyrical for what she did. I'm so used to blaming Lyrical for her death, and a part of me wants to believe she's the cause of my sister's death. I'm not saying I want to marry her but what I'm saying is, I can't fight what I want—and I want her.

I need her.

I crave her.

I've never wanted anyone the way I want her.

Those feelings I felt for her before the car accident, I can't keep them buried much longer.

I forget how much I hate her, how I'm *supposed* to hate her.

I forget she's my enemy.

Sucking in some fresh air, I close the window, then I make my way to the bed, pulling off the blanket wrapped around her body. I need to taste her, need to touch her, and I need to fuck her. Slowly, I unbutton her jeans, yanking them down to her ankles, then I toss them to the floor. She stirs but turns onto her side, but I slowly turn her on her back again, yanking down her panties. I take a good look at her glistening pussy, and she's already wet. My dick aches in my pajama pants, needing to release all over her.

She's mine.

I might not want to marry her, but I want to own every inch of her body, and I want her to realize that she belongs to me.

Placing my mouth on her clit, she moans softly, wrapping her legs around my shoulders with her eyes closed.

She wanted this. She wants me to fuck her in her sleep. She loves it when I take from her and do what I want to her sweet body.

She slowly humps my face as I slide my fingers inside of her, squeezing around every digit. She moans loudly as I spread her wide.

"S-Snow... what are you doing?" She rubs her eyes and glances down at me, sucking in a breath.

She lies back down, and I expect her to fight me, like she used to, but she takes it, like she needs it. I'm not letting her go, no matter how she feels.

She moans my name, arches her back, yanks my hair hard to the point my scalp stings.

I don't care.

Once I let her ride out her orgasm, I remove my dick from my pajama pants, slide into her slick pussy, and I fuck her so hard. The headboard knocks against the wall and she squeezes herself around me. I grip her by the neck tightly, squeezing hard. I've never been a gentle lover.

I lean down and whisper in her ear, "That's it, take this dick like a good girl. Come on my cock, Blue. Show me who this pussy belongs to."

"Harder, please," she manages to get out.

When I push inside of her as hard as I can, I pull out and do it again. I kiss her, biting her bottom lip, drawing blood. She darts out her tongue and licks up the blood.

Fuck. That's hot.

"You like taking my dick."

She doesn't respond, just enjoying this. My balls tighten and the crown of my cock tingles.

"Open your mouth, Blue."

I slide out of her and stand at the edge of the bed. Blue sits up on her knees, places her mouth on the crown of my dick, then she sucks hard. Moaning, I place my hand in her hair, yanking the strands tight. She deep throats my dick, playing with my balls. My spine tingles, and my toes fucking curl, as I empty out in her mouth, and she swallows, darting out her tongue to lick up every drop. She gets up from her knees and heads to the bathroom, but I have more plans for her. I scoop her up in my arms, bend her over, and put her ass in the air. I grab lube from the drawer and slide it along the crack of her ass.

I stick my finger inside of her ass and she squeezes it as she gasps loudly. I slide my dick inside of her pussy and using the clit stimulator I stole from her, I place it on her clit, causing her to scream.

"S-Snow, it's too much. Please, stop. I can't take any more."

I completely ignore her.

She wants this. She wants to be fucked beyond reason.

When she tries to straighten out her legs, I hold her hips, keeping her in place as I fuck her hard. She screams as her orgasm rips through her and I feel her pussy squeeze the life out of my dick.

It feels so fucking good, I can't believe I've been missing out on this. I should have fucked her the minute I laid eyes on her. I should have fucked her the night we went swimming in the ocean. I had so many opportunities to fuck her and I didn't.

She sags against the bed, the side of her head resting on the sheets, all the while I continue to fuck her. Her eyelids are heavy-lidded as I come inside of her. When I pull out of her, I go into the bathroom, turn on the faucet of the tub, and I go back into the bedroom to remove her shirt before I scoop her up in my arms like a newborn baby and place her in the tub.

She casts me a bewildered look. "Have you bumped your head?"

I arch my eyebrow. "No. Why?"

She sighs at the feel of the steamy water on her skin. "Why are you being nice to me? Usually, you leave me covered in your cum."

"Let me be nice."

I slide into the water across from her, and she stares at me like I've grown three heads.

"You're up to something."

"Why do I have to be up to something for me to take care of you?"

She shakes her head, brings her knees to her chest, and stares at the tattoo on my chest. I've never been this intimate with any woman, and I've never bathed with one either.

"Whatever," she mumbles under her breath.

"What did you say?" I ask, daring her to repeat herself.

She shakes her head. "Nothing. Has Jameson found out who was sent to kill me?"

"Not yet, but he's working on it."

"I'm scared, Snow. I don't want to leave here until he is found."

"Understood."

She nods, then starts to sob. I don't like that another man made her cry.

When we catch the son of bitch, I'm going to make his death a slow one after I get all the information out of him.

"Don't cry, Lyrical. That motherfucker doesn't deserve your tears."

"And you do?"

"No one deserves to make you cry—but me."

"You're insane." She sighs. "Please, make me forget."

I pull her to me and slide her onto my dick, bouncing her up and down. She slowly rides me, not giving herself time to adjust to my size. Once I come inside of her, I bathe her body, then I wash myself.

"Chase me through the woods," she whispers. If I wasn't paying attention, I would have missed it. "Chase me through the woods, find me, and fuck me, please."

Usually, I would find something snarky to say, but I don't. She slides off of me, getting out of the tub, and water drips onto the tiles. When she grabs a towel, she rubs the cotton fabric along her pretty flesh.

"Give me a head start."

I love it when she begs me to fuck her, and my dick hardens at the thought.

"Five," I say.

Her eyes widen, and a smile creeps onto her face.

"Four."

Tossing the towel into the empty basket, she dashes out of the bathroom.

"Three," I shout.

I follow her to the bedroom and watch her put on some clothes, then I go into my walk-in closet, throwing on a black T-shirt and a pair of jeans. My heart hammers in my chest as I walk back into the bedroom, watching her tie her shoelaces.

"Two."

She stares at me in awe, biting her lips, then she walks up to me, stands on her tippy-toes, and kisses me before dashing out of the room.

"One."

I chase her.

CHAPTER TWENTY

Lyrical

THE SUN CREEPS BETWEEN THE DARK CURTAINS IN SNOW'S old room at the mansion. I roll onto my back, scroll through my IG, and a text message pops up on the screen from Winter.

> **Winter:** Are you okay? I haven't heard from you since the night you disappeared with Snow. He didn't hurt you, did he?
>
> **Me:** I'm fine. We argued and talked about it, but now we're fine.

I had to lie to her, and I'm not going to admit that he fucked me on the ground because I know deep down what I like is disturbing to other people.

> **Winter:** So are you two in a relationship?
>
> **Me:** Hell no.
>
> **Winter:** I think Snow is into you. He posts a lot of pictures of you on IG.

I leave her on read. She thinks he's into me and maybe the world does too, but I know it's all for show. For the arranged marriage and for him to have some claim on me, to let men know I'm off-limits.

I roll onto my stomach, exit out of the chat, then go back to the IG app and scroll mindlessly through my newsfeed page for the next few minutes, liking a few posts and stories.

For most of the night, Snow chased me around in the woods, then he fucked me the way I wanted him to. I'm not allowed to go anywhere until we figure out who was trying to kill me. Which I don't mind, because I don't want to take any chances of being attacked.

Why would someone want me dead? I don't know who, but Snow is determined to find out.

Once I'm finished with my phone, I set it on the nightstand and throw on some of his old sweats and a T-shirt before heading downstairs.

The scent of bacon and syrup wafts in the air, and I hear laughter echoing from the hallway. When I make it to the kitchen, I find Snow and Keanu cooking at a stainless-steel stove while Jameson and Irvin are in the open space living room playing a video game. I make my way to the island, sit on the barstool, and pour myself a glass of orange juice, gulping it down like I'm dying of thirst. When I set the glass down, Snow turns around and eyes me for a few seconds, frowning.

"Go back upstairs, Lyrical," Snow demands.

I straighten my spine and take another long sip of my orange juice. "No."

"Now."

"I said no. What have I told you about bossing me around?" I snap. "They are helping you with the person who is trying to kill me. So, I'm determined to be around them. Besides, you can't keep me from your friends forever."

"Yeah, let her stay." Keanu grins. "I've always wanted to hang out with her."

"You're not even allowed to breathe in her direction, K," Snow growls.

Jameson makes his way to the stool next to me, and Snow points his spatula at him, watching his every move.

"You don't sit next to her, that's my seat."

Rolling his eyes, Jameson gets up from the stool, giving me a weak smile. "Aren't we going to address the elephant in the room?"

All eyes are glued to him, including mine.

"What?" Irvin asks.

"About how Miss Firestarter burned down our garage?" He smirks, folding his arms across his chest. "I didn't know you had the guts to try to destroy our shit."

"You led us to believe Melvin did it," Keanu grumbles.

I glance at Snow, tapping my fingers on the marble counter. "You told them the guy I kissed did it?"

"I thought you all were going to kill her, then I would have to kill each one of you, and I didn't want a bloodbath."

That happened a month ago, so why would Snow want to protect me then? He could have let them hurt me or do whatever the fuck they wanted to do to me. Or he could have allowed them to pass me around like a sex toy. That would have been... hot.

"What would have been the consequences of my actions? Would I have been tied to the headboard, gagged, then you all take turns fucking me? Or would you all fuck me at the same time? Filling every one of my holes?"

Snow has made me feel so comfortable in my sex fantasies, and I didn't think twice as I uttered the words.

I feel my cheeks burn at the thought.

They all stare at me, except for Snow who is glaring at me.

"I knew you were a freak." Keanu winks at me, licking his lips. "When you're done fucking her, I'd like to have a turn. Those innocent-looking girls are some of the best freaks. I could gag you, tie you up to the bed, and shove a dildo up your ass while I fuck you." Keanu grins ear to ear. "Have you had that done to you?"

I blush and I bet my cheeks are redder than a stop sign. My mind quickly goes to the night Snow fucked me in the ass. It was the hottest shit he's ever done to me.

I like Keanu; he seems pretty cool and nice. I'm pretty sure he's a killer like Snow, but the way he carries himself, he doesn't strike me as one and he has the personality of a golden retriever.

I study the dark ink on his tan arm—a naked woman with a blindfold over her eyes, her hands tied behind her back, on her knees.

"What does this symbolize?"

"I like my women tied when I fuck them."

I like to be tied during sex, but I keep the thought to myself.

I rub my finger along his tattoo of dead aster flowers growing from a skull. "What about this tattoo?"

Snow grabs the pan with the sizzling bacon, slowly lifting it off the stove, ready to smack Keanu with it.

"Put the pan down and leave him alone," I snap. "We're talking."

Snow rolls his eyes and sets it back down.

I smirk at Snow. "What would happen if I would have enjoyed them fucking me?"

Jameson chokes on his drink, while Irvin shakes his head.

"You're trying to upset Snow and it's working." Keanu sighs.

"Mention fucking my friends again and we are going to have a problem." Snow grinds his teeth.

"You can throw it in my face how you will fuck Savannah while we're married, but if I even have a single thought about fucking any of your friends, it's a problem? You're a hypocrite."

"That was different, and things have changed. I wasn't planning on fucking her anyway while we're married; I just said it to piss you off." He piles food onto my plate. Slamming it in front of me, he glares at me. "Eat up." He walks around the island, leans down, and whispers in my ear, "I know what you're doing, and it's working. You want me to gag you and tie you to the bed and have my way with you like before. You keep it up, and I'll do far worse to you."

I shrug, pick up my fork, and pop a piece of bacon in my mouth. "Sounds like empty promises."

"I need to install a camera in your new house so I can jack off to you both," Keanu says.

"You don't value your life, do you?" Irvin asks.

"If I die, I'll die happy," Keanu shoots back.

"I found information on the guy who chased Lyrical off the road," Jameson says then, changing the subject.

"Okay, so where is he?" I ask, placing my over-easy egg onto toast. Snow hasn't forgotten how I love to eat my eggs. These are the little things I like about him. He remembers every detail about me and it causes my cheeks to flush.

"He's locked up in the basement," Keanu answers, before he pours himself a large glass of orange juice.

"I can't wait to hear what he says about trying to kill me," I state.

"It's not a pretty sight. I fucked him up pretty bad. It's some of my best work," Keanu says so casually like it's normal to hurt people.

Now I understand why Snow doesn't want me around them.

"I still want to see him. I know what you guys do. I know of the killings and what you have to do to protect the club and to be so powerful."

"You're not going," Snow growls. "If I catch you anywhere near the basement, Lyrical, you're going to be punished for it, and you won't like what I do to you."

I crinkle my nose. "Why the fuck not? I'm the one who he ran off the road."

"It's too dangerous and I don't want you to see what I do

to people. What we do to people. I'm driving you back to the farmhouse."

I bang my hand on the counter, not caring about the throbbing pain shooting up my fingers. "We're supposed to be a team and work together to help solve Bailey's death, and you're not being a team member."

He cups my face, stroking his fingers over my lips. "I care about your safety, and my job as your fiancé is to protect you at all costs. I don't want the bastard being in the same room as you. He doesn't deserve to inhale the same air as you. Do you know the fear I felt when you texted me asking if I was the one following you? I felt pure terror because I was worried about losing you. It damn near killed me. So, this is me protecting you. Once you see someone kill a person, you won't be the same anymore. It alters your mind. This is me protecting you mentally."

I want to say I don't need his protection, but instead, I mutter, "I can protect myself, Snow."

He doesn't respond.

Without a word, I pout, storm upstairs to his bedroom, and slam the door shut behind me.

CHAPTER TWENTY-ONE

Snow

AFTER I DRIVE LYRICAL HOME, I HEAD STRAIGHT TO THE basement of the mansion that I used to live at. When I head down the stairs, rage fills me up like an ocean.

This motherfucker is going to pay for trying to kill my fiancée.

I grab a bucket of ice-cold water, pouring it all over the bastard's face. Keanu did a number on him. Half of his face is carved up, and he has two black eyes and fresh scars over his pale chest.

I want to know who sent him after Lyrical.

The guy in the hoodie who was chasing Lyrical, Samuel, has a rap sheet of felonies. Jameson did a background check on him, and it turns out he sells drugs to the students on campus.

He finally opens his eyes and takes in his surroundings, trying to see where he's at. He glances at all four of us. Horror fills his pupils.

That's right.

Be scared.

I'm going to make what Jigsaw did to his victims look like a walk in the damn park.

"Let me go, you fucking bastard!"

He tries to wiggle his way out of the rope restraining him, but it's no use. He won't be able to get free, and if he does, he won't be able to take all of us down at once. He's too weak.

When I step up to him, I yank a fistful of his blond hair that's caked in blood and then punch him in the face, hitting the exposed wound. Biting down on his lip, he tries to keep himself from screaming.

Pure rage courses through my veins and I grind my jaw so hard, my molars ache. I need to distract myself from thinking about Lyrical. I can't stop obsessing over what she's doing. I'm not giving her space either, so she better suck up whatever feelings she has about me not allowing her to watch me kill Samuel.

I don't care.

She can't see this side of me. I know we're a team, but I'm the one who handles the nasty work. I'm doing this to protect her. She doesn't realize it.

"Why did you try to kill my fiancée?" I snap.

He screams for help and Jameson punches him in the face. The way Jameson carries himself, you would think torturing people is beneath him—you wouldn't think he would get his hands dirty like this.

But he can be more savage than I am.

I glance at Irvin; he looks like he doesn't want to be here. But it's in our code to trust and protect each other. I'm still working on the trust part. Since I drowned him, he's been keeping his distance from me, but I know the bastard well enough that he's waiting for the right time to strike back at me. I can't use Lilac as leverage to keep him in check because she told him she doesn't want to have anything to do with him anymore.

Samuel spits out blood, getting my T-shirt wet. Blood is a bitch to get out of clothing.

I've had enough of his bullshit.

"Keanu, cut of his pinkie finger," I order.

"Delighted to." He removes his Swiss army knife from his pocket and slices through the pinkie finger, causing Samuel to wail in pain as blood squirts onto the concrete.

"Please! I beg of you! Let me go!" he screams, spit flying everywhere.

"Cut off his thumb." My tone is calm and deathly.

"Fine. I'll tell you. I was paid to do it." His voice is hoarse.

His face is turning more pale, and if I don't hurry up and get all the information he knows out of him soon, he'll die on me.

"By whom?" I ask.

"He shows up in a white mask, never revealing himself to me."

"How did you get in contact with him?" Jameson asks.

"He contacted me and told me he'd send me thirty thousand in cash if I took the girl out. Kill her."

"Give us his address," Jameson asks, folding his arms across his chest.

"I-I don't have his address. He meets me somewhere."

I cock an eyebrow. "Where?"

Samuel snaps his mouth shut.

I squeeze the wound on his severed finger.

"I can't tell you," he groans through gritted teeth.

"Your life is hanging by a thread. So tell me."

"You don't understand. I have a sister. If I say anything, he will kill her."

"I don't give a fuck about your sister. You should have thought about her the moment you tried to kill my fiancée."

Tears run down his face. "We meet in Gogh Hall. Please stop the blood. Please get rid of the pain."

That is the art hall on campus, where the college's art professors hold their classes.

"Can you trust this scum for anything?" Jameson asks.

"What choice do I have?" I grab the gas can and a lighter from the shelf. "Is he a student on campus?"

"I don't know."

"What does he go by?"

He opens his mouth and says, "J-Ju—"

The life leaves his eyes then, and his mouth hangs open, like the Ghostface mask.

"Do you remember Samuel Jacobs from our senior year?" Jameson says, sliding his fingers through his hair.

I nod. He was a famous football player on campus. Unlike other dumb jocks, he graduated at the top of the class and was going to take over his father's tech company that's known throughout the United States. His father is a member of the Billionaire Club.

I look him up and down. I knew he looked familiar since he only graduated last year. What happened to him? How did he end up as a drug dealer?

"Where is his phone?" I ask.

"I already got it, Snow," Jameson says.

I drench gasoline all over Samuel's dead body and then hit the button on the lighter, setting him on fire. I watch his flesh burn, the smell making my head hurt.

I've got to keep Lyrical safe, no matter what happens. Whoever the masked man is, I'm going to find and kill him slowly.

"What do we do next?" Keanu asks, folding his arms across his chest.

"Get rid of his body," I state.

"I'm going to hack into his phone and find the person who hired him to kill Lyrical." Jameson says. "In the meantime, keep an eye out on Lyrical and tell her to change up her routine. I'm assuming he's going to send someone else to finish the job."

My phone buzzes in my pocket, and a notification pops up showing me she's at her parents' house. She can't sit still to save her life—I told her to stay at the farmhouse.

"We can set him up, pretend to be the guy, and tell him that job is done, and when he's ready to give the cash, we'll torture him until we get answers," I state before heading upstairs. "I have to take care of Lyrical," I mutter just as I'm leaving the basement.

CHAPTER TWENTY-TWO

Lyrical

OPEN THE DOOR OF MY CHILDHOOD HOME AND WALK TO THE living room, spotting my mother reading a *Better Homes and Gardens* magazine. I haven't stepped foot in here in several months, but I note that my mother has kept the smell of lavender in the air. I eye the new furniture my parents now have: leather brown couches and matching end tables.

I clear my throat. "Hi, Mother."

I haven't heard from her since our phone call, and I have to admit, I've been avoiding her because she wants to speak about planning the wedding.

"Lyrical. Did you get my text messages about the wedding?"

I shake my head. "No, I haven't. I've been busy," I lie. "I'm here to see Dad. Where is he? He's not answering his phone."

"Clemon is in his study, dear. Next week, I need your approval on what type of cake you would like."

"You can pick it ou—"

"I hope we will use this time as bonding. We barely spend time together anymore, especially after you started this semester."

Shame washes over me like a tidal wave, knowing I let her down. We never talked about the car accident, even when I stayed locked up in my room all summer after rehab.

"Okay, Mother. We can have lunch next week and speak more about the wedding."

She waltzes up to me, bringing me in for a hug. I squeeze her tight. I do miss her so much. Her fruity perfume engulfs me.

Turning on my heel, I head upstairs, open the door to my father's study, and find my father typing away on his computer. My phone rings and Snow's name pops up on the screen, but I hit the Decline button. I don't want to deal with his shit right now.

I'm so tired of him dictating what I do. Controlling my every move.

"Father." I clear my throat.

"Hey, sweetheart." He pushes himself from the chair, walks toward me to give me a hug, and drops a kiss on my forehead.

I flop into the leather chair in front of his desk. "How come you're not picking up your phone?"

"Busy with work." He sits on the edge of the table. "What brings you here?"

I pull out a picture of Bailey and the guy, handing it to him. "You recognize this tattoo?"

My father's face scrunches up, and he nods. "Where did you get this picture from?"

"Bailey's stuff. She was seeing the man in this photo."

"He's part of the mafia in South Haven. They sex traffic women. It's their symbol, but since his is marked out, it means he was kicked out of the organization."

I frown.

"We don't allow membership at the club to them. The last time we had one of their members there, they were kidnapping college girls from North Haven and selling them off. They got busted with the FBI. We had no idea."

"When did this happen?"

"Four years ago, the semester before you started. That's why I told you to wait before starting college. I was worried they might traffic you," he tells me. "So, you're saying Bailey was dating this guy?"

I nod. "I think he abused her, and she was worried he was stalking her. I found some disturbing pictures she had drawn. I think our accident was set up because I remember getting pulled over by a cop, but I don't remember what happened after he reached my window. Next thing I know, I'm in a hospital bed and told I was in a car accident."

"Are you sure you were drugged? You and Bailey used to take substances."

"How did you know that?"

"You don't think I know what goes on with you? I know everything about you, I don't let you know because I want you to trust me."

I sigh. "Father, I was drugged. We were both drugged and no one believes me. Not even Snow."

"If you say you were, I believe you. Let me look into your medical records. I know a few people who work with the North Haven police department. I'll see if I can find the guy."

"Don't tell Mother about this. I love her but I don't want her to have any part of this."

"Okay. If I find out someone was after Bailey or you, I'm going to make them pay."

My father never gave me the impression that he killed people. They aren't allowed to speak about it to their family and loved ones.

"Do you kill people? Have you ever killed someone?"

My father sighs and runs his hand through his hair. "What makes you ask that?"

I want to say Snow, but I also don't want to rat him out.

"I heard things about Snow's dad and the other owners."

He grabs my hand. "Listen, sometimes I have to do wh—"

"I'm not spooked, Dad. If you do, I want the truth."

He sighs. "Yeah, I do. Not because I want to, but because I have to, and I'll kill for you and your mother if I have to. I have killed for your mother before, and I'll do it again. I'm not ashamed of what I do or did, sweetheart."

I nod as he clears his throat.

Snow sends me a message in that moment.

Snow: You need to come home.

I roll my eyes and shoot him a message.

Me: No.

Snow: It wasn't an option. Come home now.

Me: Hell. No.

Snow: If you don't show up, I'm going to turn your ass black and blue.

His words turn me on. I like the dirty shit he does to me, and I want to be punished—but at the same time, I need to stand my ground with him. I don't have to bow down to him or any man.

Me: Do your worst.

Snow: *devil emoji*

I say my goodbyes to my father and give him a big hug, then I leave my parents' home.

Once I make it to the farmhouse, I kick off my shoes and set them on the rack. Needing something to eat, I head to the kitchen.

Just then, Snow flips on the light switch, stalks up to me, and tosses me over his shoulder.

"It's time to play, Blue."

CHAPTER TWENTY-THREE

Snow

CARRY HER UP THE STAIRS AND TOWARD OUR BALCONY THAT'S in our bedroom. She bangs her tiny fists onto my back, screaming at the top of her lungs for me to let her go. I'm tired of her playing games and not being open about what she wants—me. She lies to herself all the time, trying to convince herself she doesn't want me, but I'm sick of her not understanding that she doesn't have any control over her life anymore.

"I hate you, Snow!"

"No, you don't. You keep telling yourself that."

She snaps her mouth shut.

I place my hand on her ass, squeezing tight, and she squeals like a schoolgirl.

Once we make it to our bedroom, I unlock the balcony doors and push them open.

The cool nightly breeze drifting from the sea tickles my skin.

I can see the crescent moon hovering above tall palm trees from here.

I set her over the balcony rail, her ass facing me. She grips the rail as hard as she can, but I'll never drop her, though I need her to believe I will so she can admit to me what she wants.

"What are you doing? Don't kill me." I hear the fear in her tone, but that's not what I want to do to her.

If I wanted her dead, she would have been dead already. I use one hand to grip her hip and the other to unbutton her pants. After I unzip them, I yank them down to her ankles. When I remove her cotton panties, I slide my fingers inside of her pussy and she lets out a squeal.

Damn, she soaks my skin, causing my dick to ache in my pants. I knew she would get off on me controlling her and putting her life in danger like this.

"P-please, Snow. Let me go. I don't like this."

"Your pussy says otherwise. You're soaking my fingers, Blue."

She lets go of the rail and I have to hold her tighter.

"Grip the rail or you will fall."

I use my other hand to yank out my dick from my gray sweatpants, stroking it.

"We're going to play a little game," I tell her.

Despite the cold, my dick aches with the need to be inside of her.

"Snow, this is crazy! I'm not playing no goddamn game! Put me down, I'm scared!"

I ignore her. "If you don't play, I'm going to drop you."

She shakes her head, so I push her farther, causing her hair to fall over the rail. "W-what?"

"You heard me."

"This is insane. You're going to kill me because I won't play with you."

I ignore her. "Who do you belong to?"

She snaps her mouth shut, grinding her teeth, and I lean her over the rail some more.

She screams.

"Snow! You're going to drop me!"

"That's the idea."

I get on my knees, holding her in place and putting my mouth on her clit, licking her like I'm dying of thirst.

"Keep going, Snow."

I pull away from her, and she lets out a moan. Interesting. I knew she was an adrenaline junkie, but this only confirms it. She's getting off on the thrill of me having full control over her life.

I inch her farther over the rail. She's lightweight, easy for me to grab and hold on to.

"Who. Do. You. Belong. To?"

Tears well in her eyes and drip off her face.

She doesn't respond.

"Not talking, huh?"

Digging my nails into her hips, I shove my dick inside of her, while her juices drip down my balls. Her pussy grips me, milking me hard. She comes from the adrenaline rush alone.

I thrust into her as hard as I can as she moans my name.

I'm going to switch tactics.

"Who do you want?" I say, grinding my teeth.

She tries to keep herself from leaning too far over the rail, but I'm the one who has all the power here—her life is in my hands as we speak. It's up to her to admit that she wants me. Just a simple answer.

I reach over and stroke her clit, and she screams my name—loud.

"Answer the fucking question."

I lean her over the railing even more.

"You! I want you!" she says with tears in her eyes.

I fuck her hard.

"You look so beautiful when you cry, Blue. Such pretty tears for a pretty woman. You look even better coming for me on my dick."

I fuck her harder, grinding my teeth, all the while her pussy squeezes the life out of me.

My spine tingles, and my balls tighten as I pull out and shoot cum all over her ass.

I turn her around to face me. She has mascara clumps around her eyelashes, pure fear filling her eyes, and her face is pale. This is how I like to see her—scared, crying, at my mercy. I knew I could get her to bend to my will.

I pick her up and slam my mouth to hers, kissing her roughly. She stares at me as if in a daze before finally kissing me back. I place her on the cobblestone wall next to the balcony and slide my dick back inside of her, finding her slippery for me. She grips my neck hard, digging her nails into my flesh. I love the pain she inflicts on me.

She kisses me deeply again, then removes her mouth and says, "I want you. I've always wanted you."

Her words are music to my ears.

I've been waiting years for her to utter those words to me.

She yanks my hair hard, making my scalp burn, and I come inside of her this time. Thankfully, she heeded my warning when I told her that her pussy was mine, because she got on birth control not too long ago. I empty out inside of her, then pull out, letting her down on the hard concrete.

I tuck myself back into my sweatpants and carry her to the bed. Then I fuck her again.

She whimpers, moaning at the same time. I come inside of her once more, and she watches me as I pull out of her.

Complete shock washes over her a moment before she slaps me across the face with tears in her eyes. She tries to hit me again but I catch her wrist in midair, then I pin her down, pulling her hand above her head.

"How long have you wanted me, Blue?"

Digging my nails into her skin, she tries to turn her head to the side, snapping those beautiful lips shut.

"Answer me, Blue."

"Go to hell," she spits.

"You lie to yourself so much, Lyrical. Your desires, your wants. Sometimes you behave like a deprived, starved woman." I place my hand around her throat, squeezing tight.

"Please d-don't k-kill me."

This is the only way I can get her to admit her own feelings.

"You look so beautiful with fear in your eyes." I squeeze tighter, cutting off her airway. I don't want her to die on me. "Tell me and I won't kill you," I whisper in her ear.

Tears stream down her face. "Since I met you!"

I grab the handcuffs from the nightstand, and I flip her over, placing her arms behind her back.

"What are you about to do to me, Snow?"

I don't answer as I grab the clit stimulator from the drawer. I place it on her clit, and she screams at the top of her lungs, trying to move away from me.

"Who do you belong to?"

She bites down on her bottom lip, so I keep the stimulator on her.

"Motherfucker! Asshole!" she screams.

I yank the stimulator from her pussy, and tears leak down her face.

"P-please let me come. Don't torture me like this."

"Who do you belong to?"

My dick aches seeing her like this, so I grab some lube and put it over my dick and her ass crack before I lift her up on her knees.

"Please, no."

I ignore her and slide my dick in her ass. She groans, pushing on my dick, like she wants me to fuck it. She squeezes so tight around me, it feels like she's trying to push me out, so I shove forward. I'm not all the way inside of her yet.

"Please… Please… Fuck!"

I place the clit stimulator back on her clit, and she screams at the top of her lungs. I slide deep into her, making sure she gets every inch of me inside of her ass.

She's going to take this dick whether she likes it or not.

I yank her ponytail hard. "Who. Do. You. Belong. To?"

"You! I belong to you!"

CHAPTER TWENTY-FOUR

Lyrical

NOW THRUSTS INTO ME, AND I COME SO HARD, TEARS RUSH down my cheeks. When I feel him pull out, warm cum is sprayed all over my ass cheeks. He removes the clit stimulator, tosses it to the floor, then disappears to the bathroom, and walks back with a wet rag. Once he finishes wiping his cum from my ass, he wipes off his dick and he throws the washcloth into the basket. My legs feel like jelly, and I'm completely exhausted. As my eyelids feel heavy, I yank the soft blanket over my naked body.

I'm sore.

So sore.

I like it when he makes me sore.

And I'm scared of him, but it's a good fear, I suppose. I think deep down Snow's feelings for me are more than a silly crush and his behavior seems odd. He made me his sex toy, using me when it's convenient for him. He used my sketches against me, to make my fantasies real, and he is always so protective over me. I wasn't ready to admit to him that I want him, but he forced it out of me, giving me everything I want.

I like being his sex toy.

I like him dominating me.

I like every essence of him.

This is what I always wanted from Snow.

We started this school year as enemies, with him hating my guts, and I hate him for the way he treated me. I'm not sure if he thinks I killed Bailey. He made me admit my true feelings, and I don't like it. My feelings for him are spiraling out of control.

Our relationship is spiraling out of control.

I want this man.

The fucked-up version of him.

Why?

Because I've seen the ugly parts of him, and I know what I'm getting, so whatever he shows me, I can easily accept it.

I'm a glutton for the pain he inflicts on me.

The way he dangled me over the rail of the balcony, fucked me senseless, made me feel the adrenaline that I never experienced in my life, and I loved it.

He cocks his eyebrow, leaning in, stroking his knuckles against my cheek. "You keep staring at me? Why?"

He's so beautiful and unhinged at the same time. I keep staring at him until a smile tugs at the corners of his mouth. His smile makes me melt, but I school my facial expression so he can't read me.

Sighing, I bring my legs to my chest, resting my chin on my kneecaps.

"Did you always have a crush on me?"

His eyes narrow as he runs his fingers through his silky hair, keeping his gaze glued to mine. This is the first time in a long time Snow has taken forever to answer any of my questions. The silence stretches between us.

"Are you going to answer me?"

He twitches his mouth, biting the inside of his cheek. "I think it's pretty obvious that it was more than a crush."

Confusion rises within me. Bailey always told me he had a crush on me, but I never suspected he actually *liked* me.

I straighten my spine like a needle. "Then how did you feel about me before the accident?"

"Some words aren't meant to be shared."

I cock a brow. "What's that even supposed to mean?"

He sits up on his knees and our lips are so close that if I moved an inch, he could kiss me.

He grips my chin, stroking his fingers along my jaw, then his gaze goes to my lips. "You don't need to know."

I place my hands behind me, thrusting my tits in his face, but I didn't mean to. He looks down at them. My heart beats frantically in my chest as my pulse accelerates.

"I wouldn't ask the question if I didn't want the answer."

He's quiet for several moments. "I worshipped the ground you walked on back then." He yanks me by the hair gently, eyeing my lips. "I would have died for you, and I would have killed for you. Is that a good enough answer?"

I gasp at his words because I had no idea he felt that way toward me. "Now, how do you feel?"

"It's complicated. I don't know."

His words twist up inside of me, and the way he says it makes my heart beat faster.

"Are you still mad at me about the car accident?"

"I don't know." He sighs. "What were you going to ask me that night?"

I don't want to admit to him that I was going to ask him to take my virginity and to help me navigate my sexual desires, or the fact that I wanted to tell him I was in love with him.

I remember the feeling clearly as day, hoping he wouldn't reject me. "I was going to ask you to take me skating."

He shakes his head, then places his hand around my neck.

"Liar. The last time I asked you, you told me you wanted takeout from your favorite restaurant."

I shrug. "I was going to ask you to take my virginity."

I glance away, though I'm not ashamed of what I like anymore. Snow made me accept that part of myself and helped me come out of my shell. He taught me to like that side of me, and I'm forever grateful for him for that, but I'm not about to admit to him that I was in love with him at the time. I don't want to complicate our relationship any more than it already is.

Bewilderment creases his face. "You wanted me as much as I wanted you back then." He says it more to himself, as if he's confirming it for his own benefit. I don't reply because it's true.

He squeezes my neck hard, and my core dampens the silk sheets. Usually, shame comes from me liking it rough, but it doesn't come this time.

"Ask me what I always wanted from you, Lyrical. Ask me what I always wanted, and I'll reward you like a good girl."

I don't want to hear his answer, but if I don't, Snow is going to force me to ask. I'm exhausted from all the sex, and even though I want to go for another round, I don't know if my body can handle it.

"What did you always want from me, Snow?" I swallow thickly, and it feels like cotton in my mouth.

"You wanting to be mine."

CHAPTER TWENTY-FIVE

Snow

I SPEND THE WHOLE NIGHT FUCKING LYRICAL LIKE A MADMAN. I needed more of her and have gotten addicted to her so easily. She's what I think about when I first wake up and the last thing I think about when my head hits the pillow at night.

I watch her paint in her art room that I built. She loves it, and like old times, she would paint as I watch her in her element while reading a nonfiction book. She's more beautiful than anything I have ever laid my eyes on.

Once she's finished painting, I tell her we need to talk. I make my way to the couch, Lyrical covered in dried-up paint.

I always thought she was the prettiest in her natural form: no makeup, hair tied up into a bun, wearing one of my old T-shirts. She hasn't changed and she still steals my hoodies and clothes. Though I'm not going to lie to myself, I don't mind. I'd rather her wear my shit than wear another man's clothing. She flips through Netflix, biting her bottom lip while trying to find something to watch. When her eyes veer up, a slight flush creeps up to her cheeks.

I take the remote from her hand and set it on the coffee table. Her lips are red and bee-stung and I want those lips wrapped around the crown of my dick.

"Why were you at your parents' place a few days ago?"

"I knew it. You have a tracker on my phone."

"Yes, I do."

"For how long?"

"Since the first day I met you when we were told that we were going to be married. Are you spooked?"

She shakes her head. "No. It's hot that you're obsessed with me. I figured you had a tracker on me so you could keep track of me when you can't follow me on campus." She pauses. "I showed my father the picture of Bailey and the man." She nibbles on her thumbnail. "The symbol represents the mafia family but the crossed-out snake means he's not part of the mafia anymore. Also, they disbanded the sex trafficking ring."

I don't believe what I hear, so I crinkle the corner of my mouth. "That doesn't sound like Bailey, dating a mafia man."

She nods, dusting off her T-shirt. "I went through her clothing because I wanted to see what I wanted to keep of her things, and she had a shirt with the Viper logo, so I looked it up and the mafia owns it, an infamous underboss who goes by the name Dante. It's a strip joint. I have a theory, though, but you won't like it." She sits on her knees. "She was working at this strip club so she could save enough money to run away from her home. She hated Tim, by the way. She hated the whole arranged marriage deal. And she mentioned it in a joking way that one day she was going to leave everything behind and run off with her prince."

Her words are a blow to the chest and I don't want to believe them, but, deep down, I know she is right. My sister wasn't happy, and I wasn't there for her like I should have been, too busy trying to get my father's approval to hand me the Billionaire Club. I tried my best to help her with her mental illness as much as I could, but nothing I did worked. She rebelled against me.

"I wouldn't be surprised if Bailey was whoring herself to get paid, or the guy was pimping her out to feed her drug habit, too. Even though we made a pact to never do drugs again, she still did it and the last fight we had were about her popping Molly. It was about two months before the car accident. I told her we're getting married soon, that we need to get clean. I only did drugs with her so she felt like she wasn't alone, Snow. She felt like everyone was against her and I didn't want her to feel like I was too. I didn't want her to feel like no one loved her. You have to believe me, I te—"

I nod, twirling her hair around my finger. "I believe you, Blue."

This is so much to process. Since Bailey was dealing with a human trafficker, my parents weren't paying enough attention to her. In a sense, they neglected her. My baby sister was suffering in her final years, and it pushed her into the wrong hands. Whoever the guy is in the picture with the tattoo is going to suffer. I want his blood spilled. The more I learn about Bailey, the more I feel as if I failed her. I should have been there for her, protecting her.

My parents failed her—*I* failed her.

My sister needed me, and I turned a blind eye because I couldn't see her suffering. Instead of being a big brother, I shut her out.

Lyrical's eyes suddenly light up and a smile spreads across her face. She faces me with her legs crossed, and I tuck a strand of her hair behind her ear.

"I have a stupid, crazy-ass idea." She beams.

"We go to the strip club, talk to Dante, and ask questions about Bailey."

There is something that hasn't changed about Blue. She doesn't think things through. When she wants to get shit done, she never thinks about the outcome. It could be another target on her back, because the mafia doesn't like people asking questions about people they dealt with.

I grit my teeth. "No, Lyrical."

"Please, Snow."

"It could be another target on your back."

"It won't," she tells me. "Be right back."

She climbs the stairs and comes back not a minute later with a skimpy dress, suit, and a blonde wig.

"They won't know who we are if we wear a disguise. I bought this yesterday."

The idea sounds good, and she is so sure that this would work. I wouldn't forgive myself if something happened to her. My number one priority is protecting Lyrical.

"I can get Jameson to hack into their computer."

"They won't have Bailey's information on who she was dating at the time, but if we can get names at the club, we can narrow it down."

"No," I state.

"You told me we can work on this together, but you're not playing as a teammate."

I told her that, but it's my job to handle this.

"I said, no."

She frowns. "You get to have control over me in the bedroom, Snow. But you don't get to control my every move. I'm going— with or without you."

My eyes darken and rage courses through my veins. "I'll lock you in this mansion, Lyrical. Don't test me." I exhale, feeling annoyed. "Jameson and I will take care of it. We will handle it. Like we will handle the white mask man who was after you. I'm not risking your life, Lyrical. I do control your life; everything you do."

"You're not my dictator, Snow."

She pouts, and it's cute, so I grab her chin for her gaze to meet mine. "I'm the guy who is fucking your brains out every night. I'm the guy whose dick you come on all the time. You're going to have my last name soon, so yeah, I own you. Every inch of you. I catch you anywhere near the strip club, I'll punish you, Blue."

She peels my fingers from her chin. "You're unbelievable."

"You're mine. And don't forget it." I pause. "I'm hiring Russell as your bodyguard when I'm not around. He will walk you to and from classes when I can't. Until we find the white rabbit."

"Are you fucking serious, Snow? I don't need a babysitter."

"Yeah, you do. Either that or you do your classes online. The choice is up to you."

All the guilt I feel for taking my anger out on her eats at me, but I don't let it show. She was right the entire time about some-one coming after her, but I still don't know whether she did drugs and got behind the wheel that night or if she's using this as an ex-cuse and feels guilty. At this point, I don't know what to believe. She would have done anything Bailey told her to out of guilt be-cause she wanted to make her best friend happy. Sometimes, my sister would use her mental illness as a weapon to control people if she didn't get her way.

She rolls her eyes. "I'll take the bodyguard."

"Good girl."

Her phone buzzes and she grabs it from the coffee table, smiling.

"I got a D-plus on my algebra exam."

She wraps her arms around my shoulders, hugging me tight, and I slide her into my lap, squeezing her ass.

"Professor allowed me to use the notes you gave me on my exam. I wonder what made him change his mind?"

The professor kept true to his word, but I'm still keeping those photos just in case he slips up.

I gaze at her smile that was worth blackmailing him for. I'll do it all over again to see that smile on her face.

"I really didn't think I was going to pass." Tears wet her eyes. "I'm really going to graduate, thanks to your study guides. Let's celebrate! Let's go barhopping."

CHAPTER TWENTY-SIX

Lyrical

WE BARHOP, VISITING ALMOST EVERY BAR IN TOWN, AND BY the time we get to the last one, I'm ready to call it a night. Though I don't want to go back home.

Snow pours vodka down my throat. This reminds me of old times when we used to go barhopping all night and went to our respective classes the next morning drunk as fuck. Well, I would, not Snow. He has always been more responsible than me.

I pour a bottle of whiskey down his throat as he grabs a fistful of my ass, then I flop down on the leather cushion and set the bottle on the table. He pushes a strand of her hair behind my ear, then grabs me by the neck and kisses me hard before taking me to the bathroom and fucking me against the wall.

Once we're done, we leave, and my bodyguard drives us to the iconic cliff which is thirty miles away from North Haven. People from all around the world come to visit.

The sea is calm and the salty air tickles my nose. I sit on the hood of Snow's car, and he follows suit as we look at green and blue streaks of light in the pitch-black sky. Crickets chirping in the background. It's a little chilly, so I wrap my arms around myself, trying to keep warm.

Snow gets off the hood of his car and strolls to the trunk, pulling out a hoodie. When he sits next to me, he hands it to me. I yank the soft hoodie over my head, pulling it down and inhaling it.

It smells just like him, sandalwood and cinnamon.

We're quiet for a while and I bring my knees to my chest.

I can't believe I'm actually passing my college algebra class and graduation is only months from now, then I'll be getting married to Snow. I didn't expect things to spiral out of control between us the way they have, but things feel like they are back to normal between us. Living with him, I learned so much.

He's more unhinged and he's a lot sweeter than I initially thought. He has to be in control, and now I know the reason why he used to act like a possessive boyfriend whenever I talked to other men.

He wanted me.

I remove a fine strand of hair from his face, and he grabs my hand, kissing the inside of my palm.

He smiles at me. "Life is so funny. I used to crave for you to acknowledge me as the man you're going to marry instead of your best friend."

Snow is truly drunk because he doesn't usually speak about his emotions like this.

Shocked, I run my fingers through his silky hair, my gaze dropping to his lips. "I did have a crush on you," I answer honestly. "For a while. I used to get mad when you blew me off for a chick you were going to bang. I used to think, why couldn't you use me instead? Why cou—"

He places his fingers over my mouth. "The only person I fucked since I met you was Savannah."

I lean my head to the side. "What about high school? Taylor told me you two were banging."

I remember that day. I was in the locker room, and I tried so hard not to bang her head against the locker when she was bragging about Snow.

"That's a rumor she started to make herself popular. You're the only woman I always wanted."

My cheeks heat, and we're both quiet again.

How would things have been if we both admitted we wanted each other? I understood where Snow came from when he told me he didn't want to ruin our friendship. I always wanted to be accepted by him and never disappoint him.

"I accepted whatever you gave me," he reveals, gripping my chin. "I used to accept whatever piece of yourself you had given me."

"When did you know you like to dominate women in the bedroom?"

"I went to the Billionaire Club when I was seventeen and watched a man do it to a woman. In some part of the club, there is a sex room where you can watch people fuck, but the wall is a one-way mirror."

"Oh."

My skin feels heated from all the alcohol I consumed. My eyes venture to Russell, who stands by a tree, eating. I forgot he was here.

Just then, my phone buzzes in my pocket and I grab it. Glancing down, my mother's name pops up across the screen, and I hit the Decline button.

"Why are you ignoring your mother's call?" Snow stands between my legs, placing his hands on either side of me on the hood.

Tears well in my eyes but I don't want to cry. Maybe it's the alcohol in my system, but I want to know why she really doesn't support me in my dreams of opening my art gallery.

Art is supposed to be shown to the world and helps people

get out of their slumps and make them forget their worries. I always wanted to have a relationship with my mother, the way I see others have bonds with their mothers, but we never see eye to eye on a lot of shit. The only thing that makes her proud of me is my marriage to Snow. She wasn't a bad mom growing up, she supported me in whatever I wanted in life... financially. She and Daddy paid for dance lessons, piano lessons, whatever I wanted, but more than anything I crave emotional support from her. My father has always encouraged me to do my own thing, have my own hobbies. Sometimes they would bump heads because they both had different goals. Yes, my father believed in arranged marriages, but he also encouraged me to go after my dreams. But my mother? She had a stick up her ass when it came to any dream I wanted to pursue.

Snow strokes my cheek, wiping away my tears with his thumb.

"She's not happy I'm in college. She thinks my duty is to lie down and have your children and be a trophy wife, but I don't want that. There is more to life than being your trophy wife, no offense. I want to travel the world and be kid-free, maybe until our thirties at least." I shake my head. "Sometimes, I think my dreams are silly. When I told her Bailey and I wanted to start an art gallery together, she was livid. I feel as if she wants to put me into a box and keep me there."

He shakes his head. "I think she wants what's best for you, in her own way."

I tilt my head to the side. "How? She doesn't know what's best for me. How could lying down for a man, bearing a child for him, and losing myself be best for me?"

He strokes the back of my hair, tilting my chin to look at him. "Do you know why we have arranged marriages in elite societies and the Billionaire Club?"

"Because of greed. It keeps the money going."

He nods. "Yes, but they do it to build structure and image.

Without a family, the gentleman's club would go up in flames because there needs to be a structure."

"Then why aren't women owners of the club, why does it have to be all men?"

"Because when it first started, women didn't have rights and men brought on so much power. I think if my father wasn't married to my mother, the Billionaire Club wouldn't be as successful. We wouldn't be able to have the structure it now has."

"I thought it was like a boys' club for rich snobs who want to get their dicks wet."

He chuckles against my forehead. "Yes, Blue. It is. And to network with other rich people, so they can keep their generational wealth going."

He plants a kiss against my skin, and butterflies dance in my stomach.

"You can't fuck around on me at the club."

"I've never had the thought before." He crinkles his nose. "Speak to your mother and tell her how you feel. She has her reasons for how she feels. Trust me."

"I don't know if I'm ready to speak to her."

"If you don't, I will," he warns.

"Fine. I will."

"Good girl."

My gaze meets his. "Do you believe in my artwork? Do you believe it will be possible to have a successful art career?"

"Yes, Blue. My girl can do whatever she puts her mind to," he says before he kisses me slowly.

CHAPTER TWENTY-SEVEN

Snow

MY FIANCÉE THINKS SHE'S SLICK. SHE PURPOSELY LEFT HER phone at home so I won't track her every move, but little does she know that when she pulled that stunt with Melvin, I had my family doctor give her a shot under the skin of her right ass cheek, and I can track her everywhere she goes just in case she loses her phone. It's a precaution, so if she goes anywhere I tell her not to go, she will be punished for it.

She's having dinner with Professor Carter without informing me because she knew I wouldn't approve of it, so I smooth out my tie and wear my dark, navy suit. I want to match her navy dress she decided to wear for this so-called dinner. When I saw her getting dressed, I asked her where she was heading, to which she replied she was having dinner with her friends.

Once I make it to the restaurant, which is located on the other side of town, I spot her sitting next to him, along with two other girls.

I want to cut off his tongue and watch him choke on his own blood for having my girl's attention. For her putting her hand on his shoulder and throwing her head back, laughing. Shit isn't that damn funny for her to be laughing the way she is. She's only supposed to laugh at my jokes. I might kill him for putting that smile on her face, because no other man should put a smile on her face *but me.*

I maneuver my way to the crowded dining area, then pull up a chair from an empty table and squeeze in between Lyrical and Professor Carter. Frowning, he smooths out his dark hair.

I drop a kiss on her forehead. "I'm sorry I'm late, baby. I had some shit to take care of."

Lyrical glares at me as if she wants to poke my eyes out. "What are you doing here?"

I bring the back of her hand to my lips and plant kisses on her knuckles. "I'm here to support you. He's displaying your artwork in his art gallery, right? I thought I'd show you my support."

Her heel mushes my loafer, and I lean down, whispering in her ear, "You're going to be punished for having dinner with another man."

She digs her heel into my loafer harder, and I bite down on my lip from the pain. When I glance at Carter, his smiles deflates, and when my gaze veers to the other two women at the table, they blush.

The waitress places a bowl in the center of the table. I grab the warm buttery bread, tear a piece, and feed it to Lyrical as she glares at me.

"Are you Revi 'Snow' Williams?" one of the women asks.

She's wearing a minidress with her tits barely covered up, so I'm assuming she's using her body to get what she wants.

I spot Lyrical eyeballing the one who asked me the question. "In the flesh."

"Can we get a picture of y—"

"Hell no," Lyrical snaps. "If you want a picture of him, you need to look online."

Jealousy looks good on her. I actually love it.

"Not right now," I say. "You're not wearing your engagement ring, Blue."

She hid her engagement ring and I looked everywhere for it. She's going to admit she's my fiancée sooner rather than later.

"You give me back my sketchbook, and only then I'll wear my ring," she whispers in my ear. "Excuse us," Lyrical says to the rest of the table, tugging on my arm. I follow her outside of the restaurant as people casually scroll along the sidewalk, the streetlamps illuminating the pavement. "How did you find me?"

I grab her phone from my back pocket and hand it to her. "You forgot this."

She folds her arms across her chest, pushing up her breasts. "I didn't forget it, I knew you would act crazy if you knew I was having dinner with another man, so I didn't want you to read into it."

I did a background check on Professor Carter. He likes them young—college age young. I had Jameson hack into his personal laptop, and he has endless footage of himself fucking different college-aged women.

"You don't think it's odd that he only invited girls to this dinner?"

"No, they are all in my art class, and Professor Carter is married and has a child. He wouldn't hit on me."

Yeah, I don't believe it. He's looking for his next victim. And he's not married—not according to the background check. He's not in a relationship with anyone else, nor does he have a child.

"If you're going to sit with me, shut up and don't ruin this for me. I need my art in this gallery."

"I don't understand why you don't want to use my connections or your parents."

She places her hands on her hips. "Because my identity is not going to be tied to you or our families. I want people to actually love my artwork."

I get what she says. She wants her own identity.

"Behave, Snow. Please, for the love of God, don't threaten him. Or try to harm him."

"No promises."

"Ugh."

I follow her back to the table, sitting between her and Professor Carter, and pull Lyrical so close to me that she's damn near on my lap. She looks animated, telling him why she wants a spot in the gallery so bad.

It pisses me off the way he keeps looking at my fiancée's breasts.

I ball my fists under the table.

I have to behave; I can't cut his head off with a bunch of witnesses around.

Do you know how hard it is for me to not punch the bastard for keeping his eyes glued to her?

"Excuse me, I have to go to the ladies' room." Lyrical stands up, and I watch her disappear along with the other women until they are out of earshot.

"This is what's going to happen, you're going to choose my fiancée's painting to go inside of the gallery."

"With all due respect, you don't tell me what to do," Carter snaps.

I yank him by the collar, bunching up his shirt.

"With all due disrespect, I did a background check on you, and you're not married. So you lied to her. I don't know what your endgame is with my girl, but if you lay a finger on her, or if so much as a hair is out of place on her head, I'll gut you like a fish. You keep your contact with her to a minimum. Keep your eyes off my fiancée's breasts or I'll cut you up into pieces, then dump your remains in the ocean." I let him go. "Fix your fucking face before she comes back to the table."

Before he can respond, the girls are back, taking their seats, and Lyrical sits next to me, eyeing me suspiciously, before her eyes go to Carter.

"Is everything all right?" Her tone is skeptical.

I nod and then step on Carter's shoe under the table.

"Yeah. Um, sure," Professor Carters says before standing up from the table. "It's been an evening, but I have to go." He buttons up his dress jacket. "See you ladies later."

I watch him make his way to the front entrance.

"I could use a drink, too," the blonde girl says.

"Me too," Lyrical agrees. "We're having a girls' night for my bachelorette party and you two are welcome to come."

"Really?" The dark-haired girl's eyes beam.

"Yes, the more, the merrier."

I tilt my head to the side. "What bachelorette party?"

"The one Winter is hosting for me. She wants to bring male strippers to serve us drinks in their boxers."

She's trying to get a rise out of me because I crashed her dinner. My little fireball loves revenge just as much as I do.

A smirk forms at the corner of her mouth.

I whisper in her ear, "If you allow any man at your party that's not security, it's going to be a bloodbath."

She shrugs her shoulders and rolls her eyes. "And we're going to have good food too. Men giving us a peep show as well. My friend said she's only hiring men with big dicks. The best party ever."

"Punishing you will be so much fun," I murmur against her temple.

Once dinner is over and we make it home, that's exactly what I do. Tie her up to the bed and fuck her.

CHAPTER TWENTY-EIGHT

Lyrical

SINCE SNOW WON'T LET ME DO THINGS WITHOUT HIM WHEN it comes to solving Bailey's death, I guess I'll have to sneak behind his back and look for the answers myself. We're supposed to be a team and work on finding out who Bailey's boyfriend is together, but he's not being a team member.

So, I had Winter keep my phone with her and if Snow texts me, she'll text him back on my behalf. I'm not going to wait around on him.

I understand he's trying to protect me from harm, but I can take care of myself. I don't need him to control every aspect of my life. Just in the bedroom.

I met a girl online who worked at the strip club with Bailey, and I told her to meet me on neutral grounds at a park, because I don't want to meet her on mafia turf, let alone go to a strip club without Snow being present. They are not so kind to outsiders and people asking questions. It'll put a target on my back.

I sit on a bench, watching people walk along the trails. It's mid-October and the leaves on the oak trees are bright autumn colors.

I zip up my leather jacket as the cool breeze nips at my cheeks. A woman wearing a trench coat and fishnet stockings, carrying a backpack, waltzes up to me and holds out her hand.

"Hi, I'm Rachel."

She's gorgeous with her pastel blue hair reaching her shoulders, with two rings in each side of her nose. I slip my palm into hers and shake her hand.

"I'm Lyrical."

Nodding, she lets go of my palm and sits beside me. Her expensive perfume invades my nostrils. She smells sweet like a daisy.

"So… you knew Bailey?"

She nods, crosses her legs over the other, and stuffs her hands into her coat pockets. Her deep brown pupils radiate so much pain.

"She worked at the strip club with me. She was saving up money to leave her lifestyle, to leave her abusive boyfriend."

The fact that Bailey felt like she needed to run away leaves a gigantic hole in my chest. Why didn't she go to her parents or Snow and tell them about the situation she was in? I'm sure they would have murdered him. Maybe she was trying to protect him. I've researched abusive relationships and I read that the victims would go to great lengths to protect their abusers.

Rachel looks me up and down, and a weak smile spreads across her face. "You must have been her best friend and roommate?"

"Yes."

I watch a teenager on rollerblades glide past us. The sky is turning an inky blue, and the sound of the wind fills the silence between us for a brief moment.

"She spoke about you a lot, told me you were getting engaged to her brother."

I don't respond, and she sighs.

"She never wanted to disappoint you or her brother."

Tears well in my eyes. "She was never a disappointment to us. We just wanted what was best for her."

She pats my back. "I was helping her with an escape plan. I was in an abusive relationship, too, with an underboss. He used to be in the mafia as well as her ex-boyfriend."

"Did you get his name?"

"No, but I do know he went to North Haven University. She said he was popular on campus and they couldn't be seen in public because of her arranged marriage to a rich guy. A few weeks before her death, he found her at a bus station leaving. She said she wanted to keep her baby, but he was forcing her to get an abortion. He promised her that if she went through with it, he would treat her good. The beating got worse after she aborted her child."

Bailey suffered so much, and I wasn't there to help her, to protect her. She suffered in silence, wanting an escape from her new life. I imagine her being scared and alone, and the ache in my chest builds.

She removes her backpack and hands me a bunch of Bailey's stuff. Tears gather in her eyes, matching mine. "I feel bad. I feel like I could have done more. I… He used to force her to have sex with other men. She used to tell me how he would invite her to parties with rich men from the Billionaire Club and they would run a train on her."

I feel like I'm suffocating from her words. I suspect he was pimping her out since she was involved with someone who has no morals.

We both hug each other as tears leak down our faces, and my head hurts so much from crying. I feel worn out. I pull away from her and use the back of my thumbs to wipe under my eyes. I feel my mascara clumping around my eyelids, and I'm sure my face looks like a racoon.

"It was nice meeting you, Lyrical, but I have to go to work." I walk her to her car, where we say our goodbyes.

Once I'm in my own car, I search through the bag that Rachel gave me and I find stripper clothing, pictures of me and Bailey and Snow at a house party—and an ultrasound of a baby, I think. My tears wet the picture. There's also a key, and a sketch of a house with an address scribbled at the bottom. I toss the bag in my back seat.

I can't keep the tears at bay, no matter what I do.

With the bag slung over my shoulders, I walk into the living room to find Snow standing by the window.

Anger colors his faces and his arms are folded across his bare chest. He stalks up to me, yanks me by the arm, and assesses me from head to toe.

"You met a woman at a park? Why?"

How the hell does he know where I was when I left my phone with Winter?

Peeling his fingers from my arm, I head to the kitchen, open the fridge, grab the jug of lemonade, and pour it into a crystal glass. "I left my phone with Winter, because I knew you were tracking me. Wait. How did you know I met some girl? I used Lilac's phone to text her."

He stands directly in front of me, blocking me from leaving the kitchen. "Don't worry about it. Just know I have eyes and ears everywhere."

Slowly, I swallow big gulps of the sweet beverage. "Stalking is a crime, Snow. I don't mind you doing it, but I need my privacy."

"It's not a crime if I don't get caught."

"Spoken like a true criminal," I mock.

There isn't any point in arguing with him, he's going to do what he wants—he's been like this since we were teenagers.

"She knew Bailey. She confirmed what we already knew. There is an address Bailey had written down on a sketch and a key she gave me. I think it's to her ex's house. I'm going there."

"No, you're not. I'll do everything to protect you, Blue. Even if it means I lock you in this house."

I shake my head. "You and your controlling ways, I swear.

First, you popped up at my dinner with Professor Carter, and now you're mad because I'm sneaking behind your back. You promised, Revi, but you're just projecting your fears on losing me."

He cups my face, rubbing his fingers along my bottom lip. "What would have happened if the girl you met robbed you? What about if someone kidnapped you? The park you went to is sketchy. You're a small woman with little protection, and I'm not supposed to worry about you?"

I shrug. "I don't know, but it didn't happen. I can't live my life on what-ifs, Snow. You can't protect me from everything."

"I will and I can. You can't stop me."

We used to fight about this all the time, and though I love that he wants to protect me, he has to trust me enough that I can take care of myself.

This conversation isn't going anywhere, so I kick off my shoes, set them by the couch, then I yank the hair tie and my locks fall over my shoulders like a waterfall as I comb my fingers through my hair.

He follows me up the stairs, as I stroll to the bathroom, and he turns the golden faucet to the tub, sighing. I remove my clothes and toss them on the floor. He watches me with his hands folded across his chest.

Tears wet my eyes and I quickly wipe them away.

"What is it?"

"Bailey…" I want to cut myself again. I don't want to feel this pain anymore. I want to release my blood that's in my body because it makes me feel like I'm releasing my sins, my guilt. Keeping my eyes on the makeup bag with my razors, I quickly shake my head. If Snow found out I bought new razors and started hurting myself again, he'd be pissed. He told me he would cut himself if he found out I started again, and I don't want him to hurt himself because of me. It's an addiction that I can't shake. I need to feel the pain. The hurt. "Rachel told me she had a plan to leave, that she was in a relationship with someone from North Haven University." I can't fight the sob that wants to burst free. "You remember when Bailey said she was going to London with Tim for a few weeks?"

He nods, sitting on the edge of the tub.

"I suspect she was getting beat up so much that she couldn't show her face. She really was pregnant. She was leaving him because she wanted a better life for their child, and he found her and beat her up."

Snow doesn't respond but has a murderous look on his face, the one he makes when he wants to kill someone.

"I should have seen the signs. Why didn't I see the signs? Why didn't she tell me she needed a way out? I would have gotten her out of here, I would have given all of my trust fund money to her. I would have saved her."

Snow's quiet, staring at me.

"We both failed her." His tone is low. "Bailey always went to great lengths to protect the people she loved, and she loved him. That's why she never told us. She knew I would have killed him. When I find him, I'm going to do what I have to do to him. His death is going to be a slow one."

Snow removes his pajama pants and boxers and slides into the tub, causing the water to overflow to the tiles.

I need a distraction from this pain. The hole in my chest has grown to the size of the Atlantic Ocean. I fight the urge to not harm myself.

"Use me as your fuck toy."

He strokes my cheeks, kisses me roughly, then he grabs my neck, squeezing hard and coming close to cutting off my airway. He knows I want to be dominated by him, for him to have full control over my body. He lets go of me, yanks me by the arm and out of the tub, and carries me over his shoulders before tossing me on the bed. Snow grabs some zip ties and duct tape from the drawer and restrains my arms and legs. He presses the tape against my mouth. When he flips me over onto my front, he bends my knees into the soft mattress, positioning my ass in the air. I feel the head of his dick nudging the entrance of my pussy, and I groan. Snow has been my addiction, and I love when he uses me like he wants, giving in to my fantasies.

He slides inside of me, hitting a wall, then he slides out, yanking my hair so hard my scalp stings, fucking me until tears flow down my cheeks.

CHAPTER TWENTY-NINE

Snow

JAMESON WALKS BEHIND ME AS I OPEN THE DOOR TO WHITE Rabbit's house with the key Lyrical received from Rachel. This happens to be the exact same address which was written on Bailey's sketch.

I use my fingers to close my nostrils, because it smells like cat piss and shit in here. The place is fucking dirty and moldy food lies on the table. I make my way to the living room, finding someone sitting on the recliner facing the opposite direction. I remove my gun from the back of my pants and aim it at him. Jameson does the same. When we walk in front of the chair, I find June's mouth hanging open, a gigantic hole through his forehead. Maggots and flies feast on his rotting brain. He's been sitting here for a while.

Slowly, I lift his shirt, and I see a snake tattoo with an X over it, just like in the picture Lyrical told me about. So he's the one who was abusing my sister. He probably was hanging around Lyrical so he could kill her as well, which makes sense as to why they were at a football party before they came to mine the night of the accident.

Rage fills me, so I shoot fresh bullets into his chest. I don't care if he's already dead, and now I feel like my revenge was robbed from me.

"Someone got to him before we did," Jameson murmurs.

This sucks because I can't torture him and figure out why he wanted Lyrical dead. Why did he have a hit on her? Lyrical believes he thought she knew too much about Bailey's death. I glance around the room, and I spot a cat hissing at me. Shaking my head, I walk farther down the hallway, and I don't know what I'm looking for, but I'm hoping to find some answers to my sister's death.

"Snow, come back here. You want to see this," Jameson shouts.

I follow his voice and I walk into a room with different computer screens and a file cabinet. Jameson shoots the cabinet open, and I grab a file and see pictures of different women and their information. This motherfucker was a stalker. I search through the files to see if my sister's information is there, and I find it. I spot a few photos of her chained to the bed, ones where she's giving a blow job while getting fucked in the ass, and I want to vomit.

When I flip the file open, it has a record of her abortion clinic, and how many men she has been with.

"He was Bailey's boyfriend," I tell Jameson.

He's completely speechless, not knowing what to say, so he picks up a chair, tossing it against the wall. I suspected Jameson was in love with my sister. When she was alive, he often looked at her with love in his eyes. He wasn't brave enough to voice his feelings because she was already promised to someone else, and if he had ever gotten close to her, I would have killed him.

Jameson breaks in to the computer and finds pictures of Lyrical, but there's no evidence of a car accident. I check over and over again, searching through the files.

Maybe she was high on Molly and believed she saw someone. It's okay if she was, but I need for her to admit it to herself.

Sometimes, when people are traumatized, they don't remember doing things and tend to block out certain memories or form false memories to cope.

When I tuck Bailey's folder under my arm, we head outside, and I sit on the hood of the vehicle as Jameson grabs a gas can from the trunk of the SUV.

"I'm going to torch the place so it won't leave any evidence we were here." He disappears inside, and several seconds later, he rushes back outside. It's a good thing June lives out in the middle of nowhere away from North Haven. My phone buzzes in my breast pocket and a message pops up from Lyrical.

> **Blue: We're waiting for you. The photo shoot is about to start.**

I almost forgot we have a photo shoot with *Vogue* magazine for our engagement.

> **Me: On my way.**

I see red as I ball up my fist, digging my nails into my palm. I want my revenge, but whoever killed him must be seeking their own justice. Now, I feel defeated for not making June pay myself.

Thirty minutes later, Jameson drops me off at my parents' mansion and I make my way to the backyard, seeing the camera crew setting up the equipment.

Lyrical looks gorgeous in her beautiful black dress and I watch as Nora speaks to Clemon. I spot my mother and father hugging each other. My father sees me and stomps my way.

"Where ha—"

"We need to talk. Now," I snap.

The entire time I tried to tell him that Bailey had a boyfriend, but he didn't listen. Sometimes my father lives in a bubble and refuses to acknowledge what others are going through.

"I don't have time for your foolishness. Let's take these damn pictures and ge—"

"Get the fuck out," I yell at the camera crew. "We have to do this another day."

"What has gotten into y—"

"I found Bailey's boyfriend. He was killed," I scream at my father's face. I never raise my voice at him.

Everyone remains silent, and Lyrical comes up to me. I hug her tight.

"Let's take this conversation inside," Father demands.

We follow him to the living room, and I sit on the couch. Lyrical tries to sit next to me, but I place her on my lap instead. She looks sheepishly at her father.

"What did you find?" my father asks, leaning against the mantelpiece.

I offer him the folder from my seated position, and he flips through it.

"There are pictures of Bailey and Lyrical. He was following both of them. June Jones was her boyfriend." I look at Lyrical and her face turns pale. "He wanted to kill you for a reason, maybe he thought you knew something about him abusing Bailey."

"Why didn't you let me know?" Clemon asks, folding his arms across his chest, watching my arm around Lyrical's waist.

I always had a lot of respect for my future father-in-law, and he always treated me like I was his son, even when he used to catch me sneaking into Lyrical's bedroom. He used to tell us to use protection and close the door.

"With all due respect, Lyrical is mine to protect. She's no longer yours to protect, not since the moment we first met."

He nods and straightens his spine. "Understood. But anything that goes on with my daughter, I should be the first to know. Are we clear?"

"Yes, sir."

Nora sits next to us, wrapping her arms around her daughter and crying silently. My mother looks so distraught, tears falling down her face.

My father keeps his eyes glued to mine.

"Did you find out something about the car accident? Any proof we were set up?" Lyrical wonders.

I shake my head. "I have a theory, but you're not going to like it."

"What is it?"

I tuck a strand of hair behind her ear and stroke my knuckles across her delicate face. "Maybe you weren't drugged. Maybe you told yourself you were to cope with your trauma."

"Bu—"

"I think he's right, sweetheart," Clemon says, interrupting me. "I called every precinct in town, and no one pulled you over. There wasn't any evidence of your tags being ran in the system. It's okay to admit that you made a mistake. We're not holding it against you."

"But… but… I wouldn't make this up. I wouldn't lie. I don't remember taking any drugs before driving." She sobs uncontrollably, so I pull her head close to my shoulder, stroking her back and squeezing her gently.

My father frowns in disgust, while my mother looks away. Nora strokes her shoulders, soothing her close friend.

"We handled the situation. You went to grief counseling and rehab. We forgave you," her father states, hugging her tight.

My mother gives her a hug as well, then she keeps her eyes glued to my father who walks out of the living room.

"I lost my first daughter; I don't want to lose my second daughter," my mother whispers. "We will get through this. I've been taking my antidepressants and working on my depression to help with the grief. We'll heal in due time."

Lyrical cries hysterically, shaking her head no. She wanted to believe her story so bad, and it's okay. I've been too hard on her, I realize, and I didn't take the time to think about how the car accident affected her. I was blinded by rage, because I felt like she took something from me—but not anymore.

I bring her chin to face my way so she has to look at me. "I forgive you, Lyrical. It's okay."

CHAPTER THIRTY

Lyrical

I LIE IN THE TUB, STARING AIMLESSLY AT THE CEILING. THERE wasn't any evidence I was drugged or proof I was pulled over. Everyone back at Snow's parents' house thought I was losing it, except for Snow's father. He looked at me with disgust and left like his ass was on fire. I'm disgusted with myself too.

All the pain I felt over Bailey's death comes crashing inside of me.

Rage.

Sorrow.

Guilt.

The fucking guilt.

It was all in my head because I didn't want to come to grips with the fact that I killed my best friend—that I'm responsible for the car accident. I've never had a bad trip when taking drugs before. I've never experienced hallucinations. I don't remember anything about the car accident. Maybe I'm losing my mind.

I killed my best friend.

It's all my fault.

There isn't any excuse for my actions. I let everyone around me down, and I need to pay for what I've done. I'm glad of Snow's wrath, because I deserved it.

His mother wouldn't be depressed, trying to kill herself.

My parents wouldn't have to look at a fuckup.

I step out of the tub, grab my cotton towel, and wrap it around my body as I glance at myself in the mirror. I look at the broken girl who wants to feel something other than empty and numb.

I need to cut myself. I need to make this pain go away, so I tear the plastic wrapper, remove the fresh blade, and slice the inside of my thigh. I feel pure euphoria and relief, so I do it again. I slice my tender flesh, watching the bright red blood drip down onto the white tile floor. It feels so good to redirect my pain, to relieve myself from the anger, the guilt, and rage that I feel. It feels as if all of my emotions are draining out of me, along with my sins.

But this is temporary. This feeling of ecstasy, of relief, will only last as long as I continue to cut myself. I'm trying to catch a high that I will never reach and every time I cut myself, the wound has to get deeper and deeper.

The door flies open and Snow strides in.

"What do you…" He trails off, his eyes dropping down to the blade in my hand, then the blood on the floor.

Shame covers me like a cozy blanket, so I toss the blade into the sink and turn the faucet on to clean it off. Staring at him through the mirror, I notice he doesn't take his eyes off me. I expect disappointment to shine in his mismatched eyes, but it doesn't show. His face is blank.

"What did I tell you about what's going to happen if I catch you cutting yourself?" His tone is firm, smooth like expensive bourbon.

Tears rush down my cheeks, and I don't even realize I'm

crying until I dart out my tongue and lick my lips, tasting the salty drops.

"Please leave me alone. I don't need a fucking lecture."

He doesn't respond, only pulling me into his arms, kissing my forehead, resting his chin on the top of my head. We stay glued to each other for several seconds, but it feels like forever.

When I pull away, I wrap my arms around my chest, ignoring the agony of pain from my wounds.

"I destroyed our lives. I... I... Bailey... How could I be so stupid? June... he was right up under my nose, and I didn't find it weird that he was into me. Or he was being too nice to me."

I couldn't believe it when Snow told me he was Bailey's boyfriend; he was smiling in my face as if he didn't even know who she was. God, I was so fucking stupid. It explains why he was hellbent on trying to get close to me, even when Snow threatened him to stay away from me. I figured he didn't value his life, or he was just fearless.

Snow ignores me, takes the blade from the sink, and slices his forearm. The bright red blood decorates his tan skin, dripping onto the counter. Shaking my head, I grab a cotton towel and wrap it around his forearm.

"Snow, why would you do that? Don't harm yourself because of me!" I yell.

"I meant every word—if you bleed, I bleed, Blue."

I thought he was only saying that to get me to stop. He studies my inner thigh and counts how many times I sliced myself, then he proceeds to cut his arm two more times.

Tears well in my eyes as more blood drips. At least the cuts aren't too deep to the point he needs stitches. I snatch the blade away and toss it into the trash can.

"You're a stupid man," I yell at him. "I don't like to see you hurt."

"Now you know how I feel."

I wipe the tears with the back of my hand. "Fine. I won't cut myself again. Just please stop hurting yourself because of me. I'm not worth it."

He cups my face, stroking his thumb over my bottom lip. "You're worthy of me to bleed for, Blue. You're worth the pain I inflict on myself."

His words turn me into a puddle of goo.

We stare at each other in silence for several seconds before Snow disappears from the bathroom. He comes back with a pair of handcuffs and secures them on my wrists, the silver metal digging into my flesh, drawing pain. He removes the towel from my body, tossing it to the floor.

He leads me to the bedroom and he pushes me forward until I land on my back. Fear rushes through me like a tidal wave because I don't know if this will be the time he pushes me beyond my limits. He grabs melting wax from the nightstand that I didn't realize he was burning.

My eyes light up in horror. "What are you about to do to me?"

"There are safer ways to inflict pain without you harming yourself."

I crinkle my nose. "This doesn't feel safe."

"Neither is cutting yourself. How far are you going to cut yourself… until you kill yourself? Until you cut an artery and bleed out?"

He does have a point. The more I cut myself, the more the wound gets deeper and deeper. It's never enough. After every cut, I feel like it's not enough.

He slowly pours the scorching hot wax onto my breast and blows on it. It's so painful that I bite down on my lip to keep from screaming at the top of my lungs. The wax starts to cool off and it feels warm, clinging to my skin. I didn't know I would like it so much.

"Do it again," I whisper.

He pours a little bit onto my nipple and it's just as painful, but once it starts to cool off, it feels so good. Snow wraps his fingers around my neck and spreads my legs apart, removing his dick from his boxers.

"I love to see the tears in your eyes from the pain I inflict on you. You're going to take this dick like a good girl."

"Please."

"Already begging for me, I see. I love seeing you beg."

He kisses me down to my breasts, then licks my nipple without the wax, and I become so soaking wet. Desire blossoms in my stomach and my core tingles. He pours more wax on my nipples, and I thrash like a fish out of water.

"So beautiful. So mine."

He thrusts inside of me, not giving me time to adjust to his length, and I shake my wrists, wanting the handcuffs off so I can run my fingers through his hair.

I wrap my legs around his body as he takes long, deep strokes inside of me as I scream his name. My nipples tighten and I feel the wax flaking on my skin.

"You take this dick like a good girl."

Several moments later, he pulls out and comes all over my stomach. He maneuvers me so I'm on my knees and shoves his dick inside of my mouth, hitting the back of my throat. I choke and gag, spit dribbling down my chin, and every time I swallow, I feel his dick get deeper and deeper.

"That's it. Choke on my dick, babe."

He grabs a fistful of my hair and pushes me hard on his cock. My scalp stings in a way I love.

I'm struggling to breathe, so I inhale through my nose as bile threatens to come up.

This is the wrong time to puke.

"Fuck. Your mouth feels so fucking good, Lyrical."

He fucks my mouth until my throat is sore, then he yanks out and comes all over my face.

"Such a pretty face."

My core is wetter than the ocean. When I try to swallow, I feel as if I have a sore throat.

"Such a pretty little toy. Lie back down," he orders.

I do as he says, lying on my back.

"Don't ever cut this beautiful body again."

He kisses the wounds on my thigh, and a shiver snakes up my spine as he makes his way to my clit. He slides his fingers inside of me. He licks my clit as if he's in need, and instantly, I come so hard, exhaustion overtakes me.

My core throbs as he licks me up as if he's dying of thirst.

And before I know it, my eyes are closed, and I slip into a deep sleep.

CHAPTER THIRTY-ONE

Snow

MY FATHER TOLD ME TO MEET HIM IN HIS STUDY AT THE mansion because he needed to speak to me about something important. I hate coming here; it brings back memories of him beating me when I disobeyed him. It brings back memories of Bailey. We both hated living here and we often talked about burning this place down to the ground once the mansion is handed over to me.

I roll my shoulders back and exhale. I don't want to deal with his shit. I push the wooden door open to his office and spot him standing in front of the floor-to-ceiling window with his hands behind his back, gazing out at the sea.

"You wanted to see me?"

He turns around and eyes me up and down, then flops down in the leather chair. He grabs a bottle of his whiskey and downs it like he's dying of thirst. I notice there are hickeys on his neck, and I want to know if my mother knows about the affairs he has at the club. Most men go there to cheat on their wives, living a double life. When I become the CEO of the company, I'm not touching anyone except for Lyrical.

Speaking of Lyrical, she has gone into a bout of deep sadness and blames herself for the death of my sister. I feel hurt for her, and rage about the fact I couldn't get my revenge on June. I should have been the one to watch the life leave his eyes. I was too focused on Professor Carter that I didn't think June would be the one who killed my sister. I just thought he was an arrogant-ass jock who couldn't take the hint that Lyrical belonged to me.

"Your mother is going to stay with her sister in San Francisco for a while," my father says calmly.

Good for her, I'm glad she's getting away from his sorry ass. I glance around the office, noticing he still has his degree that he received from North Haven University hanging on the wall. Yet he removed all the pictures of Bailey, as if she didn't exist, with only pictures of himself displayed. He's truly not a family man. Sometimes, I suspect he regrets having a family. But the rules are, if you want to have a share of the club, you have to get married. A stupid-ass rule, in my opinion.

"Your sister suffered so much, we didn't pick up the signs that she was abused." He opens his drawer and hands me pictures. "This is what June was doing to her."

I search through them: pictures of Bailey with a black eye, busted nose, split lips. He yanks out his phone and shows me a video of a tall man, raping her, so I snatch his phone from him and slam it against the desk.

"Where the hell did you get this stuff?"

"The PI I hired found these in the shed in the back of the house where June lived. The ex-mafia men never really stopped selling women, they just got good at hiding it. My PI said they are still kidnapping girls from South Haven, their own turf. The person who killed June was Dante. He found out what he was doing to the girls at his strip club." For the first time in my life, my father looks defeated. "Our family hasn't gotten the justice we deserve. We didn't know she was being abused, but it doesn't change the fact that Lyrical cost me a thirty-million-dollar deal."

I frown in confusion, running my fingers through my hair. "How did sh—"

"The car accident. Bailey's arranged marriage to Tim. I was going to give Bailey to Tim for thirty million dollars and forty percent of his parents' business."

My father never cared about our well-being, as long as he made more money. We're just dollar bills for him to use to gain capital.

"Are you still seeking revenge on Lyrical for the car accident?"

His words catch me off guard. I had no idea he knew what I was doing to her. I don't feel as much rage as I did at the start of the school year. And no, I'm no longer mad at her.

"How did you know?"

He picks up his crystal glass, smells the liquor inside, and downs it, before slamming it against the desk.

"Because you were taught to seek vengeance on anyone who harms our family."

He leans back into the leather seat and rests his hand on the armrest.

I shake my head. "No, not anymore. I'm going to be married to her soon, and I don't want to spend the rest of our lives hating each other."

"You have a duty to protect this family." He rocks in the chair. "You're going to kill her. I'm giving you until the end of the semester. You will marry Savannah instead. She will be your new bride. Her parents are offering me a better deal for her. They are giving me forty percent of their business as well as fifty million dollars."

I'm not going to kill Lyrical, and I'm definitely not marrying Savannah. He's out of his rabid-ass mind if he believes I will agree to his bullshit. I need to kill Savannah because she's now getting in the way of my arranged marriage to Lyrical.

"She has cost this family a great deal of pain. That girl deserves to be in a body bag." My father pours himself more bourbon and sips it slowly this time, watching me carefully above the rim of the glass, daring me to challenge him.

"I'm not going to kill Lyrical, and I don't want Savannah."

"You will, or you won't inherit the club."

I smooth out my tie and grip the armrest until my knuckles turn white. "Fuck you and your club."

I get up from the chair, turning my back to him.

"You've got until the end of the semester," he reminds me.

I turn around, trying to keep my cool and not bash his skull in, attempting not to murder my own father out of pure rage, but we don't need another scandal. If I kill him, his friend who works for the DA would bury me in prison, and the other owners of the club won't take too kindly to me killing him. I need to find a way around it. I go up to him, grab him by the collar of his shirt, and slam him against the glass wall behind him.

"I said fucking no."

He cocks an eyebrow. "You're getting bold."

"What? You're not going to strike me like you did before, because this time I'm not going to be so kind. The last time I held off was because you're my father, but I'll kill you if you go anywhere near Lyrical."

Rage grows in his orbs. "You would choose a bitch over your own family?"

I showed him my weakness, and he knows that Lyrical is my Achilles' heel, but I don't care.

"Yes. I'll choose her over you. Fuck you, Revi."

He shoves me off him.

"Listen to me carefully, son. You have two options. You kill her or I kill you both. The choice is up to you."

CHAPTER THIRTY-TWO

Lyrical

T HE CLUB IS SO LOUD I CAN'T HEAR MYSELF THINK. LILAC
and Winter decided to throw me a bachelorette party at the
club, and I have so many guards posted, watching me like a
hawk, and Snow wouldn't tell me the reason why I need a security
detail around me. He said there may be a new threat arising and
he is being precautious. I think he's hiding something from me
but doesn't want me to worry.

"What's with the security?" Lilac asks, before sipping her
beverage.

She wears a black halter neck dress with matching heels, and
her hair is tied up in a neat bun.

Nothing gets past her.

I shrug. "It's for extra protection. Snow hired them."

The music is so loud my chest vibrates along with the beat,
and lights flash from green to orange to blue. I dance with Winter
and Lilac, and the girls from the dinner with Professor Carter the

other night can't make it. It's like they all disappeared. When I asked Professor Carter about them, he told me one dropped his class because he wouldn't sleep with her, and the other one transferred to another institution because her family couldn't keep up with the tuition fees.

Shaking my head, I head to the bar and I ask for a Long Island iced tea. I watch the barman pour a glass, then hand it to me. I down most of it and slam the glass onto the bartop.

A guy sits next to me, flashing me his pearly white teeth. He's beautiful, with dark hair and big brown eyes. He wears a beige suit with a black tie. I don't want any of the security to report to Snow that I'm talking to him, or any guy for that matter, because it will be a bloodbath. I fucked up when I kissed Melvin, and I don't want him to send me another body part. I got the hint. I need to stay away from the opposite sex, so I leave the bar.

When I make my way back to Lilac, I bump into someone, and the guy looks familiar. The scar across his face…

My heart hammers in my chest, and I feel bile rising to the back of my throat. I place my hand over my chest, because it's hard for me to breathe, so I clutch my dress.

He looks like the cop who pulled me over on the night of the car accident, but that can't be right… because it didn't happen, it was all in my head.

No, it can't be him. That wasn't real. My mind is playing tricks on me.

Someone taps me on the shoulder, and I turn to see it's Snow staring down at me, but when I turn back around, the cop guy disappears into thin air.

"What's wrong? You look like you just saw a ghost," Snow asks, gently stroking my chin.

I would tell Snow who I thought I saw, but I don't want to sound crazy, and I'm exhausted. Knowing Snow, he would have looked into it if I asked him to, but I don't want to waste his time chasing someone who is fictional.

I need fresh air, so I head straight to the back door, straight into the alley where there isn't anyone outside. I lean my back against the brick wall, trying to catch my breath, slowly inhaling and exhaling, so I can lower my heart rate. Snow and one of his guards follow me out back.

"Don't worry about it. I'm fine," I say.

Snow places both arms above my head, caging me in, and I inhale a heavy dose of his masculine cologne. "Are you sure? Did the guy at the bar say something to you?"

"No, he didn't. Just drop it, Snow. Mind your own business."

He places his hand on my neck, squeezing but not cutting off my airway. "I'm your fiancé. You come on my dick and mouth every night, and you have the audacity to tell me to mind my own business?"

"I'm your toy, that's all I am to you, remember?"

He lets me go, and I breathe in deeply.

"You and I both know you are more than just a toy to me."

I'm so fucking irritated.

"What's with these guards? Why don't you tell me what's going on, Snow? We already found out who Bailey's boyfriend is."

"Don't worry about it."

"Just tell me."

"No."

I move past him, swinging the door open, but Snow grabs me by the arm and ushers me to the car. My phone rings, and I hit the End button, sending a message to the group chat and letting them know I'll be there in a second.

"You're ruining my bachelorette party."

He strokes the side of my cheek. "I can't believe you think you're still my toy. I told you I wanted you, and you're not comprehending it. You're my fiancée."

"We're not in a relationship, Snow," I bite back.

"You're my property and I own every inch of you. Your tits

and the holes between your legs are mine. Everything about you is mine."

"I'm not that important if you won't tell me what's going on. You're hiding something from me." He doesn't respond, so I go on, "If you want this relationship to work, whatever this is—"

"Engagement," he corrects me.

"Whatever. You're going to have to be honest with me." I fold my arms across my chest.

"I will. When it all blows over."

Whatever he's hiding, I'm going to find out. It's frustrating that he won't tell me what's going on, that he keeps me in the dark about stuff.

"Fine, Snow."

I'm not about to allow him to ruin my bachelorette party, so without a word, I step out of the car, but not before Snow grabs me by the neck.

"I need you to trust me, Lyrics. Trust that I have everything under control, and trust that I will do anything or kill anyone to keep you safe."

Without another word, I go back into the club, and I drink until I'm drunk off my ass.

CHAPTER THIRTY-THREE

Lyrical

SOMEONE KNOCKS ON MY DOOR, AND I RUSH TO OPEN IT. My mother stands in the archway with an overnight bag in her hand and a box of pizza in the other. This is a surprise, because I wasn't expecting to see her until our lunch date next week.

The guard eyes my mother cautiously, and I place my hand on his shoulder. This is another reason why I should be concerned about whatever Snow's hiding. If he feels like someone is after me, I need to know, so I can protect myself.

"It's okay. This is my mother."

Snow is freaking me out with the guards, and he's been paranoid lately, making sure I have a guard following me whenever he's not around. He won't tell me what's going on, and I feel like I'm alone where everyone else is in on this big secret. No matter how many times I ask him what's going on, he won't tell me. It seems like nothing has changed with him.

"What are you doing here?"

She strides inside, amazed at the decor of the farmhouse, and I shut the door behind her.

"You had the farmhouse built exactly how you like it."

"Actually, Snow had it built for me as a wedding gift."

"That was thoughtful of him." A smile stretches across her face. "I'm here to spend the night with you. Snow informed me he didn't want you to spend the night by yourself." She crinkles her nose. "Where is he, by the way?"

"Bachelor party with his friends."

I show her to the dining room to set the pizza on the table. Grabbing a slice, I gobble it up as I show her to the guest room so she can get settled, then I head back to the living room and grab my phone from the coffee table to shoot Snow a text message.

> **Me:** Why did you send my mother over?
>
> **Snow:** To keep you occupied. You keep googling 'what type of secret my fiancé is hiding'.
>
> **Me:** Stalker. One day I'm going to find out what app you are using to spy on me. Are you still not going to tell me what's going on?
>
> **Snow:** NO. You will never find the app.
>
> **Me:** Insert middle finger emoji. Maybe I should put a spying app on YOUR phone.

I tuck my feet under my butt as I scroll mindlessly through IG.

My mother strides in, wearing a silk gown and a pair of house slippers. She flops down on the couch next to me and it's so awkward that I don't know what to say or do. Some days, I wish I were close to her like I was when I was a little girl. Our relationship has been distant and we've become detached, especially after the car accident.

I look at Jameson's story to see strippers are giving him a lap dance, while Keanu and Snow are by the bar, downing shots.

I send Snow a message.

> **Me:** How come I wasn't allowed to have male strippers at my party, but you can have strippers at yours?
>
> **Snow:** I didn't hire them, Keanu did.
>
> **Me:** That's not fair. I wanted men shaking their dicks in my face.
>
> **Snow:** If that would have happened, I would have sliced their dicks off and shoved it down their throats.
>
> **Me:** Jealous much?
>
> **Snow:** Very. You already know how far my jealousy takes me.

"Do you want to watch a movie?" my mother asks.

I nod, snatching the remote from the coffee table, and I put it on her favorite. *The Notebook.*

I never know what to say to her, we never spent time with each other, other than going to lunch dates, and she has never been in my personal life unless it's involved my marriage to Snow.

"Snow told me you had dinner with your professor to have one of your paintings in his art gallery. That's nice."

She never complimented me on my art before, so what's the catch? Did my father put her up to it? They used to fight all the time about her not being a supportive mother when it comes to my dreams and hobbies.

I raise my eyebrows and straighten my spine. "That's nice?"

She brushes a few strands of hair from my forehead. "Yes."

"You don't have to care about my artwork, it's okay. I know you only care about me being taken care of."

She sighs, picking at the invisible lint on her gown. "It's not that I don't care about your work, sweetheart. I've been projecting my trauma onto you and that's not right. I've been talking to a therapist, and she told me I did a lot of projecting that I wasn't aware of."

She glances out the window at the pitch-black sky. This is what I love about this place, it feels secluded and peaceful.

Snow bought this land so we could be away from people, which I don't mind. He wanted to move to New York City and be close to one of the locations owned by the Billionaire Club, but I'm not one for the city life. It's too loud, with too many people.

"What do you mean?"

She frowns. "I never told you about my childhood and what it was like for me."

"You grew up in a wealthy home. Nana and Papa love you so much."

She shakes her head. "No, I grew up poor, jumping from home to home. My birth parents traded me in for drugs. I was in foster care up until I was thirteen years old, then your nana and papa adopted me. My parents aren't your real grandparents." She removes her house slippers from her pedicured feet and crosses her legs. "I met your father my freshman year of North Haven University, and he was in an arranged marriage with someone else. So, he told his father that he didn't want the woman he was engaged to and convinced him to approve of us being together. His parents didn't like me, especially your nana, but they came around."

I knew Nana and my mother butted heads a few times. When we used to go over there for holidays, the tension would be so thick, I could have cut it with a knife. My nana said mean things to my mother, and my mother would ignore her.

"Your father wanted the trailer trash girl and not the rich girl whose parents had a billion-dollar empire. I had to prove I was good enough to be here. I guess I was making sure you were taken care of like I was. I had dreams too, Lyrical."

This is the first time my mother has actually opened up to me about her past.

"What were they?"

"I wanted to be a defense lawyer, but your dad's father gave me an ultimatum: give up my dreams and follow the traditions of the

Billionaire Club or leave his son alone. I chose your father. I will always choose your father. Your grandfather helped my adoptive parents become billionaires too." She sighs. "I grew up poor and as a nobody, and no one loved me until your father came along."

I bring my mother into a hug. I had no idea the life she had to live through. I had no idea she had a rough childhood. It's a shock that my mother's parents aren't my biological grandparents.

"I don't understand why you would keep that from me."

"Because I wanted to forget about my past so quickly. It's a part of me that I'm ashamed of. They gave me a lot of hell because of my background, and for a while, it ate away at my self-esteem to the point that I wanted to hide it from you. I wanted to protect you because I didn't want you to look at me as a failure. I didn't want you to look at me as less than. I want to give you the life I never had. I wanted you to fit in, because I know what this life-style entails. It can be corrupt, and I wanted to make sure you are taken care of. I didn't support your career because it wasn't part of the tradition of being among the elite. I was like you, filled with dreams and hopes, but then I realized I'm not the broke, unloved girl anymore. And you have more love than I ever did."

"I'm sorry, Mother. And I don't see you as a failure. I just want you to support my dreams and be happy about what I want."

"I understand. So, if your artwork is picked, then I want to be there at the showing."

"Really?"

"I'm sorry I wasn't supportive of your goals and dreams before."

"It's fine. I understand now."

She smiles, and I'm so glad she's supporting me because that's all I wanted from her.

I might be a disappointment to her, though, if she knew that I used to cut myself. I frown.

"What's wrong, darling?"

Tears leak from the corners of my eyes, and slowly, I roll up my shirt sleeve, exposing the faint scars on my arm.

"I've been cutting myself instead of dealing with the pain of losing Bailey."

My mother gasps as tears gather in her own eyes, then she brings me into a hug, and I cry on her shoulder.

"Snow helps me deal with it in other ways. He's actually helping me a lot." My mother doesn't need to know how he hurts me and that I love the pain he inflicts on me. "I still think about her. I can't believe I made it up that someone pulled me over and drugged me. I don't remember taking a drug, but I must have. It's my fault she passed away."

"Accidents happen and we all make mistakes, you shouldn't beat yourself up about it."

"But I'm the one who got behind the wheel."

"Yeah, you did, but you will go insane thinking about the what-ifs. Bailey wants you to be happy. She wants you to go on with the dream you have and live a great life. She doesn't want you to be sad about something you had no control over. She knew both of you took a drug and she didn't stop it. Just don't do any more drugs."

"I haven't touched a single one since."

She kisses the top of my head. "Good." She inhales deeply, then exhales.

"Did you know Dad killed people?"

"Yes. He has killed for me. It's what he was trained to do since he was a teenager."

"Why did he kill for you?"

"One of my foster dads raped me. I told him about it, spilling my guts. I was just opening up about some of the things that happened to me, but I thought nothing of it. And, the next day, I saw my foster dad on the news, about how he died from a gunshot wound. I asked your father about it, and he told me he did it and the man deserved it. I agree with your father."

217

I hug my mother tight. Now I understand her a lot more than I did. I used to not understand why she is the way she is with me. All this time my mother was fighting her own battles. Hearing what my mom went through brings me great sorrow.

"I'm sorry, Mother. I'm sorry for how I was acting toward you. I wish you had a better childhood."

She nods, kissing my forehead.

"I'm proud of you, Lyrical. No matter what you do in life, I will always be proud of you. Don't you forget it."

CHAPTER THIRTY-FOUR

Snow

I T'S BEEN THREE WEEKS SINCE MY MEETING WITH MY FATHER. I already made a choice, and I choose Lyrical. I should have chosen her from the beginning; I should have been on her side since the car accident, but I was blinded by rage and needed to blame someone. I was so pissed at her because of a careless mistake. Lyrical and Bailey are both at fault for the car accident, they should have been careful and made wiser decisions.

He wants me to take away someone I love? I'm going to take his life. I'm sick of the abuse my father doles out on me. This is about power. If he thinks he has power over me, and he thinks I'm going to choose him over Lyrical, he's more stupid than I thought. Lyrical wants to know what's going on, but I can't tell her because I'm afraid it's going to start a war between her father and me, and I don't want a bloodbath to start from either family. So, I'll take care of it myself.

Keanu, Irvin, and Jameson are throwing a party at the

mansion. Standing behind the table, I make Jell-O shots and Jameson hands them to different people. A woman stands on her tippy-toes, whispers in his ear, and he glances at her tits before telling her no. Jameson has a thing about innocent-looking women. He likes them quiet, and ones he knows he could easily break.

The music is too fucking loud for my liking, and I'm having sensory overload. I never liked crowded places, or people in general.

Lyrical is in my old bedroom, working on her papers for midterms, and I plan to join her as soon as I'm finished making the shots, then we're going to watch a movie, and afterward, I'm going to tie her up to the bed and fuck her as soon I can.

I didn't want to bring her here, but I'm worried my father is tracking my every move, sending people to follow us.

Savannah walks into the kitchen and I don't know why she showed up, but she probably heard we're having a party.

I thought she got the hint that I was done with her.

I guess the bitch has a hearing problem as well.

When our eyes connect, a smirk spreads across her face.

"My wedding planner will be contacting you soon and we need to figure out our wedding date," she says smugly.

Jameson looks at Savannah, then back at me, shaking his head. I haven't told them anything. I haven't told them about my relationship with Lyrical, and I haven't told them about my father's stupid-ass ultimatum.

When I place my hand around her throat, I squeeze tightly. I can't stand the sight of this bitch.

Jameson shakes his head before he leaves the kitchen.

"You know about my father's plan?"

She claws at my fingers, but I only squeeze tighter, making her face turn a shade of tomato red. Damn, I want to choke the shit out of her, then toss her lifeless corpse in a shallow grave.

"I overheard both of our fathers talking. I know he wants you to get rid of Lyrical and marry me instead. Yet, she's still alive. Does she know about his plans?" She pauses. "Would she be so heart-broken that her fiancé is supposed to kill her and marry the person she hates? I need to send her a message on IG informing her. I wouldn't want her to be left in the dark about her fate," she mocks.

I tighten my hand around her throat before slamming her against the fridge. Her nails dig into my skin harder, but I don't stop choking her.

"You go anywhere Lyrical, I'll gut you like a fish."

I let her go and she coughs, causing a few people to step into the kitchen due to the commotion, and I scream at them to get the fuck out.

"If I'm forced to marry you," I snap, "you wouldn't make it past the wedding night, because you would be dead by dawn."

Her face is pale as she gets up from the floor, tears falling down her cheeks. "We're meant to be together, Snow. Why can't you see that?"

She can't be this fucking desperate and delusional.

"See what? That your father is so desperate for money that he's willing to sell his daughter to a man who doesn't want her? That you are desperate for someone who doesn't like you?"

"You don't like me, yet you invited me over to this party? Are you playing a twisted game with me?"

Just as I figured, she has lost her goddamn mind.

"What? I never invited you here."

She pulls out her phone from her bra and shows a message on IG, where I'm asking her to come over.

What the fuck?

Someone clears their throat and I look up to find Lyrical staring at the two of us.

I hope she hadn't heard our conversation about my father's plan because if she did, she's going to be pissed off at me for keeping it from her.

"Lyrical, I swear I didn't in—"

Lyrical grabs the punch bowl and pours the contents all over

Savannah, staining her white dress, then she points a finger in her face.

"I invited you, you fucking bitch!"

Savannah screams, trying to stand up, but she slips on the liquid, falling on the floor again.

"That's for lying about Snow and telling me he fucked you, you dumb bitch. Stay the hell away from my fiancé."

Lyrical yanks Savannah by the hair and slams her face into the wall as she's screaming at the top of her lungs, blood dripping down her nose. I've never seen her physically harm someone. Savannah tries to grab Lyrical's hair, but Lyrical moves out of the way and trips Savannah. Savannah falls over the table, knocking over the Jell-O shots I made. She pushes herself up, holding her arm.

"Dig up a grave because you're going to need one. I'm going to be Mrs. Williams soon bec—"

I yank Savannah by the hair, pulling as hard as I can, rushing her through the crowded living room just as Keanu opens the front door. I toss her out onto the grass.

"Stay the fuck away from us. Or next time, I'll slit your throat," I warn.

I slam the door shut and hurry back into the kitchen, but Lyrical isn't there, so I head upstairs to my old bedroom.

She's perched on the bed, her phone in her hand, so I clear my throat. Lyrical looks up, glaring at me.

"What are you hiding, Snow?" She crosses her arms across her chest. "What is going on?"

I need to figure out what I'm going to do about my father. She doesn't need to know, not right now. It will only make her worry more—and make the situation worse. If I tell her everything, she'd go to her father and it will start a war between our families, which means Keanu's, Irvin's, and Jameson's families would be forced to take sides. It can cause division between us all.

I'll protect Lyrical at all costs.

She's the woman I want to marry. As far as I'm concerned,

our arranged marriage is still on, despite the ultimatum my father gave me.

My father hates losing control and power. This is a game to him.

He thinks I'm going to go through with it because he thinks I care about becoming the CEO of the Billionaire Club more than I do about Lyrical. He thinks he has me wrapped around his finger, like he used to do, but not anymore. I don't give two shits about him.

I love Lyrical. I love her more than the air I breathe. More than my own life.

I told her a while back that I used to worship the ground she walked on, and that hasn't stopped.

"Snow... please tell me what's going on. Why do I need the guards? Do you think someone else is trying to hurt me and does it have something to do with your father? I heard bits and pieces of your conversation with Savannah."

"No," I lie.

I hate fucking lying to her, and it's killing me, but it's for the best.

"Then what was Savannah talking about?"

I cup her face, stroking her cheeks as they turn a pale pink. "Do you trust me to protect you?"

"Yes."

"When this blows over, I will tell you everything."

"Why can't you tell me now?"

"Drop the conversation, Lyrical."

I kiss her lips, but she turns her head to the side, so I continue to kiss her neck as she sits there like a statue.

"Sex isn't going to change the fact that you're hiding something from me. I'm going to figure it out on my own."

"You will never find out."

"Savannah will tell me," she shoots back.

"Savannah is a fucking liar, remember? She tried to start shit between us to break us up." I pause. "I'll punish you in a way you wouldn't like. I'll fuck your ass without any lube, and I'll have you screaming for help."

I slide my hand up her dress and move her panties to the side, then I slip my finger in her pussy. At this point, I shouldn't expect her to not be turned on by my words. She loves when I hurt her, and I love that she allows me to do anything I want to her body.

"Is my Blue turned on by the way I punish her?"

Her cheeks turn a darker shade of pink as she nods.

"On your knees, Blue."

She drops to her knees, and I love that she falls so freely. Lyrical unzips my pants, removes my dick, and sucks me off as if she was made to worship my dick.

CHAPTER THIRTY-FIVE

Lyrical

TODAY IS HALLOWEEN AND I CAN'T WAIT TO CELEBRATE IT. It's one of my favorite holidays. Snow and I are meeting our friends at the festival. Every year, North Haven throws the biggest carnival in the United States and it turns into a tourist attraction during this time of the year. I'm also glad Snow doesn't have any bodyguards hovering around us, because that would make it less fun. I guess since he's with me, we wouldn't need them.

I've opted for a blue ripped dress, with fake blood splattered across the fabric, and Snow wears a Ghostface mask from the movie *Scream*.

He tried to convince me to stay at home with him, but I told him that he couldn't keep me locked up in our home. I need to get out of the house and let my hair down and have fun. I haven't seen my friends since the night of my bachelorette party.

We enter the carnival and the *Halloween* soundtrack plays in the background. People are dressed in different scary costumes, and the staff have chosen killer clown outfits. Screams fill the air from people riding the roller coasters. Red and orange lights illuminate the inky sky and the smell of funnel cake and cotton candy makes my mouth water.

Snow squeezes my hand tight, guiding me through the sea of people.

When we make it past the apple bobbing contest, he whispers in my ear, "We're not hanging out with your friends for long. I'm taking you in the woods to chase you, catch you, and fuck you."

My nipples harden at his words, and I feel my cheeks heat. "Snow. I haven't seen my friends in a while. I could use some girl time."

He traces his thumb over my palm. "Your girl time isn't cutting into our time."

"Snow, behave, please. It's just one night."

I spot our group of friends standing by a haunted house.

"What are my friends doing here?" Snow asks through gritted teeth.

"I invited them. Well, I sent Keanu a message on IG asking to hang out with us."

His eyes narrow. "You know I don't want you around my friends."

"I'm aware, but I also don't care."

He grabs me by the throat, pulling my face close to his. "Do I need to turn your ass black and blue?"

When he lets me go, I wink. "As long as your dick is inside of me, I don't care what you do."

I glance at Irvin and he's wearing a Jason Voorhees mask, Keanu has on a killer clown mask, and Jameson chose Michael Myers. All of them are shirtless, wearing jeans. I can tell by the way their bodies are built, and the different tattoos, who is who.

I try to keep my eyes off of them because I don't want to get caught ogling. They are too fucking hot. A group of women walk past us, staring at them, and they giggle like schoolgirls.

Lilac is dressed as a schoolgirl with pigtails, and when she spots me, she stretches out her arms, and I accept her embrace.

"I love your costume. You look so fucking hot." She eyeballs me.

"You do too."

Winter stands next to her, wearing a playboy bunny costume. "It's been so long since we hung out. I was worried about you."

"I'm fine," I murmur.

Irvin removes his mask and looks at Lilac, licking his lips. He strides up to her, gripping her chin.

He looks her up and down, then his eyes land on her tits, before reaching her gaze. "Why haven't you been answering my phone calls?"

"None of your business," she snaps, turning her head to the side. "I don't speak to men who are engaged."

He yanks her by the hair, forcing her to look at him. She whimpers, her light brown skin tone turning slightly pink.

"I have no control over that," he snaps. "You're mine."

She elbows him in the chest, and he lets her go.

"I'll never be yours. I'll never allow you to string me along and play second to anyone. So stay away from me." Lilac loops her arms with mine, but he snatches her away again.

"I don't want her; I want you."

"People in hell want ice water, but they don't have it."

He chuckles. "Oh, princess. You belong to me. Once I figure out how to convince my father to break the engagement with her and marry you, you'll be mine."

"My parents wouldn't force me to ma—"

He shuts her up with a kiss, and I tear my gaze away, glancing at Snow, blushing. Winter loops her arm through mine. Snow and his friends trail behind us and we decide to play some games and ride a few roller coasters. Snow wins me a few stuffed animals, and I eat all of his blue cotton candy.

The group want to break off and go to the maze.

"Lyrical and I have other plans." Before I can respond, Snow grabs my hand and leads me out of the festival into the nearest woods.

"Run, Blue."

My nipples peak and his words make desire grow in the pit of my belly. I run farther into the forest, and I hear my own pulse thumping in my ears. The icy-cold air nips at my face as I hide behind a huge bush, then I turn my nose toward the moist sky and inhale deeply. I hear footsteps approaching so I take off again, running deeper into the forest, tripping over a log. I get dirt in my mouth and spit it out.

"Surprise, Lyrical. You wanna play?" he taunts, the voice changer in his mask making him sound like Ghostface.

I yank my arms away from him as my pulse accelerates.

"Let me go!" I scream.

Snow pins me down to the grass, and I feel hard rocks rubbing against my back. Snow climbs on top of me, tearing my fishnet stockings with a silver blade, then he lifts up my dress and yanks my panties to the side. He rubs the cold metal against my inner thigh, causing both fear and excitement to override my senses.

"You're a willing victim. My little Blue."

"Yes!" My voice sounds uneven.

He leans down, darting out his tongue and licking my clit, while I lie on my back, looking at the gigantic trees and stars stretching across the sky. My hands go to his mask, down to his neck, squeezing tight, coming so hard I see stars.

Snow sits on his knees and unzips his jeans to pull out his dick. He lines himself up with my entrance before fucking me hard with his hand around my throat.

Several minutes later, I feel him throbbing inside of me. Once he grabs my hand, he pulls me to my feet, and I yank down my skirt.

"I'm not done with you," he whispers.

He scoops me up in his arms, and holds me against a tree, and slips back inside of me and I feel his semi-hard dick grow.

I bite my bottom lip to keep me from screaming and he plants soft kisses against my neck.

"Scream all you want, Lyrics, no one will hear you."

My back aches from the rigid wood and my core is slippery as I feel him stretching me wide.

He fucks me hard and long and as soon as I feel my orgasm slither down my spine, I scream and lay my head on his shoulders.

He continues to fuck me as he chases his orgasm. Before I know it, he empties out inside of me, and I feel his seed dripping down my thigh. As he sets me down to my feet, he kisses my forehead.

My phone rings, so I pull it from my bra and read the message from Winter.

"It's Winter. She wants me to meet her at the fun house."

Snow kisses the top of my forehead. "I need to speak to Keanu about something, so I'm going to meet him at the house of horrors. I'll walk you over there."

I shake my head. "I'm a big girl, I can take myself."

"I didn't hire any bodyguards ton—"

I start jogging in the direction of the fun house before he can finish his sentence.

"No, I'm fine. It's only five minutes away. What's going to happen between here and when I get there?"

Before he can respond, I rush in the direction of the carnival.

Once I make it to the fun house, it's about twenty minutes before Winter shows up, her lipstick smeared and her hair messy.

"Who were you making out with?"

Her cheeks turn rosy red as she grins. "Keanu. He's so hot."

I draw my eyebrows together. "Do you know what his kink is in bed?"

"What do you mean?"

I shake my head. "Never mind."

She has no idea what she's getting herself into with him. He'll have her running for the hills and left brokenhearted. He's the only one in the group who isn't arranged to be married because he always ends up hurting the girls, effectively scaring them off.

We walk into the fun house, and we scream, clinging onto each other for dear life as a clown pops up out of nowhere with a bat. We run through different mirrored rooms that make us look different sizes from each angle. Once we leave that area, we stumble into a room where a woman dressed like a dead doll runs after us with a machete. When we are near the exit, someone throws fake blood on us, and we scream again.

Suddenly, a woman wearing a Chucky mask shoves a knife into my side, and Winter screams and runs toward her, snatching the mask from her face, revealing… Savannah. Savannah laughs like a maniac and runs out of the back door.

I feel lightheaded and fall to the ground on my knees, my hands against the wound. It feels as if someone poured salt onto the cut and lit me on fire.

"Call Snow!!" I scream.

"Fuck! Your blood is getting everywhere." She places her hand onto the wound over mine, but blood gushes through our fingers.

I feel cold and dizzy as if I were back on the yo-yo roller coaster ride, and I want to puke. The more I breathe, the more my side burns. I empty out my stomach onto the concrete.

"You have to get up, Lyrical."

She wraps my arm around her neck, and we both get up. I keep my hand on the wound, applying pressure, hoping I don't bleed out.

Fuck! I hope I don't die like this.

We rush out of the fun house, and Winter screeches, "Help! Help!"

A staff member comes over and scoops me up in his arms.

I close my eyes then, and everything goes black.

CHAPTER THIRTY-SIX

Snow

I PACE THE WHITE TILES OF THE WAITING ROOM OF THE ER, watching Winter cling to Keanu as she cries silently on his shirt. When I found Lyrical, the paramedics were loading her in the back of the ambulance. If Lyrics dies... I can't live in a world without her. Savannah is going to pay for stabbing my fiancée. She's going to die a slow death. My father must have sent her after Lyrical to prove a point that he's in control of the situation and that I'm going to bow down to him and do what he says, but I'm done being his lap dog.

The doctor walks into the waiting room.

"The family of Miss Haynes?"

I ball my fist, embracing the worst news. "Tell us what's going on, Doctor."

"Lyrical is still sedated, and she needed snitches. She's lucky her stab wound didn't puncture an artery."

"I want her discharged."

"We ha—"

"You've stitched her up fine, now she can come home. Draw up the paperwork and I'll have my family doctor look after her."

"We have to do an investigation because of the stab wound."

"No, you don't. Keep this quiet and I'll make a fat donation to the hospital."

He nods. "Very well. I'll have the nurse draw up the paperwork."

He leads me to Lyrical's room, and the nurse monitoring her removes the IV from her arm as I reach her bed. I scoop her into my arms, and she snuggles into my chest, burrowing her face.

She stirs in her sleep. "You smell like Snow, Doctor."

I chuckle. Once I make it to the lobby, Winter drops a kiss on Lyrical's forehead.

"If you need anything, please send me a text message." Her eyes narrow. "Can you give me a ride home? I rode with Lilac earlier."

"I'll give you a ride home," Keanu says.

"Okay."

Once I make it home, I tuck her into bed, and she's out like a light. I remove Lyrical's bloodied clothes and give her a bed bath, then I put her in one of my T-shirts. The pain meds cause her to not stir.

I get into my car and drive to Savannah's place that's located in North Haven. Instead of knocking on the door, I go around the back, open the window to the living room, and slide it up slowly before climbing inside. I watch her go to her bedroom, then I follow her. She tosses clothes into a suitcase, and I assume she's leaving because she knows Lyrical survived her attack.

"Going somewhere?"

She turns around and pure terror overtakes her face as she backs up, putting her hands up in surrender.

"Snow, what are you doing here?"

She looks like a rabbit caught in the sight of a wolf. I'm ready to kill this bitch so I can send my father a message not to fuck with me. When I grab her by the hair, I toss her to the floor, knocking over a small table. She looks up at me, holding her elbow.

"S-Snow. What the hell?"

I yank her up by the hair and throw her ass against the drawer. Her body hits the mirror, shards of glass raining on her, and she groans.

"You fucking bitch. I told you what was going to happen if you didn't stay away from us."

She has a deep cut in her forearm now, and she removes the chunk of mirrored glass, tossing it to the floor, causing blood to drip onto the wooden floor.

"P-please. P-please."

I don't feel anything but rage.

Pure rage.

I place a ball gag in her mouth and tie the leather strap around her head. The entire time, she shakes her head, then slaps me across the face, but I don't flinch.

Once I grab her by the throat, I squeeze tight while she claws at my flesh, getting my skin under her nails, and I slam her against the wall two times. I let her go, and she falls to the ground.

I grab the zip tie from my pockets and force her arms in front of her, then I tie them around her wrists. Throwing her over my shoulders, I carry her to my car and place her in the trunk before closing it.

On my way home, my mind veers toward the best way to kill this bitch. I can drown her, break her neck, or toss her into a shallow grave and bury her alive, making her death slow.

Once I make it to the farmhouse, I carry her to the basement and wrap a chain around her neck that is attached to the wall.

Tears wet her eyes and fall down her cheeks.

"My fiancée decides your fate."

I kick her in her stomach, then walk upstairs to find Lyrical's eyes open. She tries to sit up.

"Savannah stabbed me," she says. "She really thinks that if I'm out of the picture, she can have you."

I want to tell her about my father and how he wants me to marry her instead.

"I have something to show you. Are you able to walk?"

She nods.

I don't believe her, so I scoop her up in my arms and I carry her down to the basement. When I flip the light switch, she looks around and her eyes land on Savannah.

Grasping, she clings onto me, as I set her on her feet, and lean down and cup her face.

"What do you want me to do with her?"

She looks at Savannah, then back at me, not appearing to be fazed by what I'm about to do to Savannah. I love that she accepts me for who I am.

She goes up to Savannah and slaps her across the face. Savannah screams into the gag, scooting away from Lyrical like a wounded animal.

"Kill her. She tried to kill me." Tears run down her cheeks. "I want to watch you do it."

There isn't any way I'm going to allow Lyrical to see what I'm about to do to Savannah. It can make you go crazy.

"No, I don't want you to watch me kill someone, Blue."

She stands on her tippy-toes and presses a kiss on my cheek.

"P-please. I want to see it. I deserve to see it. I want to see you hurt her."

"Are you sure? Seeing someone die changes you, and I don't want to scare you."

She runs her fingers through my hair. "There isn't anything you do that would scare me. Since we're going to be married soon, I need to be fully involved in your life, and not just what you show me. I accept you, Snow. All of you."

Her words cause my heart to jump.

Nodding, I grab a plastic bag from the top shelf of the cabinet and place it over Savannah's head. Her body thrashes as she kicks her legs, until she goes limp. I hold Lyrical's hand, but she snatches it away from me, and I remove the plastic bag from Savannah's head. Her eyes are bloodshot, popped out of their sockets, and her mouth hangs open.

Lyrical lifts her lifeless arm. I rub my lips against her shoulders. "How does it feel looking at a dead body?"

She shakes her head. "Shocking. I feel worry and fear. But I'm happy that she's gone."

I didn't expect her to say that.

We make it to the bedroom, where she climbs onto our bed, and I remove my clothes. I hop in the shower, then lie naked in bed with her. She lays her head on my chest and she grabs my dick, but I remove her hand.

"I'm turned on by what you did. I must be a sick person."

I lift her chin to gaze into her eyes. "You're not sick, Lyrical. It's okay to like what you like." I pause. "I don't want to hurt you, Blue."

Her gaze pleads with me. "You won't."

"We both know that I don't have a gentle bone in my body. When you heal, I'll fuck you any way you want. I'll gag you, tie you to the bed, and fuck you however I want to fuck you."

"Watching you kill her turns me on. It made me wet. Please fuck me. Fuck me like I'm your favorite toy."

"You have stitches."

"I'm fine, Shadow."

"You haven't called me that in a long time."

"Please."

"I'll give you head, but that's it."

I remove her underwear, and I slide my mouth to her clit, and I lick her until she orgasms on my tongue.

I invite Keanu and Jameson over to the house, while Lyrical is out bridal shopping with her friends and her mother. I need to tell them everything about what's going on.

They all pile into my living room, and Jameson proceeds to eat a bag of chips. I swear he has to be munching on something.

Sunlight through the window brightens up the room, and Keanu kicks up his shoes on the coffee table.

"I like your home, secluded and away from people." Keanu whistles. "I'll have so much fun with Lyrical here. Chasing her through the woods. Have her leaning over the cliff while I ram my dick inside of her."

Keanu doesn't know when to shut up and keep his thoughts to himself.

I ball up my fist. "Mention fucking my fiancée again and I'll toss your ass over said cliff."

He throws his hands up in the air and rolls his eyes. "Chill, bro. I was only joking. What crawled up your ass?"

"Why did you call us over here?" Jameson finishes off the bag of chips and tosses it into the trash can.

"My father sent Savannah to kill Lyrical."

They both narrow their eyes, then look at each other in confusion.

"Why?" Jameson wonders aloud.

"Because he wants me to kill Lyrical by the end of this semester to get revenge for the car accident." I sigh, leaning back against the wall. "Initially, I was getting revenge on her, making her my sex toy, but now, seeking revenge isn't as appealing."

"Because you love her."

I don't reply to Keanu's comment, because it's true. I love

Lyrical; I never stopped loving her. I never stopped caring about her either. What I feel for her is more than love—she's part of my being, ever since I first laid eyes on her. I was filled with rage, but now, my father's wrath is getting out of control. He's more bloodthirsty than I was and he won't rest until she's dead.

"I killed Savannah, buried her body in a shallow grave, but I'm worried my father is going to find someone else to go after Lyrical. He hasn't gotten his hands dirty in years. Usually when he wants someone dead, he'll send me to do it."

"So, what do you want us to do?" Jameson asks, smoothing out his tie.

"Protect her at all costs. I'm going to marry her despite my father's wishes. As far as I'm concerned, I'm going through with the arranged marriage."

Keanu stands up from the couch, pacing the cream carpet. "You need to kill your father. He's not going to stop until the job is complete."

There is a knock on the door, and we all look up to see my father strolling in, his hands in his pockets, grinning from ear to ear.

"So, that's your plan to get rid of me? Huh?"

I go up to my father and punch him in the face.

He staggers back, shock coloring his face.

I pin him up and punch him in the gut.

"You sent Savannah to kill Lyrical."

He falls to the ground. I'm tired of holding back because he's my father. I'm tired of trying to protect the image of the family, and I'm tired of him making me feel like I'm not good enough.

"I didn't send Savannah to kill Lyrical. She did that of her own accord."

I go to punch my father in the face again, but Jameson stands in my way, blocking me.

"You're not thinking clearly, Snow. If you kill him, you're asking for a death sentence."

"I already have a death sentence."

I push Jameson out of the way, just as my father yanks out his gun from his holster, cocking it and holding it to my head.

"Time is ticking, son. If you don't have your fiancée's head on a silver platter for me by the end of the semester, I will take action. The only reason why I'm going easy on you is because you're my son, but you do not cross me and get away with it. So she has to pay. You should have stuck to your plan and kept going on with the revenge. Now, you're playing house with the bitch. Falling for the girl you're supposed to marry for money and wealth. You're a fucking dumbass, just like your mother."

"He's egging you on. Don't listen to him. If you kill him now, you will go to prison. He's not worth the risk," Jameson whispers in my ear.

"He's worth the risk as long as Lyrical is alive," I snap.

"No, he isn't. You won't be married to her if you get locked up."

"I know you killed Savannah," my father says, smirking. "I'll have another whore lined up to serve you to be your wife."

He beckons someone into the room and a woman with brunette hair and pale skin, dressed in only a trench coat, staggers in. She looks like one of the workers at the Billionaire Club, shaking like a leaf. I wouldn't be surprised if she's one of his whores.

This bastard has the audacity to bring another woman into my home. Into my fiancée's home. Smirking, I grab my knife from my boot, slice the blade across her throat like butter, and I watch her fall to the ground, gasping for air. She uses her bony fingers to cover the wound. Blood leaks onto my floor. Seconds later, the life leaves her eyes, and her head hits the marble floor, surrounded by a pool of her own blood.

I turn to my father. "Every bitch you bring in here to try to replace Lyrical, I'll kill them. Get the fuck out of my house."

A wicked grin spreads across his face as he tucks his gun back into his holster. "You have until the end of the semester, or I'm putting a hit on both of your heads," he reminds me.

Several moments later, I hear the door shut and slam my fist into the wall, causing my knuckles to ache.

"If I kill him, then they will automatically open up an investigation case on me. My father is protected by the judges in North Haven, because he knows too much," I say, looking out the window.

"They will want to pin it on someone, and you will be the first target," Jameson adds, glancing at the dead body.

"So, what should we do?" Keanu asks.

"Make his death an accident. Those are my favorite things to stage," Jameson answers. "A car accident?"

"That sounds cliché." Keanu leans against the wall, staring at the artwork above the mantelpiece.

"If you can come up with another plan, by all means, because that's all I got." Jameson sighs.

"Get her pregnant," Keanu says, tapping his finger on the wall. "I love feeling like I'm about to knock up a wo—"

"Hell no. Lyrical doesn't want kids yet," I state.

"You need to move the wedding up," Jameson murmurs.

"Why?"

"She'll have your last name and your father can't touch her then. He only cares about his image. If he tries to kill her, then they would have to open up an investigation on her."

"He'll just make it look like an accident, and he can buy off the judges on his payroll." I roll my eyes.

"I overheard my father on the phone with Clemon the other day," Jameson states. "He's burning a lot of bridges with his connections."

"What do you mean?" I question.

"He fucked Judge Clearance's wife and forced him to watch. He's not paying his debts to the mafia in New York City, like he was supposed to. Your father is the reason why the mafia had to disband their human trafficking ring. The only reason why they got busted is because your father didn't like the fact that the underboss wouldn't let him have a woman he wanted."

I know my father dealt with the mafia in the past, but I had no idea to which extent, and I didn't know that he stopped the sex trafficking ring on campus four years ago due to selfish reasons. It doesn't surprise me, though, how he has always done things out of personal gain.

"I'm not worried about him killing you. He won't. I suspect there's more than one reason for your father to want Lyrical dead."

"What do you mean?"

"He told my father right after Bailey's funeral that he's glad she was dead. He wasted too much money on her and didn't see a return. Why would he want you to kill Lyrical out of revenge if he never cared about Bailey? His words aren't lining up with his actions."

My father only cared about the mighty dollar and I already suspect he only saw us as an asset or a liability, but to hear it from someone else hurts like a bitch. I loved my father and often wanted his approval, but not anymore. He's dead to me.

"Fuck," I muster to say.

"Yeah, marry her," Keanu urges. "Marry her and not only will she be protected by law, but she'll be protected by our families as well. Our families will go to great lengths to protect her. If something happens to you t—"

"Nothing is going to happen," I snap.

"I know, but you never know, and she will be protected by us," Keanu says. "Then you kill him, and you will automatically become the CEO of the American Billionaire Club, keeping up with the traditions, and our fathers won't come after you or try to get you fired."

"I'll stalk your father, learn his patterns, and I can stage his car accident." Jameson walks to the minibar, pouring himself a glass of liquor.

"It's a fuck-you to your father if you marry her," Keanu adds. "Flaunt her around, use her as a pawn."

"She's more than a pawn, Keanu. You say that again and I'll cut your tongue out of your mouth," I say, irritated.

"No matter how you spin it, Snow. That's all she will be. Lyrical is the target. Even our loved ones can become pawns in this type of lifestyle, and women have always been pawns to us because we use them to have our kids and keep them at home. They are always second to us."

He's right. I don't like using Lyrical as a pawn in my scheme for revenge, but she's benefiting from it too. I want her to be protected, and I will not rest until I have my father's head on a silver platter.

"I'll set up the arrangement for Lyrical and I to elope, but let's get this dead body off my floor. It's starting to stink."

CHAPTER THIRTY-SEVEN

Lyrical

Snow: Come home.

I READ SNOW'S TEXT MESSAGE, BUT I DON'T FEEL LIKE COMING home right now. I just want to have a night out with my friends. My side is hurting me from the stitches, but it's not as bad now, and my head hurts. I can't believe that I watched Savannah die and don't feel bad about it. Not at all. She tried to kill me and failed, so she deserved what happened to her. I just wish it were me holding that bag over her head. Something about seeing life leave a person's eyes changes you, in a way. I see people as bodies and not actual people with feelings after Snow killed Savannah. It sounds creepy and weird. Life is a lot more fragile than we think and in a split second, any of us can be murdered by anyone.

I now see Snow in a different light; him talking about killing is one thing, but seeing him actually do it is another entirely.

I couldn't love him more than I already do, and I accept him for who he is.

My phone dings with another message from Snow.

> Snow: You were supposed to be home resting, not at a bar.

> Me: I'm fine, Shadow. I'm just out with the girls. I didn't want to stay in the house.

He reads my message, so I know he'll be popping up soon, because Snow never takes no for an answer. He's also extra clingy. Which is another thing I love about him.

Love.

I love my best friend. I will never stop loving him, even though he manipulates me and controls everything in my life. I love the way he takes from me and dominates me in the bedroom. I love that I can freely be myself around him. He really still cares for me. He accepts me, flaws and all, and never shames me for anything. Our love is unconventional, but I don't care; the world is not supposed to understand our relationship.

I down the whiskey, and it burns the hell out of my throat, causing me to cough.

Winter pats me on the back and giggles. "Are you okay?"

I nod.

The bartender pours me another shot, and I down that one just as fast. Two more shots, and I'm tipsy and feel dizzy.

I watch Lilac make out with a guy, and Winter asks the bartender to bring the whole bottle of whiskey. By the time I get home, I won't remember what happened and I'll sleep like a dead fish.

Several minutes later, I stand up from the barstool and glance up, Snow stares into my gaze and he cups my face, strokes my cheeks, smearing my lipstick all over. I feel the stickiness of it on my delicate skin.

J. M. STONEBACK

The club is too busy for us to talk, so he ushers me outside of the building, into his black car.

Snow straps my seat belt for me and I sink into the leather seat. I inhale his woodsy cologne as he sits next to me. I'm horny and I need dick now, so I unzip his pants and whip it out, but he pushes my hands away and tucks himself back into his pants.

When I'm about to ask him why he won't allow me to touch him, I look up as we pull up to his private jet.

How long have we been riding? The alcohol in my system makes me lose sense of time and the world spins. I feel like I'm floating in the air.

"I thought we were going home."

He shakes his head. "No. We're going to Costa Rica."

Why on earth are we taking a trip across the country? I'm not big on surprises. My cheeks flush as I touch my warm face. Sobering up a little bit, I sit forward.

"No, we're not. I have to go to my classes unlike you. I have to study, especially for algebra."

The driver gets out of the car, goes to the trunk, unloads it, and wheels our luggage to the airplane.

Snow strokes my cheeks and a shiver snakes up my spine.

"Don't worry about that class. You will pass."

I fold my arms across my chest. "I don't want to go, Revi. Take me home."

"You're going with me. Whether you like it or not." He steps out of the car, then walks to my side, opening the door and holding out his palm.

He's insane—just insane.

I place my hands under my butt. "You can't make me get on a plane."

"Do you want to test that theory?"

"Snow... please. Let me go home. Why are we going to Costa Rica?"

"We're getting married."

244

I stare at him like he has three heads. There is no way I'm going to say "I do" to him this soon. Not without my parents and friends present. It's my mother's dream to watch me walk down the aisle and I'd be stealing that from her.

Where does he come up with these crazy-ass ideas?

"Why, all of a sudden, do you want to elope so fast?"

I can't wrap my head around it, he's lost all of his marbles if he thinks he can kidnap me and take me to a foreign country to marry him. But all he does is kiss my lips.

"Because I want the world to know you're officially mine. That I own every part of you, and you own me."

"They already know I'm yours. They have a hate group dedicated to me just because I'm with you!"

I love Snow, but what's up with him acting paranoid and wanting to get married out of the blue?

"It's not enough. I don't want to marry you because of the stupid-ass arrangement our families made. So, I will force you to be my wife because I want you to. You can go willingly, or you can go by force."

"You don't own me, Snow."

"Yes, I do. I own every inch of you. Being owned by me means I get to be there for your emotions, and nurturing your every need in life. Like I always have."

The truth is, I have always been in love with Snow and dreamed of being his wife, but not like this. I want my father to walk me down the aisle. So I pout, turning my head to the side.

"Suit yourself, Blue."

He yanks me out of the car, and I scream for him to let me go while he carries me bridal style.

"Help! I'm being kidnapped!"

No one stops what they are doing, not even the flight attendant. She has on a blue outfit and a big-ass grin across her face.

"Watch your step, sir," is all she says.

I feel as if I have to puke, and my face is all of a sudden hot.

"He's kidnapping me to marry him," I whine.

My eyes are pleading with her to help me, but she just shakes her head, following up the steps.

"You're complaining about it?" she asks sarcastically. "I wish a man would marry me. A rich, powerful man, at that."

Once we make it inside, he continues to carry me to a small room and throws me onto the bed.

"Get some rest, we have a long flight and I want you fully rested by the time we get to the beach."

CHAPTER THIRTY-EIGHT

Lyrical

CAN'T BELIEVE I'M ABOUT TO ELOPE WITH SNOW.

We stand in front of a pastor on a beach, the wind tickling my face. The stars and the full moon brighten up the dark sky, shining against the dark water.

Sweat blankets my forehead, and I bite the inside of my cheek as I stand across from Snow. He eyes the white dress he picked out for me to wear. It hugs my body like a glove, barely covering my tits and ass. I suspect he picked it out so when we get back to the villa, he'll be able to rip it off my body. Snow has opted for a white dress shirt and dark shorts, looking so damn sexy with his white hair spiked up. I want to tear his clothes off and fuck him.

I'm not as drunk as I was when I got on the plan, but I feel the alcohol swimming in my system.

I can't get out of the wedding, no matter how hard I try, but he's right: we do love each other, so we might as well make it official. I've been waiting for this moment since I was sixteen and it's long overdue.

And we did need to push the date up and do what we want instead of what our parents wanted. I'm getting turned on by the way he takes control over me and my body. Maybe we both needed to get away from the demands and spotlights of our family and social media.

The pastor begins his speech about love and honoring God, then he looks at me, a grin on his face.

"Lyrical, do you take Revi Williams the Second as your husband?"

My cheeks flame. "Yes."

He turns his gaze to Snow and asks him the same question. A wicked grin spreads across Snow's face. "I do."

"I pronounce you husband and wife." The pastor beams.

Snow yanks me into his arms, sliding both my engagement ring and wedding band onto my finger.

When did he find my engagement ring?

My heart flutters against my rib cage and happy tears leak down my cheeks as Snow kisses me with so much passion, my knees buckle.

He scoops me in his arms bridal style and carries me to the car. Once we make it to the villa, he sits me on the bed, and I watch him go into the kitchen, grab a glass of water, and pour white powder into it. My brow ceases as he hands it to me.

"Drink up, Blue."

"What did you put in the glass?"

"Crushed sleeping pills."

I tilt my head to the side. "Why?"

"Page ninety-nine."

My eyes widen. He's willing to give me what I want. When I used to bring up to him that I want him to completely take away my consent, drug me, and fuck me, he would ignore me. I know that the idea is uncomfortable to him. He likes to control and dominate me, but not to the point where I can't fight back. He has taken my consent away before, but it was him with covering my mouth, not when I'm unconscious. I want to be forced, I want him to have complete control over my body, and he can do whatever the fuck he wants to me, because my body belongs to him.

I stare at the glass, then bring my gaze back to his. "I know that it makes you uncomfortable to do this, and if yo—"

He tilts my chin so my eyes meet his. "I'll do whatever makes you happy. If you want me to do th—"

"I want you to be comfortab—"

"This is your honeymoon, Blue. I'll make all your dreams come true. That's why we're here."

"Are you going to record it?" My eyes widen, and I can't contain my excitement as I jump on the bed like a kid, then into his arms. "I want to see what you do to me."

"Yes, Blue. I'll record it. And we can both watch it together afterward."

I can't believe this wonderful man is mine. I'm so glad I exposed every part of myself to him because the way he accepts me makes me love him even more.

I nod, then guzzle the tasteless water. I yank the covers back, lying on the soft sheets. My eyelids feel heavy, and before I know it, I slip into deep slumber.

Snow

I watch her fall asleep.

I didn't want to do this to her. Yes, I fucked her in the past, taking her consent by duct taping her mouth, but this is different. She won't wake up and she won't remember, but she wants me to record it, and I will. If that's what she wants, I will give it to her, because her happiness is all that matters to me. I stare at my wife in her dreamy state. She looks beautiful. So fucking beautiful. Like a painting of a fucking sunset.

She's mine, and she can't escape me now. My father and the world will know it soon. This woman consumes every inch of me. She doesn't realize how much power she has over me. She brings me to my knees, and I'll walk to hell and back for her.

If this is what she wants, I wouldn't deny my wife anything. She trusts me enough for me to take away her consent and use her body in any way I want. I twirl the wedding band around my finger. I can't believe she didn't put up as much of a fight to marry me as I thought she would. I thought I'd have to wrap my hands around her mouth and force her to be my wife, but she came willingly, though it was after she accused me of kidnapping her.

I remove her dress, along with her bra and panties, and then I remove my own clothes and toss them into the chair next to the door. Once I grab a rope from my bag, I tie her wrists to the headboard, then I grab my phone and put it on a tripod before I hit Record. I start with her breasts, sucking on her dark pink nipples one after the other. I wish I could hear her moan, hear her calling me all kinds of names when I drive her to the point of orgasm. I kiss her all the way down to her pubic bone. I know she can't feel it, but I still eat her pussy and slide my finger inside of her, feeling her throbbing. Just because she can't feel, it doesn't mean I can't make her come. I remove my finger and lick her cum as much as I can, then I slip my dick to her entrance, and even though she's in a deep sleep, she's soaking wet and warm. I slide out of her and slam back into her as I kiss the side of her neck. I tell her how beautiful she is and how lucky I am to be her husband; she might not hear me now, but it's on camera, so she'll know. I fuck her so hard that the headboard knocks against the wall, and I feel the tip of my dick tingle and my balls tighten as I pull out and come on her stomach.

"Fuck," I say.

Once I untie her wrists, I look at the redness of her flesh, kissing her skin before I hit the Stop button on my phone and take it off the tripod. I place it on the nightstand on my side of the bed, then go to the bathroom to grab a wet rag and clean her up. After I put her in a night gown, I take a shower, clean myself, and put on a pair of boxers.

Once I'm in bed, I grab my phone and upload fifty pictures from our wedding onto my page and story for IG, with the caption, *With my wife.* I comment "Mine forever" five times, then I notice she posted a story four hours ago with a picture of us on the plane with the caption, *On the way to marry my best friend and the love of my life.*

After I reshare the photo to my story, I scroll through each of her posts and type "I love you" with a heart emoji. She doesn't use social media much and mainly posts pictures of her artwork, but I don't care. People are going to know she's officially mine.

A message from my father displays across the screen.

Sperm Donor: Congratulations on the marriage
knife and skull emojis

It was a threat, a threat that he's coming after Lyrical and me. My fingers glide over the screen when I send him a message.

Me: *devil and middle finger emojis*

CHAPTER THIRTY-NINE

Lyrical

MY EYES POP OPEN AT THE SUNLIGHT PEEKING THROUGH the windows of the villa. Slowly, I sit up and glance around, spotting Snow outside on the balcony with a mug in his hand, looking out at the crystal-clear ocean. My body is so sore, my core throbs and aches. What did he do to me while I was knocked out? Desire blossoms at the pit of my belly at the thought. I can't wait to see.

I toss the cover off me and slowly walk to the balcony. Wrapping my arm around his torso, I rest my head on his burning back and squeeze tight. He turns around, sets the mug on the rail, and kisses my forehead. This is the first time Snow has showed me any tenderness. He leans down to kiss my lips.

"How are you feeling?"

Those little words cause a burst of passion to grow inside of my chest.

I breathe in the crisp air, watching a group of people run on the shore of the white sand. I can get used to waking up here every day. The ocean here is more blue compared to the one back home.

"I feel good. I can't wait to watch the video. Do you feel go—"

He places his index finger on my lips. "I feel good, great even."

I love the way he took my consent away from me without judging me. I love the fact that I get to experience this with him.

Something clicks in my mind that he told me a long time ago. "You always were in love with me." He doesn't respond, looking shocked that I figured it out. "It wasn't merely a simple crush—or lust. You have always been in love with me. From the moment you met me."

Tears gather in my eyes as the salty sea mist burns in my nostrils.

I can't believe I couldn't see it before, but now I do.

The stalking.

The overprotectiveness.

Killing Savannah for me.

Anyone who he felt was a threat to my livelihood was dealt with.

The way he makes my fantasies come true and listens to me without judgment.

In response, he smiles, bends me over the railing, and slides my panties down to my ankles. His voice tickles my ear. "What I feel for you is more than love. I inhale every ounce of you, and I'm obsessed with your whole being. I can't put into words how I feel about you because there are no words that exist."

His words steal the breath from me, and I melt into his arms.

"I've been in love with you the entire time. Since I laid my eyes on you. I never told you because of the fear of rejection," I respond, honestly.

He uses his thumb to turn my head so I look into his eyes, and he bites his bottom lip before sliding his dick inside of me, and it stings and feels good at the same time that I suck in a breath. He grips me by the throat, squeezing tight as he fucks me, and my eyes roll to the back of my head until I feel myself tighten around his dick.

Several moments later, I feel him throbbing inside of me until his cum spills down my thighs. He pulls out, tucks himself back into his pajama pants, and grabs me by the arm to lead me to the bed. I'm pushed onto my back, but I scoot away from him.

My scar from the stab wound hasn't healed fully.

"I don't think I can take any more, Snow. I'm sore. So very sore."

"That's not my problem."

His words send a shiver down my spine and my core tingles.

He grabs me by the ankle, pulls me to the edge of the bed, and places my legs over his shoulders. He licks my clit until I come all over his tongue.

He lies next to me, then he pulls me into his arms.

My mind is going back to last night, of the video, and my cheeks flame.

"I want to see it," I blurt out.

Realization hits him and he nods, grabbing his phone from the nightstand. He taps the screen and hands the device to me, and I watch it, in awe of what he did to my body while I was knocked out cold. He tells me how beautiful I am and how much he loves me, and I watch him fuck my unconscious body as a huge grin spreads across my face.

He doesn't realize how much him bringing this fantasy to life means to me and I'm forever grateful.

He glances at the video, but doesn't say a word and his face is blank.

"You didn't enjoy it," I say, worried.

He arches his eyebrow. "It's not that I didn't enjoy it, it's new to me. I've never fucked an unconscious person."

"We don't hav—"

He places his finger onto my lips. "We do whatever you want, Lyrics. If it makes you happy, it makes me happy too."

My phone starts to ring.

Snow grabs it and hands it to me. "Your mother has been blowing up your phone and mine. I believe she's pissed off that we went ahead and got married without telling her."

That sounds like her. I grab the phone from Snow, tap the green button, and hold it to my ear.

"Hello, Mom."

I make my way to the balcony, close the glass door behind me, and eye the people playing volleyball in the distance.

"Lyrical Gina Haynes. Why didn't you inform me that you were going to elope with Snow?" I hear the anger in her tone.

It's always been her dream to witness me getting married, and I know what I did was selfish.

I'm not going to tell her that Snow kidnapped and forced me into it, because he really didn't—I didn't even fight him like I normally do. At first the idea sounded crazy but after I calmed down, I came to my senses and realized this is what we both wanted.

"We love each other, Mother, and we didn't want to get married because of the arrangement, we wanted it ourselves."

"Awe, baby. I wish I was there to hear you say I do."

"You will, when we have the wedding ceremony. Our families and reporters and the rest of the world will see it."

"I knew Snow always loved you. The way his eyes would light up when you're around or the way he would stare at you when you're not looking."

"You knew this whole entire time and you didn't say anything? You're a terrible mom," I joke.

Her laugh is soft and elegant, just like her. "It's something you need to figure out on your own. I'm so glad that you ended up loving the person you are arranged to because not many are happy with their spouse. Just make sure you finish college."

I can't believe what I'm actually hearing. My mother still kept her word and is being supportive of my dreams and goals.

"Where is my mother and what have you done with her?" I grin from ear to ear.

This is what I always wanted from her, for her to support my dreams. I don't want to get too lost in Snow. I don't want my life to be all about him. So many women get so lost in being a wife and they end up losing themselves, feeling empty and lonely. Not that I ever felt lonely or empty when he is around.

"I love everything about Snow, Mother."

"Even the... you know, can you truly look past that?"

She's speaking about the killing. "I don't care if that's who he is. I'm not looking to change him."

"Hold on, your father wants to speak to you."

I hear my mother tell my father that she's going into the kitchen and she loves him.

"Hello, sweetheart. I heard about the marriage. Congratulations! I'm proud of you."

"Thank you, Dad."

"Revi isn't too happy about the wedding."

"Why wouldn't Mr. Williams be happy about us? He's the one that set up the arranged marriage."

He sighs into the phone. "He won't tell me, but he asked me if we were informed about the elopement and I told him no. I think he wanted to be there for his son's wedding."

My father knows Snow's father, they are close but not best friends. Revi and Snow never got along, and my father doesn't know that Revi abused him and treated him like shit. Snow confided in me about it last week, right after he killed Savannah. I didn't know his father blamed him for the car accident and said that it was his fault because he didn't protect Bailey.

"Can I tell you something, Father? But you can't repeat it to anyone else, not even Snow. Or Revi."

"Of course," my father answers.

"Revi beats Snow."

"W-what?"

"Snow told me that his father beat him when he was a kid and every time he disobeys him. I assume the reason he's looking for him is because he wants to punish him because he eloped without telling him. Please don't say anything to Revi or Snow."

I watch Snow get up from the bed and open the balcony door.

"I have to go, bye." I tap the End button.

"What did your mother say?"

"Nothing. She's happy for us. Your father called my parents, looking for us. Do you think he's looking for us so he can hurt you? To beat you?"

"Don't worry about it. Come, get dressed. We're going out."

He still married me even though his father wouldn't approve of us eloping so soon. He's enduring pain because of me.

I head to the bathroom and lock the door. Then I cry.

CHAPTER FORTY

Lyrical

W E WENT SCUBA DIVING, WENT ON A SAFARI (IT WAS A disaster), and hung out with an older couple who has been married for some time. It feels… normal between us, and the life back home at North Haven seems miles away.

I wrap the towel around my head as I plop on the bed after coming out of the shower, going through my IG. Every other post is about us eloping, so I tap out of the app and place my phone on the dresser.

Snow's phone vibrates, and I pick it up from the nightstand. I swipe and it asks for a passcode. Is it still my birthday? When I type my birthday, the wallpaper is a picture of me sleeping. I smile.

A message from Jameson pops up, and I debate whether I should click on the icon. I don't want him to think I'm snooping through his phone, but I'm curious about who's after me now. My gaze scans Jameson's message.

Jameson: The plan didn't work.

What plan? I scan above and see messages of him and Keanu and Irvin congratulating him on our wedding. Keanu makes jokes about cutting someone's tongue off and forcing them to eat it. Doesn't surprise me, he seems like the type to make jokes about his victims. Their chat group is boring. Irvin asks about parties, Keanu makes jokes about killing people, and Jameson sends memes. I click out of it and type in Savannah's name and their messages pop up. It's mainly her talking to herself because Snow never responds back.

A message from his father displays on the screen, demanding him to answer his phone calls, and I scroll further and see his father congratulating us using knife and death emojis, then Snow sent him back a devil emoji and a middle finger. The rest is mainly messages of his father demanding him to do something and Snow responding with "Okay." The phone vibrates with his father's name across the screen, and I hit the green button. Revi screams in my ear.

"You married Lyrical out of spite to get revenge on me! I told you to kill the bitch. You were supposed to marry Savannah! You completely went against my wishes and did the oppo—"

I tap the End button before tossing the phone on the bed. The walls around me are caving in, and my heart beats a thousand times a minute. Snow was supposed to kill me? Is that why he married me, to spite Revi? I thought his father was going to hurt him for marrying me, but it turns out he was supposed to kill me. Why does he want me dead? That is why Savannah wanted me dead—she was supposed to replace me in the arranged marriage. Her words come crashing down on me... *Dig up a grave because you will need one.* She was referring to Revi's plan to kill me.

The blood in my face drains, and I feel lightheaded and dizzy. Bile tickles the back of my throat, and I grab the trash can by the bed, emptying out my stomach.

Snow walks into the bedroom, wearing a T-shirt and denim shorts.

"Lyrical? Are you okay?" He gently holds my hair as I continue to vomit.

When I sit up, Snow disappears into the bathroom, then he comes back with a white washcloth to wipe my mouth.

The pain I feel in my chest burns like lava and I don't know what to say and do. For the first time in my life, I feel completely broken that I truly married my enemy. He kisses me on the forehead, but I flinch and slap him hard across the chest as tears stream down my cheeks.

I trusted him.

I trusted him with my heart.

I trusted him with my body.

I've never felt so betrayed in all my life.

How long was he going to keep this secret from me?

He grabs my arms and holds them to my sides, but I can't stop the gigantic hole in my chest from getting bigger and I feel like I can't breathe.

"What's wrong, Blue?" I hear the panic in his voice.

"How long?" I say, trying to gather my thoughts. "How long, you motherfucker?!" I scream at the top of my lungs.

"How long, what? Blue? What the fuck are you talking about?"

I swallow hard, and my head hurts. "How long were you going to wait to tell me that your father wanted to kill me? When were you going to tell me that Savannah was supposed to marry you and be my replacement?"

Snow lets me go, guilt flashing in his eyes. He hangs his head. Fuck Snow!

I fell for the lies, thinking that he loved me. That he actually gave a fuck about me. I slap him again.

"I thought your father was mad at you because you moved the date up for our wedding, but it turned out that he was pissed off because you married me."

"So what if he is fucking pissed? I'm handling him," he snaps, folding his arms across his chest. "How the fuck did you find out?"

"Don't worry about it!" I yank the ends of my hair. "When were you supposed to marry Savannah instead of me?"

"After I couldn't prove that you were drugged, he wanted me to kill you. I told him no and he told me that if I don't kill you, he'll kill us both."

"In the beginning of the semester, did you have plans to kill me?"

"No. I wanted to, but I fell in love with you—again. I never stopped loving you, Lyrical."

"Bullshit! You were in a pissing game with your father, and I was just a pawn to you."

Defeat fills his pupils, and I realize I will always be second to him in his revenge. If it's on me or his father or the next person. He doesn't care if it affects me. And I'm so sick of being second to him.

He grips my chin. "I married you to protect you. He can't touch you now because—"

"Your last name carries so much power," I finish.

I can't stand the sight of him. His father can't hurt me because I'm protected by Snow's last name. Completely protected. It doesn't stop the betrayal. It doesn't stop the fact that he would have never told me and he always leaves me out of the loop.

"It doesn't matter. All of this was a lie. Our marriage. You said that you loved me. But you chose your revenge over me."

"No, I didn't."

"No? Why didn't you tell me the real reason why you married me?"

"I married you because I love you and needed to prot—"

"I don't need your damn protection. I need your honesty, I need you not to keep shit from me, Snow."

"You would have gone to Clemon, and he would have started a fight between our families. I didn't want a bloodbath."

"Yes, my father would have, as he should."

"That would have ruined the business image."

"Fuck you and the American Billionaire Club! All you men

worry about is your goddamn empire. It doesn't matter if you hurt the ones you love. It doesn't matter how far you guys hurt someone as long it serves you. Unless it protects your precious empire."

He's never going to change, I realize. Snow has always been this way, and I put up with it for so long because I love him. The secrets, the lies… and I'm tired. I'm tired of looking the other way when he does something that I don't approve of. And I gave him too much power over me, letting him control everything I do. He will always keep me in the dark about the important things, and instead of telling me and treating me like I'm his equal, he acts like he's my dictator.

Snow cups my face, rubbing his index finger along my bottom lip. "I was going to get revenge on my father and find a way to kill him."

"You always leave me out, and you never include me in anything that you're plotting. We're supposed to be a team, but we're not. You chose revenge over me. Whether it's on me or on your father. You chose that. I'm always second to you as long as you're seeking blood. You're never going to change."

Admitting it out loud hurts even more and makes me burst out in more tears. I wipe them with the back of my hand.

For the second time, my heart is breaking. The first time was when he walked away from me in the hospital after I told him I was set up, and now this. But at least I have control over this heartache. At least I'm standing up to him and saying no.

I remove my wedding and engagement rings and toss them at Snow. He grabs them, staring at the rings.

"I'm going home, and I want a divorce, Revi."

Rage colors his face.

"You're not going anywhere and if you ever mention divorce again, we're going to have a fucking problem." He blocks the entrance of the door. "You're never going to leave me, and I'll never let you go, Lyrical. I'll tie you to the headboard, keep you here until you come to your senses. We're just fighting. Couples fight all the time."

He doesn't get it. He doesn't realize how badly he has hurt me.

I shake my head, my pulse accelerating under my skin as I throw on a white T-shirt and a pair of jogging pants. "You don't understand how bad your actions hurt me. I'm not going to be second to anything. You already made your choice on which is more important. Your revenge. You need to let me go, or I'm going to hate you. If you keep me here, I'm going to hate you, Snow."

He doesn't move, keeping his eyes on mine. He's daring me to move past him.

"You're my wife and we're going to work it out. I do understand, but you're going overboard with your reaction. You can hate me now, but we both know it won't last long."

"Wow! Way to minimize my feelings."

"I'm not trying to minimize your feelings, Blue. I love you. I'm not trying to hurt you intentionally."

I know he's not trying to hurt me intentionally and I know he loves me, which makes walking away from him ten times harder.

"There isn't anything to work out."

"My father wants us to break up, and if you leave me, he'll win. I'm not letting him win."

I laugh humorlessly. "You don't get it, do you? You care more about winning and beating your dad than you do about me."

I toss my belongings into my suitcase, zipping it up and yanking it behind me.

"If I don't come second to your revenge on your dad, then stop trying to get revenge on him. I'll tell my father, and he can help you—us. My father can protect us. He has the same connections as Revi. Do it for me."

"You're not giving me a fucking ultimatum, Lyrics. This is between me and my dad. I'm not involving your father in my family bullshit. Not when it's something I can fix myself."

"Prove to me that I'm not second to your revenge. Me or revenge on your father."

"You're being fucking unreasonable!"

"You're being an asshole! You're too consumed by your rage against your father," I snap. "I want off this island and away from you. I don't want to be around you anymore. I don't want to stay married to you! I want a fucking divorce, and I mean it!!"

"I'm not going to change, so you have no choice but to deal with it."

"You've just made my decision so easy," I lie. "I'll see you in court."

"If you have someone serve me divorce papers, I'll cut their hands off and send them to you. Don't fucking test me, Lyrical."

"Until you learn that I come first, then it's over between us. Please, let me go. Give me this one last thing, and let me go!"

He searches my eyes to see if I'm bluffing, and he frowns. I've never seen his face fill with such sorrow, but I have to do what I have to do for myself. He steps aside, and I open the door.

Then I leave, not bothering to look back.

CHAPTER FORTY-ONE

Snow

I WATCH LYRICAL SLAM THE DOOR IN MY FACE, AND I GO TO MY suitcase and toss my stuff into it, zipping it up. Usually, I wouldn't let her go, but I have to because I don't want her to hate me for the rest of our lives together. The look of defeat and hurt on her face made me realize just how much I fucked up. She thinks I chose my revenge over her and she's second on my list of priorities.

But she's wrong.

At the beginning of the semester, when I was blinded by rage and anger, she was just a pawn I wanted to use. But she's become more than that. I didn't marry her to piss off my father initially; I married her because I truly love her and want to protect her. Yes, I knew it would hit the mark with my father, and a part of me did marry her to get back at him. Show him that he doesn't have control over my life.

I glance at the rings and I put them in my pocket.

She has another thing coming if she believes that I will actually sign the divorce papers. She's going to be wasting her time finding a lawyer and serving me those papers. I meant every word—if she sends someone to serve me divorce papers, I'll slit their throats and send their hands to her.

I told her before that I'm not letting her go, and I meant it. There is a way to fix this mess that I made. I've broken her trust, but I'm going to earn it back somehow. I should have been upfront and honest from the beginning.

My father would just love for us to break up so he can find a way to kill her. He doesn't want to kill me, otherwise he wouldn't be sending women my way for me to marry them. He wants me to get rid of Lyrical because he's pissed off that she made a mistake. Now, all of sudden he cares about Bailey? Yet when she was alive, he treated her like a liability. He was happy to announce her marriage to Tim because he was getting something out of it.

How did Lyrical know about the revenge plan against my father?

I pick up my phone from the bed and see a text message open from our chat group. Jameson sent a message informing me that the plan didn't work, so I close out of it and pull up my call log. My father is the last person who called, so she must have answered. He must have told her what's going on. I should have been upfront and honest with her from the start, but I kept her out of the loop in fear of losing her.

I click on my father's name and hold the phone to my ear. It rings three times before he picks up.

"I'm not killing Lyrical, and I'll have your head once I'm done with you."

I tap the End button.

When I get on the plane, I fly back to North Haven. Once I make it to the mansion on campus, I walk in to find Jameson and Keanu sitting on the couch playing on the PlayStation Five. Keanu takes out his gun and points it at me, but when he realizes who I am, he places his gun back on the coffee table.

"Motherfucker, have you heard of knocking? I could have blown your head off. You're back early from your honeymoon trip." He gets up from the couch.

A girl is naked with her hands tied behind her back. A blindfold covers her eyes and a gag is in her mouth. Dried-up residue smears her face and I'm assuming it's cum. She's propped up on her knees with her head bowed.

I raise my brow.

"This bitch stole three million dollars from me, so I'm using her body as payment. Before I kill her," Keanu answers, slapping her across the face.

"How did she get a hold of your bank account information?" I question, folding my arms across my chest and leaning against the wall.

He yanks her by the hair. I realize it's the same blonde chick who asked to be my pet earlier this semester at a party.

"She waited until I was asleep and stole my credit card."

Jameson tosses the controller onto the end table and gets up from the couch.

"Where is Lyrical?"

"She's staying at her parents' house because we had a fight."

When I checked the tracker on my phone, that was her last location, and she hasn't left since.

Has she told her father everything? It doesn't matter at this point. I'll have to prepare for the worst, for when her father attacks me, when I show up there begging to talk to her.

I'm not going to tell Jameson and Keanu that she's threatening me with divorce, because she isn't going to get it.

"The plan failed. Your father noticed a tracker on his car. I wouldn't be surprised that he is on to us." Jameson pulls a bag of Skittles from his pockets and pops one in the mouth.

"He sent me messages saying he's going to take care of me for marrying her. He knows that since I married her, he can't touch her unless he wants there to be a full investigation. I'm sure he's looking for a loophole."

"I followed your father while you were gone," Jameson says. "He has been conning the mayor out of money. Screwing over people at the club. And he meets at some mansion out in the middle of nowhere. I can't get close to it because they have cameras everywhere."

"We have another problem. Lyrical knows about my father wanting her dead, so she might tell her father and it might start a bloodbath between our families. I don't want my mother to be caught up in the middle of it, nor her mother. My father won't hesitate to kill her parents, and her father will do the same thing."

Keanu removes his gun from the coffee table and scratches his head with the butt of it. "What's the plan?"

"I'll talk to Clemon, if he'll let me. Then we'll go from there. Until then, keep a lookout for my father. He's filled with rage and is unpredictable."

Keanu puts the gun to the girl's head and pulls the trigger. Her lifeless body hits the floor, getting brain matter on the cream carpet and staining it with blood.

"Got it."

CHAPTER FORTY-TWO

Lyrical

I T'S BEEN TWO WEEKS SINCE I BROKE UP WITH SNOW. HE SENDS me text messages every day, telling me how much he misses me and loves me, and he follows me everywhere I go. I almost feel sorry for him, but I remind myself that I have to be strong, and he needs to learn that he can't keep things from me. That I'm supposed to be first in his life.

When I was out with Winter and Lilac last night, he broke a man's hand for grabbing my arm. Every time a guy would speak to me, he blocks their view and scares them off with threats. I don't say anything. I wasn't entertaining any of the guys, they were only trying to strike a friendly conversation.

I expect this behavior from Snow; he has always been controlling and manipulative—and revengeful. But I thought we agreed that we were a team. I knew he was getting revenge on me by making me his sex doll, but I didn't know that he had an order to kill me. That he was supposed to marry Savannah. His father wanted to kill me because he wants revenge for Bailey's death, which makes sense why he looked disgusted at me when it came out that I actually killed her.

I'm always going to be second to Snow.

And it hurts like hell that I can't talk to him.

I sit on my old bed in my room at my parents' home. They don't know why I'm staying here, but they suspect I had a fight with Snow.

Tears wet my eyes and I bring my legs to my chest, resting my chin on my knees.

Most days, I sit in my room, trying to catch up on homework and painting.

There is a knock at the door and my mother barges in. She takes in my tear-streaked face. When she sits next to me, she wraps her arms around my shoulders.

"Why are you crying?"

I don't want to tell her what's going on, but if I don't now, she'll call Snow, so I might as well admit it.

"I'm divorcing Snow."

"I'm sorry, baby." She pulls me into her arms and kisses my temple. "What happened?"

I want to tell her what's going on, but I need advice from my father first. He's the president of the company and knows how the men are built to run the Billionaire Club. It's more than a business and a secret society, and they have a set of rules that the owners have to follow.

"Where is Father?"

"He's in his study on a business call."

I get off my bed, stride downstairs, and I walk into his office. My father speaks using the Bluetooth, his arms folded and wrinkling up his gray dress shirt.

Once his gaze lands on me, he tells whoever is on the other line that he will call them back.

Dad rolls up the sleeves of his crisp dress shirt, stands in front of his desk, and crosses one loafer over the other as he leans against it.

"Did you and Snow have a fight?"

I tilt my head to the side. "How did you know?"

"Snow sleeps under the tree by your bedroom window. He does that every time you two have a fight."

I try to keep the tears from falling down my cheeks, but I need to tell my father what is going on before I end up dead. So I blurt it all out.

"Snow's father ordered him to kill me over Bailey's death. His father blames me for it. And it is my fault."

I see the look on my father's face, full of rage.

"Was Sno—"

"Going to go through with it? According to him, no. He was plotting a revenge plan to get back at his father. To kill him. He said that he married me to protect me, but he kept me in the dark. I broke the marriage off, Father. I'm sorry your daughter won't be married to an owner of the American Billionaire Club."

"You will be. I'll find you another husband."

I flop down onto the chair in front of him. "Am I always going to be second in my husband's life?"

"Sometimes. This is our lifestyle. I can't change the rules." He sighs. "Snow is only following the rules, even though he's not the CEO yet. I can understand why he didn't tell you."

"So you're on his side?"

"Never, sweetheart. I'm always on your side. His father won't get anywhere near you. I promise. I'm going to kill him myself." My father leans down and kisses me on the cheek. "I'll take care of Snow. Do you want him gone?"

I don't reply, but he takes my answer as a yes, so he heads toward the front door. I follow after him as he finds Snow sleeping under the tree.

"Get up!" my father yells. "My daughter told me about your father wanting her dead. Why the fuck are you even here?"

Snow looks at me and my father. "Because I can't be away from Lyrical, sir."

"Go before I kill you, Snow. It's over between you and my daughter. She doesn't want you."

"You can go ahead and kill me if you must, but I'm not going away until she orders me away, sir."

My father looks at him, then back at me in confusion. "Has he always been this clingy?"

I nod my head and Snow rolls his eyes, crossing his arms.

"You've got to the count of thr—"

"You can't keep me from your daughter. So go ahead and kill me. Slice me up, toss me in the ocean. Then go after my father because he wants her dead."

Without taking his eyes off of Snow, my father says, "Let me speak to Snow alone."

I do what he says and go inside the living room, where my mother is now sitting on the couch. She's watching *The Golden Girls* and I sit next to her, biting my nails. I don't want my father to kill Snow.

"Are you going to tell me what's going on?" My mother props her feet onto the coffee table.

I tell her everything, leaving out the revenge part.

"In this lifestyle, you will have to be a pawn to your husband and be second sometimes. I'm not telling you to accept it, but we were always supposed to be their trophy wives and bear their children. Snow should have told you about his father, but they live by this code of conduct. They are not supposed to tell you what's going on."

I hang on to her every word, and she's right, but it doesn't stop the betrayal and pain I feel about how he lied to my face. I lay my head on my mother's lap and cry for several moments.

My father and Snow walk into the living room, and I sit up quickly, wiping the tears from my eyes.

"Snow and I have an understanding. He will be staying here until we kill his father."

"What the fuck?" I yell.

"Until his father is dead, Snow has our protection," my father says.

Snow shrugs, and I push past him. He turns on his heel and follows behind me, up the stairs.

"Lyrical."

I stop, trying to keep the tears at bay—trying to be strong here.

I don't turn around, afraid I might give in to my feelings for him.

When I don't turn around, he says, "I'm sorry."

Those words go straight through my heart.

"It's not enough," I answer.

"I know."

He moves past me and walks to the guest room, which is the room across from mine. We have several guestrooms in this gigantic mansion, yet he chose that one.

Moments later, he shoves my sketch journal into my hands—the one he stole from me, all those months ago.

I run my fingers over the worn leather and flip through the pages fast, noting that Snow wrote on some of his favorite sketches. When I land on the last page, I find a drawing of us as stick figures, with a gigantic heart around us and the caption, *Snow and Lyrical forever*. My tears splash onto the page. I didn't even realize I was crying again.

Is he giving it back to prove that he's sorry?

"I'm sorry this isn't enough, Snow. I love you, but this will never work between us. After we find your father and you kill him, it's over between us."

CHAPTER FORTY-THREE

Lyrical

ODAY IS THE DAY THAT I'M SUPPOSED TO SHOWCASE MY painting in the art gallery. I can't stop the butterflies in my stomach or my palms from sweating. I rock on the edge of the curb in front of Gogh Hall as I watch students and staff walk in and out of the building, bundling up my jacket over my white blouse as the wind blows. It's chilly and the fresh, crisp air stings my nostrils. Next month is the last month of the semester, and I can't wait. This semester has been both hard as fuck and stressful. I hope after this semester, when I'm officially out on my own, life gets easier, but for now, I'll take it one day at a time.

Snow is at class, so I'm glad that he's not coming with me to this event. I need space, and him living under the same roof as me just makes things worse. He tries to talk to me, but I ignore him, so he uses my parents or my friends to send me messages for me to speak to him. He even broke into my room a few times and I caught him sleeping in my lounge chair. I don't have anything to say to him other than the fact that he broke my heart. I'm not going to lie, I miss him like crazy and I thought about slipping into the guest room and fucking his brains out, but I don't. I need to be strong and hold my ground.

My father told me that I need to listen to Snow and hear him out. He should be on my side, not his. My father doesn't see it because he and Snow will never change. As long as he's seeking blood and revenge, I will always be second to him. My feelings won't ever matter to him. The entire time he never treated me as if I could take care of myself, but he has always been good to me. He protects me in a way I don't know how, and he pays attention to every detail about me. The man built me my own dream home and he started hurting himself when he found out that I was cutting again. I know Snow loves me, I never doubted it, but I can't get behind the lying and the secrets.

I can't get behind that I'm a pawn to him.

It hurts. God, it hurts not being with him, but I have to do what I have to do. I just want to be heard and seen by Snow.

Lightning splits the sky in half and a few droplets of rain splatter across my forehead.

Without a word, Professor Carter pulls up to the curb of the street, and he gets out, opens the passenger door, and before I slide in, I gaze around looking for by bodyguard Russell, but he's nowhere in sight. He'll just meet me at the gallery. I doubt Snow's father will attack me with someone around me. Plus, Professor Carter and I can discuss other opportunities for me in the future. He grabs my painting and places it in the back seat.

Once he slides into the driver's seat, he straps his seat belt over his large frame, then he pulls out of the parking lot and drives through campus before emerging onto the main road.

"Is that painting of you and Snow?"

My cheeks heat. I painted a picture of Snow's hand around my neck, his lips pressed against my temple and a grin spread across my lips. It's in black and white, an oil painting.

I nod, leaning against the soft cushion.

"I like it. People are going to eat it up like candy."

When I glance in the back of the car, I notice a car seat isn't there. I quickly forgot that he had a wife and a kid.

"Does your wife know that you're picking me up?"

"I don't have a wife. I have a girlfriend."

"But the lady at the engagement ball?"

"Was my sister."

"I saw a wedding band on your finger." I glance at his ring finger and the ring isn't there.

"I only wear that ring so women leave me alone."

We drive away from the city near North Haven and my heart sinks, and my pulse accelerates. Why do I feel so nervous? Why are my spidery senses going off? And why do I feel dread in the pit of my stomach? I glance at Carter, noting he has a wicked grin on his face.

"You'll go for the highest bidder." He twists his neck to glance at my body, his words catching me off guard.

"I hope so. I want my paintings to be worth at least three thousand."

He places his hand on the back of my neck and chills travel up my spine.

"When people really know how much you're worth, you're going to make me a lot of money. You're going to be my favorite muse."

Pure terror overrides my senses. My heart pounds in my ears, and I feel the blood in my cheeks draining.

"You see. Bailey had that same look on her face when I told her the same thing."

"How do you know Ba—"

He taps his finger on the steering wheel. "I'm her boyfriend."

The entire time, June was set up.

Fuck!

"My business partner approached me about wanting me to

sell her, get his money worth and at first, I didn't want to because I already had feelings for her when Bailey was in my class a few years ago. Everything was good between us in the beginning. Fighting the urge to sell her, because I loved her. I was taught that women are more valuable because they have holes between their legs. That's what we learned in the mafia. She's my girl, always will be, but after the mafia was disbanded, I lost a lot of income and my business partner knew her so well, so he suggested I make a profit for the both of us."

The car feels small, and bile rises in the back of my throat. Placing my hand on the door handle, I pull hard, and when that doesn't work, I kick the window, but it's no use.

Carter burst out into laughter. "The way you think you can get away is comical."

"You drugged us at the football party, you spiked our drinks."

"Bingo. You're smart." He smiles as if he's proud of himself. "The guy that Snow killed at his party for spiking your drink? It was all a setup. I told him to approach you two so he can distract Snow, and I knew Snow didn't like you and Bailey at his parties."

"I didn't see you at his party."

"I was there watching the whole event."

"How did yo—"

Tears gather in my eyes and I try to resist the urge to cry.

"You staged my car accident to make it seem like I was driving under the influence."

"You're smart. Very smart."

"You set June up. You had him ki—"

"I paid him to follow you around and act like he was interested in you, and when you were on to us, one of my partners killed him and planted evidence on him. Rachel is one of my whores and I paid her to meet with you at the park to give you that stuff. She told me you sent her a message on social media."

Tears fall down my cheeks, and I clench my fist to my chest, trying to breathe.

"Please, Carter. Let me go. I won't tell anyone."

He grabs my chin, digging his nails into my flesh. "I will let you go once I sell you to someone else, and he'll do what the fuck he wants to you."

I grab my phone from my purse and try to hide it under my butt, but he snatches it from me. After he hits a button on the side of the door and the window rolls down, he tosses my phone out.

"Please, let me go. Ju—"

"Shut the fuck up and sit back and I won't end your life."

Time passes by slowly… the drive seems so long. He pulls up to a mansion made out of dark brown cobblestone. The lawn is overgrown with weeds and neglect, and I try to remember every detail so when I escape, I'll know where to run, like the white statue with a naked woman with water coming out of her nipples in front of the door, next to a row of expensive cars.

Once he kills the engine and slips out, he opens the car door for me, so I get out and elbow him in the chest. Before I can get anywhere, he yanks me by the hair, causing my scalp to sting, and I feel cool metal against my temple.

"If you try to run from me again, I'll put a bullet through your brain."

With his hand wrapped around my hair, he walks inside the mansion. He drags me to a basement. Glancing around, it looks familiar, like I've been here before.

"You're going to stay in here," he says, slamming the door shut.

I go to the window, trying to push on it, but it's no use. It's filled with dust mites and it looks like it hasn't been opened in years. I look around the dingy basement, spotting a girl strapped to a filthy mattress in the corner.

Slowly, I walk up to her. Her brunette hair is matted and unkempt and her face is dirty like she hasn't bathed in a while. She is naked with bruises and welts all over her body. The girl is thin and I can see every rib beneath her skin.

I cry hysterically as I pull on the chain, trying to break her free.

"I'm going to get you out of here," I promise. "Get us both out of here."

A familiar pair of hazel eyes gazes into mine, and they narrow. Tears leak down her face as she smiles sadly at me.

My heart catches in my throat. "Oh my God! Bailey? What has he done to you?"

CHAPTER FORTY-FOUR

Snow

I KNOCK ON THE DOOR TO CLEMON'S STUDY ROOM AND HE tells me to come in. He's on the computer, typing away, not acknowledging me. I sit in front of the desk, waiting for him to face me. He wanted to speak to me before we meet Lyrical at the gallery to support her on her big day.

I know she's pissed off at me, but that doesn't stop me from wanting to support her. It's hard sleeping in the room across from hers. Ever since she tried to leave me, she gave me the silent treatment, and she won't even acknowledge me at the dinner table. I still follow her, and I have guards to follow her around just in case my father hired someone to take her out. The hole in my chest is big enough to fill the ocean. I'm trying to respect her boundaries but it's hard. I have to tell myself that she will come around. I want to prove to her that I changed and I understand what she's saying.

She has never given me the silent treatment before. I have been still stalking her through the app on her phone and she hasn't contacted a divorce lawyer, so either she chose to heed my warning about me killing the fucker or she doesn't want a divorce. I'm hoping for the latter.

I'm going to continue to stalk her until I can prove to her that I'm sorry.

"You wanted to see me?" I ask, crossing my ankle over the other.

He sips from his mug before setting it down onto the desk. "Your father disappeared. I had my team of people to look for him, and Kyle and Julian informed me that they haven't heard from him. He hasn't been in the office in a week."

Kyle is Jameson's father and Julian is Keanu's.

I smooth out my tie, leaning forward in the chair. "That doesn't surprise me."

"Do you know where he would have gone?"

My father has enough resources to make himself disappear and not be found, but something isn't right because he doesn't back down from a fight, especially when his ego is bruised. He was so pissed that I chose not to get revenge on Lyrical.

I shake my head. "He could be anywhere—and I mean anywhere."

"Do you think your father backed off? Do you believe he's gone?"

I stretch out my legs. "No. He's biding his time for something. I don't know what."

Russell bursts through the study with a panicked look on his face.

"What?" Clemon asks.

"Lyrical is missing."

Rage clouds my thoughts and my hands shake. If the motherfucker lost my wife, I'm going to put a bullet through his head.

I jump up from the chair, walk up to him, and grab him by the shirt. "What the fuck do you mean she's missing."

"I went to the bathroom and when I got to Gogh Hall, she was gone, so I drove to the art gallery and wa—"

Before he can finish his sentence, Clemon shoots him in the head. Blood and brain matter splatter across my face. I let go of his limp body and it falls to the ground with a thud, and seconds later, a pool of blood surrounds his lifeless body.

My father must have taken her. He waited for an opportunity to grab her.

I fish my phone from my pocket, check her location, and find that she's out in the middle of nowhere. No one goes to that part of North Haven. It's nothing but open fields and trees.

Clemon makes a phone call asking someone to clean up the body.

"I found her location."

"How?"

"I put a tracking device inside of her body, just in case she went missing."

"You put a tracking device inside my daughter? What the fuck, Snow?"

"I told you my job is to keep your daughter safe and protected, and I'm a man of my word."

Clemon presses a button on his desk and the bookcase opens up, leading to a tunnel.

"We're going have a talk about your obsession with my daughter, but for now, we're going to fucking kill your father."

I follow him down the stairs to a room equipped with so many guns, it looks like a store. I grab an AK-47 and a 9mm revolver, tucking them in my holster.

My father is going to wish he hadn't fucked with Lyrical. He will be meeting his maker today.

I grab my phone again and post a message in the group chat with her location.

Me: Lyrical is here. My father kidnapped her.

Jameson: Your father has been to that location before. It's the mansion in the middle of nowhere where I can't look into because it's secured.

I dial his number and he answers on the first ring.

"Why does he go there?"

"That's where he's staying, and for some reason, he's working with Professor Carter and another guy with a scar across his face."

"We've got to go. Meet me there. Call Keanu and tell him to come."

When we make it to the front entrance, we find Lyrical's mother, placing fresh flowers on the table in the foyer. She eyes the guns strapped to our bodies.

"What's going on?" she asks.

Clemon leans down and kisses her on the forehead. "Go to your mother's and don't come back home until I tell you to."

"But I thought we're going to support Lyrical on her big day at the gallery? We have to be there in twenty minutes. If you miss this, she won't for—"

"Lyrical is missing, Nora," I state. "My father has her. You need to leave now, just in case he sends someone here to murder you while we go to get her back."

"Bu—"

"Please, Nora. My love. Do what we say." He kisses her lips. "We'll get our daughter back."

She nods as tears fall down her face. "You go get our baby and be safe. The both of you."

We leave and get into the car. Clemon pulls out of the driveway and takes the main road.

What if he's put his hands on her?

What if he is torturing her?

Why is my father hanging out with Carter? I knew something was wrong with Carter, and I should have known that he was after my girl, but I couldn't find shit on him—on his background. It's like he appeared out of thin air. I even followed him to his apartment, searched through it after Lyrical had dinner with him, but I couldn't find anything. I'll kill him too, and the other guy."

"Jameson told me that Professor Carter and another guy are at the location that Lyrical is at. Why would he be there?"

"I did a background check on all of Lyrical's professors." He rubs the back of his neck. "There was a rumor about Carter." When I don't respond, he continues, "For years, people said he was associated with the mafia, trafficking girls." He hits the gas pedal fast, bypassing a dump truck. "We couldn't prove it because there wasn't any evidence of it. So, the dean let it go.

"I believe he's still doing it. When Lyrical came to me months ago about the car accident, she said she believed it was staged, so I checked into everyone's backgrounds. Everyone who was close to her. I found nothing. If the rumors are true about Carter, your father is using him to get back at you by selling her to someone because he couldn't get the money for your sister. In my book, that is worse than death."

CHAPTER FORTY-FIVE

Lyrical

TARING AT BAILEY, HER EYES NARROWING FURTHER, THE first thing I notice is a few of her teeth are missing. My chest hurts and I cry uncontrollably.

"Bailey... what have they done to you?"

Her face is blank and she stares at the ceiling, watching the fan turn. I try to remove her restraints, but it's no use; they have a lock pad on the chain. I grab her by the shoulders in an attempt to shake her to her senses but she doesn't budge. She's drugged up, so out of it. Her pupils are the size of saucers. Finally, she turns her head to look at me, a weak smile spreading across her battered face.

"Carter told me I'll never see you again, that I'm going to die here for being a brat."

"What has he done to you?"

She doesn't respond, then her eyelids close, so I glance around the basement again, trying to find something to help us get out of here. It's bare, dirty, and stinks of piss and shit. The pictures of her sketch journal come to my mind. This is the exact same basement she used to draw. This is where he used to bring her to torture and rape her. The beautiful person whose smile lights up the room is gone. She's like an empty shell because she fell in love with someone who couldn't treat her right. Someone who wanted to use her for a quick buck. Carter is just like her father.

I wish he hadn't thrown my phone out of the window because Snow has a tracker on it. Does he realize that I'm missing? I'm sure my parents showed up to the gallery and noticed I wasn't there. Hopefully, they will find us, but I'm not going to sit around and wait for them. By then, I will be sold to some creepy-ass man.

I lie next to my best friend.

"I'm going to get us out of here. Somehow."

Her eyes pop open as tears leak down the sides of her face to her temples and her dull eyes meet mine. No hope for the future. No shine in them. Lifeless.

"Carter will never let me go, Lyrical. He makes pretty promises and does the opposite."

With that she closes her eyes once more.

I hear the steel door to the basement open, and I scramble to my feet, standing in front of the bed in order to protect Bailey. If they put their hands on her, I'll go down swinging. He already destroyed her, and I'm not going to allow them to do any further damage.

I'm going to get us out of here, even if I die trying.

Carter and the cop who pulled me over that fateful night walk in. I recognize him. He was at the club when I had my bachelorette party.

My stomach twists and bile rises in my throat.

"You're the one who pulled me over. The one who pretended to be a cop."

The guy doesn't respond but looks at me like I'm a piece of meat, darting out his tongue and licking his lips.

"If you hadn't been trying to figure out what happened to

Bailey, none of this would have ever happened. Snow informed his father that you suspected the car accident was fake. Your husband and your father snooped through my place, running background checks on me." Carter claps. "Good job. Now she will die and you will be sold off to a rich guy who's going to kill you." He turns to the other guy. "Drake, leave the room."

Drake stares at me for a moment. "I want my chance."

"You will when I'm done with her."

Fear burns in my chest at his words.

Carter unzips his pants and yanks out his fat dick. "I need to test the product. On your knees, whore."

"If you stick your dick in my mouth, I'll bite it off," I grit through my teeth, backing away from him.

"If you bite it off, bitch, I'll fucking skin you alive."

He grabs me by the arms, forcing me down to my knees by pulling my hair. My head throbs, and he nudges his dick between my lips, and the tip hits my teeth. I turn my head to the side.

He slaps me across the face, and the pain travels all the way to my forehead.

"I. Said. Open. Bitch."

When I open my mouth, tears fall down my cheeks and I bite down hard, sinking my teeth into the flesh, biting a big chunk of his dick, chewing like I'm dying of hunger.

I continue to bite until it's completely ripped off, and I spit the flesh and blood into his face. The warm blood tickles down my chin and onto my blouse.

He kicks me in the wound where I had been stabbed by Savannah, and I scream at the top of my lungs as my shirt turns bloody red, and I fall to the ground.

"You fucking bitch!"

He kicks me again and yanks my hair, then he punches me in my face, tossing me to the ground. My nostrils burn as I breathe in, trying to catch my breath. I don't know how I have the strength to get up, but I do. I knee him in the balls and he falls to the floor, then I stomp on them. My face feels as if I've been hit by a bus.

I search his pockets to find several keys, so I test each one of them and try it on the locks. Finally I find one that works, and I unlock the padlocks and I pick Bailey up. She's so malnourished that I can lift her and carry her over my shoulders. When I breathe in and out, my rib cage hurts and I feel weak. My head throbs and my stab wounds bleed uncontrollably, and I don't know if we can make it to the front door. I hope I don't bleed out before then.

When I open the basement door and step out, there is a long-ass hallway, so I keep going, tripping over my feet and dropping Bailey along the way.

She groans and tries to push herself up, but she's too weak. My heart pounds in my chest, and I wrap her arms around my shoulders, lifting her up with as much strength as I can. I'm weak as well but we have to keep going. We will not die here. I need to find a car to steal. I spotted a few when Carter brought me here.

We make it to the front door, and I turn the knob to find it's locked from the outside, which is strange. Why would it be locked from the outside? I set Bailey down on the floor, and she groans.

"Lyrics, I don't feel too good."

"I'm going to get us out of here, okay? I promise."

I don't believe my own words, but I need her to hold on to hope. I finally got my best friend back and I'm not going to let her go. She's not going to die here, and her story doesn't end in this place.

Once I grab a small chair, I toss it at a nearby floor-to-ceiling window, then I duck my head as the glass shatters in a million pieces. When I pick Bailey up, my hair is pulled back and my gaze clashes with a pair of mismatched eyes similar to Snow's.

Pure terror overrides my senses as I stare at Revi. A wicked grin plasters his face and it gives me chills.

Is he working with Carter?

"You couldn't mind your business, could you, bitch? Always shoving your nose into shit that has nothing to do with you."

He drags my body across the floor, a sharp glass sticking into my calf. I try to yank my arm from his grip but it's no use, he's too strong.

"You're pathetic." He pulls me into a room, slamming the door behind him.

He takes out a gun, placing it to my temple. "If you do anything to escape or hurt me, I will put a bullet through you."

"What are you going to do to Bailey?"

"I'm going to kill her. She's no use to me now that you're here. I'm not going to kill you just yet, I need money and you're going to spread those pretty legs!"

How can he treat his daughter this way? Hurt her?

"Why would you want to sell your daughter?"

"She's a liability. Just like you. You turned my son against me. He chose you over me, over his own family. I worked so hard to make him the machine he is today, to make him do what I want. Now, he thinks he has power and can do whatever the fuck he wants." His eyes narrow. "I almost forgot, pull down your panties."

I shake my head.

"I'm not going to fuck you, bitch. You're not my type. And I'm not going to ask you again." He pushes me to the ground.

With tears in my eyes, I lift up my skirt, pull down my panties.

He yanks me up on my feet, forcing me onto the bed and flipping me on my stomach. I turn to look at him to see he has a knife. Several seconds later, I feel a sharp pain below my ass cheek. I scream, begging for him to stop.

Blood runs down my thigh.

"My son had a tracker inside of you. Stupid ass went to our family doctor to help him."

So Snow might be on his way? I'm so happy that he put a tracker inside of my body.

I sit up, crawling to the head of the bed, wrapping my arms

around my legs. My hand grazes at the sharp glass that's currently imbedded into my skin.

My body aches and my eyelids are heavy.

Drake walks inside and slams the door shut.

"The other girls have arrived and Bailey is back in the basement."

This is a trafficking business, I realize. They never stopped trafficking women after the policemen busted them.

Revi whispers in Drake's ear, and when Drake turns his back to him, Revi pulls out his gun and shoots him in the back of the head. He falls to the ground, then Revi turns to face me, and I sob uncontrollably.

With that, he steps over the body, leaving it in the room with me, and shuts the door, locking it.

CHAPTER FORTY-SIX

Snow

WE PULL UP TO THE MANSION, AND I SEE MY FATHER'S Porsche next to Carter's car in the driveway.

Clemon comes to a stop and before he kills the engine, I jump out of the car, remove one of the guns from my hostler, and head straight to the front door. I turn the knob and it's locked, so I glance around and see a busted window and crawl through it, trying not to cut myself on the shards of glass.

Glancing around, a trail of blood leads me to a hallway, then there isn't any sign of life. The mansion looks abandoned.

First things first, I need to find Lyrical and get her out of here. Then I'll handle my father. I'm going to put a bullet through his head. Damn the consequences of what's going to happen to me. I'll rot in jail before I'll allow him to do whatever the hell he wants to do with Lyrical. It'll destroy my mother, but I don't fucking care. My father and Carter need to die a slow death.

I hear someone walking behind me and I turn around, aiming my gun at Keanu, so I slowly lower it.

"Clemon and Jameson are checking upstairs. They will let us know if they find anyone."

"Let's search this floor, then we will search the basement. Kill anyone on sight."

He holds up his gun. "I love a good bloodbath."

We reach a hallway, where there are multiple doors on each side. I tell Keanu to check the ones on the left, while I take the ones on the right. I turn the knob on four doors, and the ones that are locked, I kick them down. All of them are empty bedrooms. When I turn the knob on the last door, it doesn't budge, so I slam my shoulder into the wood, trying to push whatever is blocking my way. Once I'm able to barge inside of the room, I step over a dead body. Lyrical tries to swing the lamp at me, but I block her.

"Blue, it's me. It's Snow."

Recognition shines in her blue eyes and she throws her arms around my neck, squeezing hard and sobbing like a newborn baby.

"I thought you were your father."

She falls to the floor, and I take in her bloody shirt as she passes out.

"Wake up, baby." I shake her but she doesn't budge. "Please, open up your eyes, Blue. Wake up. Stay with me! Don't you die on me. Please! I love you."

Fuck! I can't live without her. There isn't a world without my beautiful wife.

Terror burns in my chest and my hands shake like leaves as I scoop her up in my arms, head toward the door, then I make it to Clemon's car. Once I strap her inside, I get in and drive off. Thankfully, the ignition is push to start.

What if she doesn't make it?

I drive in full speed, bobbing and weaving through the highway. I slide my fingers through her cold fingers, kissing her palms.

My heart thumps in my chest, and I feel as if I'm having a heart attack.

"I'm sorry, Lyrical. For everything. I'm going to make it right. You're going to live. You're going to make it. I promise."

Once I pull up to the parking garage of the hospital, I scoop her in my arms to find she's drenched in blood. She's losing blood from the back of her legs.

I rush her to the front desk.

"She's been injured. Treat my wife, now. She needs help!"

A lady in blue scrubs comes up to me and says, "Follow me. We need to get her to the ICU."

Once we get to the floor, I lay Lyrical down on the bed, and a doctor and a few nurses rush inside the room and check her wounds.

"You need to leave so we can treat these wounds. She lost a lot of blood and she's in a state of shock."

I fill out some paperwork for the nurse in the meantime.

"Who are you?"

"Snow Williams. I'm her husband. Fix my wife."

"We will."

With rage swimming through my veins, I drive like a maniac back to the abandoned mansion. I need to find Revi and Carter.

I pull up to the driveway, get out, only to find dead bodies surrounding the property. My father must have called in people to help him take down Clemon, Keanu, and Jameson.

When I look around, my father's Porsche is gone, which means he's now left the premises.

My phone rings and it's Jameson, so I put it to my ear.

"Where are you? I found Bailey."

Did he just say what the fuck I think he said?

My heart thunders in my chest. "What are you talking about?"

"Come to the back. There are different girls here. Your father and Carter were running a sex ring. Some of these girls are dead and a few of them are injured."

I hit the End button and I see him carrying my sister in his arms.

Pure shock covers me as he places her in my arms, and I move her hair out of her face. They beat my sister to beyond recognition, she has bruises all over her body and she's so pale. If I could cry, I would. Seeing her face brings such relief to me. I kiss her forehead, bringing her to my chest as much as I can. She's weak, fragile, and if I squeeze her hard enough, she'll break.

"Bailey, my sweet baby sister. Why would my father hurt you? What have they done to you? You didn't deserve any of this."

Pure rage washes over me as I rush back to the car and place her in the front passenger seat, with Jameson hopping into the back seat.

"Have you found Carter?"

"Yes, I have him locked in the closet. I figured I'd take him to the basement so we can torture him for answers before you kill him. Your father left. Keanu tried to hunt him down, but it was too late."

As I put the car into gear, Clemon steps outside with a woman in his arms and three others behind him. I recognize two of the girls, they're from the night Lyrical had dinner with Carter.

Bile rises in my throat. This fucker is still trafficking women.

"Did you find Lyrical?"

I nod. "She's at the hospital, I drove her there. She's lost a lot of blood, but the doctor didn't tell me if she will be okay."

Once we get to the hospital, I take Bailey straight to the ER, and they take us to a room right next to Lyrical's. Relief hits me. I hope my sister makes it. They hook her up to an IV and the doctor checks every part of her body, then puts a breathing tube into her nose.

The doctor walks up to me, his hands on his hips. "She has broken ribs, lost a lot of blood, and is dehydrated and malnourished. Bailey also has an infection due to a fever."

"Can you save her?" I ask.

"We don't know. She has a lot of wounds on her body, and we don't know how bad the infection is." With that, he goes into her room and debriefs the nurses.

My father knew this entire time that my sister was alive. He watched my mother suffer and try to commit suicide as a result of my sister's fake dead. He blamed me for her death, knowing he had her locked up, beaten, and used by Carter.

Sick motherfucker. I'm going to skin him alive when Keanu finds him.

I punch the wall, pain shooting up to my wrist, all the way to the tips of my fingers.

The nurses stop to stare at me, and one woman has her hand on the panic button, I'm assuming to call security. I rub my eyes, exhausted as fuck.

I pace the floor as my hands shake like leaves.

Jameson places his hand on my shoulder, and I push it away. "May I say something? I know it's going to get me punched in the face."

I cock my eyebrow at him.

"Your sister."

"What about her?"

He doesn't say anything but rubs the back of his neck, then he finally says, "I'm in love with Bailey."

That catches me off guard. I suspected he had feelings for her in the past, but I'll never approve of him. I'm her brother, I get a say so in whether she takes part in an arranged marriage or not, and the answer is no. I don't want her to ever feel like she has to do that again. This time, I have a second chance of making everything right. To give her freedom. To give her what she wants.

"What are you saying? Because you love her, you think I'm going to hand her over to you for you to marry?"

"Yes, and you should. I'll protect her and take care of her, get her the help she needs. She should have been engaged to me. I'll protect her. If your father had taken my father's offer, then I could have kept her safe."

I push him. "Stay the fuck away from my sister, Jameson. I mean it. I know what you're into. I know what you like, and she's already been broken. I don't need someone else trying to break her as well."

He shoves me. "You can't keep me away from her."

"I'm going to ignore your last statement to save our friendship, but if you go anywhere near Bailey, I'll slit your throat and watch the life leave your eyes."

I walk to Lyrical's room, pulling up a chair next to her bed. The sounds of the machines beep and I place my palm in her cold hand, squeezing tight, but she doesn't squeeze back.

CHAPTER FORTY-SEVEN

Snow

AFTER I LEAVE LYRICAL'S ROOM, I GO STRAIGHT TO BAILEY'S and plant a kiss on her forehead. I'm so pissed off that I need to drive to the mansion on campus. Once I make it to the basement, I find Carter there, chained, naked, bruises and cuts all over his body. Keanu carves into his skin with a knife, and I place my hand on his shoulders, so he leaves the room.

I cross my feet over the other and I don't know who I hate more, him or my father. He used my wife's dreams against her so he can sell or kill her, then on top of that, the motherfucker was Bailey's boyfriend, keeping her locked up like an animal, and he did whatever the fuck he wanted to do to her.

I piece it all together. It makes sense now.

His face is blank, no emotions on display.

Grabbing the knife from my ankle, I place it on his neck, drawing blood, itching to slice his skin like I'm carving a turkey.

"What did you do to my sister?" I demand.

He eyes me a second too long then closes them, before laughing. "I treated her like all the other whores we had down there in the basement. We used them, fucked them, then we sold her body; they do what they want to the girls and bring them back, but your sister was my favorite. At one point I did love her. She knows how to suck d—"

I slam my fist into his stomach, shutting him up.

"Why was my father at the mansion?"

He takes several moments to catch his breath before answering. "He's the one who told me to pimp Bailey out and sell her, so I got her hooked on any kind of drugs to keep her high. I told her she was pretty, made it seem like her family hated her, until she tried to leave me. He was the one who told me to start dating her because she was rebellious against her arranged marriage to Tim.

"Your sister came to him, wanting out of the arranged marriage, and she threatened to run away so he told me to groom her, keep her drugged, make her a slut for my dick and then sell her.

"Your father is behind the girls being sold in the basement. He wanted to start his own ring to traffic girls and since I used to be part of the mafia, he paid me a large amount to find girls for it.

"When your father told me Lyrical came to you about someone else having something to do with the car accident, that's when he told me to get her next, so I sent Samuel to kill her."

It takes every ounce of my being to not slice him into two. I shove forward, nicking his neck, blood dripping down his flesh.

"The car accident was your father's idea. He's the one who had me drug both of them at the football party, and Drake pulled over the girls, pretending to be a policeman. He took Bailey out of the car, replaced your sister's body with someone else and pulled Lyrical out. He rolled the car into a tree, set Lyrical's unconscious body next to the tree, then he set the car on fire. Revi knew his daughter was a junkie. He knew that if he blamed you for the car accident that you would want to take your revenge out on Lyrical. He didn't want Lyrical dead because of revenge for your sister, he wanted her dead because he knew Lyrical realized the accident was staged. The body that was in the car belonged to one of the girls we sold—she looked like Bailey.

I remember going to the morgue, looking at a burned body—a dead body that wasn't my sister's. I feel like shit, like the walls are caving in. Lyrical thought that it was a setup. She knew and I made her believe that she made it up in her head, that she was hallucinating. She doesn't remember taking Molly because she didn't. She was drugged. No one believed her. When I checked through footage of the car accident, there was none, and I thought it was strange. Clemon checked with the NHPD and the medical records, but it turns out it was all forged. Lyrical was in the crossfire of it all, and I need to apologize to her. I did choose my revenge over her—instead of taking it a step further and investigating it, I believed what I thought were facts. It makes sense how my father had pictures of Bailey in the basement. They staged June's death because he was the perfect setup. My father needed me to believe that Lyrical was making it up so I would kill her and go to jail.

"Whose house was it that we found June's body at?"

"Your father's. He owned it."

I don't buy the story my father told me that Dante killed June. It has to be a cover-up story.

"Who really killed June? He was already dead when I found him."

"Your dad had Drake do it. When we found out you had killed Samuel, we knew you were close to finding out what happened and your father was afraid that June was going to rat us out to you. Since I paid June to follow Lyrical and act like he was interested in her."

I've had enough of his shit and I'm going to be the one who takes his last breath, then I'm going to find my father and make him pay.

I grab Carter by the hair, then what's left of his botched dick and balls, and I slice them off. He screams at the top of his lungs.

Blood sprays across the concrete as he bellows, calling me all kinds of names.

"You will never hurt another woman again." I lean down. "No one is going to save you, and I don't want to hear from your fucking mouth."

I take a thick thread and a needle from the top shelf of the cabinet, and I sew his mouth shut.

"Now, you're going to watch me saw off all your limbs. One by one."

His eyes widen.

I start with his arms, cutting through flesh, then bone, tossing them onto the floor.

"You hear that? The sound of your flesh getting cut. That's music to my ears."

Next, I cut off his legs. Carter bleeds out, smearing his body with his own blood as he tries to move, and before I know it, he stops wiggling.

And I watch the life leave his eyes.

CHAPTER FORTY-EIGHT

Lyrical

THE BEEPING NOISE FROM THE MACHINE STIRS ME OUT OF my sleep and I look around the room, the lights blinding my eyes. Relief washes over me to find that I'm safe in a hospital. My body feels like it's on fire. Exhaustion overtakes me as the room spins. I glance down at my fingers intertwined with Snow's. I've never been so happy to see him more than I am now.

I'm forever grateful to him for rescuing me from his father and Carter. Snow sits up, rubs his eyes, and when he sees I'm awake, he immediately cups my face and kisses me deeply. I allow him to kiss me long and hard.

I miss his lips on mine.

I miss being at home with him.

I miss him controlling my body.

Tears rush down my cheeks, and he brings me into his arms, stroking my hair.

"You're safe, Lyrical. You're so beautiful and brave."

I've never felt safer than I do now. He lets me sob uncontrollably on his hoodie. When I pull away, he uses his thumbs to wipe away my tears.

He whips out his phone and types on the screen before tucking it back into his pocket.

"I texted your parents to let them know you're okay." He brushes his lips against my forehead. "How are you feeling, Blue?"

"Where is Bailey? I want to see her."

"She's right next door."

"Take me to her, please."

I can't wait to see her and hold her in my arms, I miss her terribly. When we get out of the hospital, we're going for milkshakes, and I'm to help her however I can so she can get through her trauma of dealing with her father and Carter.

"What happened to your father and Carter?"

Snow grabs a bag from the corner, pulling out a sweater and some sweatpants. He removes my gown and helps me into my clothes, trying not to touch the stitches on my side and the back of my leg and below my ass cheek.

"Carter is dead—I killed him. I can't locate my father, but Clemon and Keanu are working on it."

Good. I'm glad Carter is dead. He deserves it. And his father needs to be killed too.

My legs burn so Snow picks me up, and I snuggle up in his arms. My face feels like it's lit on fire from being punched earlier. Even though we've broken up, I like the fact that he's still taking care of me.

He carries me to Bailey's room, and I sit on the bed next to her.

She's thin and weak. I hug her and kiss her forehead as tears continue to run down my cheeks.

"I can't believe you're alive," I whisper. "I'm so happy to see you. I missed you so much. The last several months have been hell without you. When you get out of here, we're going for ice cream, and I'll catch you up on the latest gossip, and you'll meet Lilac and Winter too. They are cool friends. We can have a girls' night out."

Snow stands behind me, wrapping his arms around my waist.

Bailey stirs awake and her eyes land on us, then she smiles weakly. Her eyes drink in the way her brother clings to me, and he holds her hand, squeezing. She glances around the hospital, then back at us.

"Hey." Her tone is weak and low.

I slip my fingers into her other hand, and I kiss her palm.

"We're going to get through this together, Bailey. I promise we will. We love you and we miss you so much."

"I'm... tired."

She lets go of my palm and slips back into sleep, and the monitor makes a beeping noise before all of the numbers say zero.

Realization hits me like a ton of bricks as I shake her shoulders.

"Wake up! Please, Bailey, wake up!!" I scream as I sob uncontrollably.

Doctors and nurses push us out of the way as I stand there in shock, but Snow drags me out of the room while I keep my eyes glued to the window, feeling numb, unable to breathe, clutching my sweatshirt and trying to catch my breath. I turn to Snow, wrapping my arms around him as he keeps his eyes glued to the window.

The nurses turn off the monitor and remove the IV and breathing tube. A moment later, one of them states Bailey's time of death. The nurse places a white sheet over her body.

The doctor walks up to us and places his hand on Snow's shoulder.

"The infection in her body was too great and she was already severely malnourished. I'm sorry."

I collapse to the ground, screaming, while Snow just holds me in his arms.

Snow

I drive Lyrical to the farmhouse because she told me she didn't want to be bothered by anyone. She sobs the entire ride. I'm trying to be strong for her, but I'm also trying to fight the urge to spaz the fuck out. It feels like someone took a sledgehammer to my chest. I thought for certain Bailey would survive after we found her and that I got my sister back.

Sometimes fate feels as if it's fucking with us. My sister had a tragic life. I didn't protect her like I was supposed to or stand up to my father like I should have. Maybe I could have prevented all of this and my father would pay for his crimes. Once he is found, he's going to suffer in the worst way.

Once I pull up to the driveway, I carry Lyrical into the living room, laying her on the couch, then I sit next to her. Eventually, she cries herself to sleep.

There is a knock at the door, so I grab my gun from under the couch, slowly walk to the door, and look through the peephole. I sigh in relief to see my mother, so I tuck the gun in the back of my pants and unlock the door before opening it.

She throws her arms around me, hugging me and sobbing. We stand there for several moments, but it feels like eternity.

I walk her to the kitchen, and she sits on of the barstools with neither one of us saying anything.

"The hospital called and your sister... your sister passed away... again."

She doesn't know anything that happened between my father and me, so I tell her. I tell her everything about what Carter told me, and that I have to find Revi.

"My poor baby," my mother says, her eyes bloodshot from crying. "I'm so sorry, Snow. I failed you and Bailey."

"You did the best you could w—"

"I chose Revi over you, and I shouldn't have. He blamed you for something that he staged because he's filled with control and power. I should have protected you two. I should have left him when I had the chance, but instead I allowed your father to treat you and Bailey like shit because I didn't want to be a single mother."

I don't respond because I don't know what to say to that. I always felt like she always took his side, and I understand that she was staying to survive. My mother gets up and holds out her arms, and I embrace her. She wraps her tiny arms around me, squeezing tight.

I sit on a barstool, and she sits back down, next to me.

"So, how is marriage with Lyrical?"

"She wants a divorce but I'm not giving it to her. I don't want to lose her. She feels as if I put her second and she thinks that I won't change for her. She thinks I chose my revenge over her."

Mom smiles sadly at me. "I understand where she is coming from. Your father was always putting me second. When he was out for blood, nothing stood in his way. Stop choosing revenge over her. Choose her over the Billionaire Club. I know your father taught you to serve the club, but that is what drove a wedge in our marriage. It drove him to cheat." She runs her fingers through my hair. "I'm sorry."

I watch her in bewilderment, but she goes on.

"I'm sorry for choosing your father over you and taking his side. I'm sorry for blaming you for your sister's death—the first time. I'm so sorry, my sweet boy. I'm sorry that I was a neglectful mother and I'm sorry that I allowed your father to destroy our lives. That's why I had to move to San Francisco. I couldn't take the guilt. I had no idea that your father did what he did. Do you forgive me, son?"

"I do. You don't have to continue to say you're sorry."

"I want you to hear it."

I nod. I love my mother, and I already lost my sister a second time; I don't want to lose her too.

I need to make up for my behavior toward Lyrical. I should have believed her in the first place when she said the car accident was staged, but I couldn't see past my rage. Instead of choosing love, I chose my rage—my revenge over her—but not anymore. My revenge got us in this predicament. I'm going to change by picking her. Going forward, I will always pick her no matter what. She deserves an apology from me again, I owe her that much. And I'm going to spend the rest of my life making it up to her.

Lyrical limps into the kitchen, and my mother gets up from the barstool and hugs her, cupping her face. Mom drops a kiss on her forehead. "Thank you for loving my kids."

She turns on the ball of her heel and says, "I'll be in the guest room."

Lyrical stares at me for what seems like forever.

"If you need anything, ask me. Don't be walking on your injured leg, you could tear your stitches."

"I'm fine, Snow."

"I need to talk to you," I tell her, pulling out a barstool and helping her sit on it. "How are you feeling?"

"Tired."

"What kind of revenge do you want me to exact on my father?" I ask, resting my elbows on the breakfast nook.

She gives me a puzzled look. "Come again?"

"I want your help getting revenge on my father. So, what are your ideas of how you want me to kill him?"

"You want to include me in your plan for revenge against your father?" she asks, skeptical.

"Yes."

"Why?"

I tuck a strand behind her ear, and her cheeks turn a pale pink. "Because I'm not the only one who lost Bailey, you lost her too. For a while, I didn't take any consideration of how you felt about her death. This revenge isn't just mine, it's yours too. We're a team, Lyrics."

Her eyes water, and she wraps her arms around my shoulders. "Really?"

I nod.

She squeezes my hand. "Thank you. It's all I wanted, to be seen and not be second to you."

Tears tickle down her bruised face and I use my thumb to wipe them away. Leaning forward, I brush my lips against her forehead.

I grab her by the neck and squeeze tightly, kissing her deeply, and she moans against my mouth. God, I miss my wife.

My phone dings with a message, so I grab it from my pocket.

Keanu: I found your father.

Me: Send me his location.

"Keanu found my father, are you ready to pay him a visit?"

She wraps her arms around my neck. "Yes. Let's show him who he's fucking with."

CHAPTER FORTY-NINE

Lyrical

I CAN'T BELIEVE SNOW IS GOING TO INCLUDE ME IN THE revenge plan against his father, allow me to watch him kill Revi. I'm so excited and I can't wait to see the look in his eyes when Snow kills him.

I feel worn out and pissed off that I lost my best friend twice. The pain of what happened will never go away. Bailey went through so much, but maybe she can finally rest. Snow told me everything that Carter said. I wish I were the one who chopped his body parts off and watched him die.

Revi is hiding out in a cabin in the middle of nowhere.

We pull up to an abandoned driveway nearby, Jameson and Keanu pulling up beside us just in case we need backup. Snow and I hop out of the car. He grabs my hand, squeezing tight. I know this was hard for him, for me to be involved in this. He set aside his feelings for mine.

Maybe he's going to change.

My face, side, and leg hurt, and I feel as if I was hit by a bus.

We rehash what is exactly going to happen. Hopefully, we will be successful.

"I disabled his cameras," Jameson says.

Snow gives him the thumbs-up and when we walk around the back door of the cabin, he leans down and kisses my temple.

"You stay behind me, Blue."

I nod. Snow picks the lock and slowly pushes the door open. The place is clean and empty. His father has his phone glued to his face, speaking to someone about helping him leave the country.

"Just have my fake passport and ID ready, so the other owners of the American Billionaire Club can't track me. I'm pretty sure my son is looking for me and I'm fucked if he finds me." He taps the screen and places the phone on the mantelpiece.

Pure rage consumes me. How can he betray his own family like this? I want to attack him and go ahead and end his life. I've never hated anyone as much as I hate him.

I breathe in and breathe out as we continue to watch him.

Snow removes his gun from his holster and points it to the back of his head. As his father slowly turns around, pure terror colors his face, and he throws his hands up in the air.

"Sit," Snow orders.

He doesn't move, so Snow hits his father's head with the butt of the gun, causing Revi to stumble back.

"I said, sit."

Slowly, Revi sits at the dining room table and stares at us.

"You won't get away with this. I'm important, Snow. If I go missing or get killed, they will look at you two as the suspect."

"Where were you going? You're such a fucking coward. I don't know why I wanted to impress you all my life. You destroyed everyone's lives and didn't give any fucks about it. I should have killed you a long time ago."

"Everyone is a dollar sign, Snow. You will see that when you're older. Falling for this bi—"

That's enough, I don't want to hear any more, so I walk up to him and punch him in the face. My small knuckles sting, but I don't care. Revi holds his face as I walk back to Snow.

"That's all you got, bitch? I should have kidnapped you myself, used your body however I wanted, and allowed my men to take turns on you. Then have my son watch. You whore."

Snow grabs a zip tie from his back pocket and ties his father's hands up.

"You will never get away with what you're about to do to me," he says. "The FBI will hunt you down like the dogs you are, and you will be in jail."

Snow yanks a fistful of Revi's dyed hair. "Your business partners know what you did to Bailey, and they are going to help us cover up your death. They told us to do what we have to do to get rid of you."

For the first time, his father is completely speechless, panic coloring his face. I've never seen him look so scared in my entire life.

"Please, don't kill me. I'll give you more money than you can imagine."

Snow hands me the gun, his palm gentle against my cheek. "Do you want to be the one to pull the trigger, Blue?"

I look at him in complete shock, my mouth hanging open. "You would let me pull the trigger?"

He nods. "It's not just my revenge, it's your revenge too, Blue. I killed Carter, but you can have my father. I saved him for you."

Now I'm the one who's speechless. He's really trying to include me in his plans and is allowing me to kill him, not leaving me in the dark. I know how badly he wanted to get his revenge on his father and be the one to end his life. I never thought he would sacrifice his own need to make me happy. For the first time, I feel heard and seen. For the first time, he's putting me first.

"I never killed anyone, Snow."

"Don't worry about it, my wife. I'll walk you through it. But I have to warn you, you won't be the same, Lyrical, if you do this."

"I know."

I really do. I know once I shoot Revi that my life will never be the same and that's okay. I accepted what I have to do and I already know how my future might be. It might make me go mad and I might be fine, but it doesn't matter because getting revenge will be worth it in the end. Justice for Bailey will be worth it.

I stare at Revi, and I see the fear in his eyes and, for a second, I hesitate, because part of me knows he's a human being, but when I remember how poorly he treated Bailey, death is the only way to stop the bastard.

Snow shows me how to aim as I place the gun against Revi's forehead. Fighting the urge to close my eyes, I pull the trigger.

Once we get back to the farmhouse, my father is waiting in the foyer, and I hug him tight.

"It's been done," Snow tells my father.

"Good," he answers after kissing me on the cheek.

He takes one good look at the blood and bits of Revi's guts all over my face and clothes, gritting his teeth.

"You allowed my daughter to get anywhere near a gun and a dead body?"

"Fath—"

"Yes. She wanted to. An—"

"I don't give a fuck," my father snaps.

"If she wants to help me get revenge on someone, then she's allowed to." Snow keeps his eyes glued to me. "What she wants will always come first, even before me."

His words make me melt, and I want to kiss him but the smell of Revi's blood starts to make my head swim. I need to clean myself, so without a word, I head to my bedroom and remove my bloody clothes before hopping in the shower.

The scorching hot water runs down my body, and I feel numb. I ignore the throbbing stitches on my side and calf. I actually killed someone, and I don't feel any remorse for what I did to Revi. He deserved it. Snow told me that killing someone would change me, and it has. I see this world in darker and grayer colors; the world is as cruel as I once thought it was. I'm both exhausted and relieved from the events which recently happened.

Now, Bailey's death has been avenged and she can finally rest—be free from the hellhole she was in.

Sometimes being alive is hell and death is heaven.

Snow included me on the plan to get revenge on his father, making me trust him. He's proved to me that he's serious about our marriage. He apologized, but will he go back to his old ways? If I live a life without Snow, then I'm going to be miserable—so miserable. I close my eyes and try to picture my life without him, and I draw a blank, and an empty feeling hits me like tidal waves but when I imagine our lives together, I'm filled with happiness and joy. I picture him coming home from a long day, and he's telling me about what he has to do at the Billionaire Club and we have dinner, then he does whatever he wants to my body. That is what I always envisioned how our lives would be—in complete happiness. There isn't any doubt in my mind that he loves me. I can't live without him, and I know he can't live without me. The fact that he's actually giving me a choice says a lot, because the old Snow didn't give me choices. He's not perfect, but he's trying and that's what truly matters.

I want him in my life, and I never stopped loving him.

I scrub my skin raw and watch the blood swirl on the tiles. Once I step out of the shower, I dry myself off with a cotton towel, then I put on a robe, tie the sash, and I head to the living room. My father is looking out of the window as he and Snow speak about him becoming the CEO of the Billionaire Club next month.

I lean in the archway, clearing my throat.

"Can I talk to you for a second?" I say to Snow.

My father looks between us and goes into the kitchen.

I stare at Snow as he walks up to me, placing a strand of hair behind my ear.

"What is it, Blue?"

"Thank you for rescuing me from Carter and Revi and including me in your plan for revenge. It means a lot to me."

He cups my face, and my cheeks flush, butterflies dancing in my stomach.

"I'm sorry. I fucked up. And you shouldn't come second to anything in my life. I chose revenge over you, but now I'm choosing to put you first. Always. You have my word, Blue. I promise to inform you of everything and to never keep secrets from you. I'm sorry I chose to exact revenge on you, and I'm sorry I chose my revenge on my father over you. You didn't deserve my wrath from the beginning. I should have believed you when you told me you didn't do any drugs."

I slip my fingers into his pocket and grab my wedding and engagement rings, sliding them on my finger. "I want to stay married to you, Snow. I want to work this out."

"I wasn't going to let you get a divorce. I wasn't going to sign any papers. We would have to just live separate lives until you decided to take me back."

I shake my head because that part hasn't changed about him, and I never would want him to give up on us. I love my obsessive, stalker husband.

"I know your intention wasn't to hurt me, Snow."

He grabs me by the nape of my neck and kisses me deeply, and I kiss him back. His kiss is filled with so much love and passion, my heart melts.

"I love you, Snow."

"I fucking inhale you. Every fiber of your being. I'm obsessed with you. What I feel for you is far deeper than love." He grabs my hand, leads me upstairs to our bedroom, and removes my robe. Grabbing some zip ties, he slaps them around my wrists, then he secures a gag around my face.

"I'm going to fuck you until you can't handle it anymore, my wife."

Yes!

Yes!

Yes!

I nod my head, tasting the rubber ball in my mouth.

He lays me on my back and slides inside of me, keeping his promise by fucking me until we're both out of breath.

EPILOGUE

Last Day of the First Semester

Snow

STAND IN THE FOYER OF THE MANSION ON CAMPUS. LYRICAL and I slept over because we had a Christmas party the night before and we didn't want to drive all the way home. So we stayed in my old room, where I tied her to the bedposts and fucked her brains out. We're going to her parents' for winter break, then we're flying out to San Francisco to spend New Year's with my mother. I'm so fucking glad that this semester is over with, and maybe next semester will be better.

I started working as the CEO of the American Billionaire Club, and next semester, I'll be attending night classes to complete my master's degree.

The townspeople of North Haven whispered about my father's death; they don't believe he committed suicide. But the business partners kept their word and had our back. No one but us know what really happened to Bailey, and my family and I want to keep it that way. I don't want people to remember her as this sad, tragic person. Now that I have found out the truth about my sister, I can finally breathe, while she can finally rest.

Lyrical rushes down the stairs, wraps her arms around my shoulders, and kisses my lips as I slide my fingers under her leather dress, squeezing her ass.

"Did I mention how much I love you?" she says, grinning from ear to ear.

I tuck her hair behind her ear. "Yes. You tell me every hour."

"I tried looking everywhere for my Christmas gift at the farmhouse and here. Please give me a hint so I can stop trying to kill myself over it."

"You're never going to find it," I shoot back, holding her hand.

We're going to have our own Christmas dinner at the Billionaire Club, then I'm taking her to the part of the club where the sex club is, where I'm going to fuck her. Her second gift is the building she wants to turn into her art studio and gallery, our first investment. It's the place she's been eyeing for so long, and I saw it on her Pinterest boards.

Keanu walks down the stairs with his bag in his hand and Lyrical meets him at the bottom of the steps, wrapping her arms around him. Setting his bag down, he spins her around like he's some fucking Disney prince and she's his princess. The scene where the girl gets the prince. It takes every ounce of my self-control not to slit his throat, but if I kill Keanu, Lyrical will never forgive me because she considers him her "friend." So he can keep his life—for now. He's supposed to be on my side, but it seems my wife's got him wrapped around her finger. For the last month, they got close, hanging out, going on these so-called friend dates. It makes me sick. A week ago, when I was at the club, she texted him to bring her a bag of gummy bears and they watched a movie together. I watched them through the camera I planted in the farmhouse. I hate their fucking friendship. I'm the only male friend she needs.

I stand between them, bringing Lyrical to my side, and Keanu smirks.

"Where are you going for winter break?" she asks, rocking on her heels.

"My parents'. Though I don't want to because they are going to be hounding me about getting married."

"You're still not in an arranged marriage to anyone?" she asks.

He shakes his head. "I tend to scare the prospective wives off with the shit that I'm into. Plus, marriage is not my thing. I like to be free to stick my dick into anyone I want to. I see how Snow acts with you, and I'll be damned to be pussy-whipped because of a woman. No offense, Snow." He eyes me.

I roll my eyes, folding my arms across my chest.

Lyrical crinkles her nose at him. "Will you be able to become CFO after graduation? I thought you had to be married to inherit your proportion of the business."

"My father is planning on giving it to my brother if I don't." With that, he slaps me on the back. "I'll see your crazy ass next semester. Take care of my *bestie*."

"She's not your best friend, K. I am, remember?"

"I replaced you with Lyrical. She's more fun and doesn't have a stick up her ass like you. Maybe you need to peg him a fe—"

"Keanu. Leave before I slit your throat," I growl.

Lyrical opens the door for him, and we both watch Keanu throw his bag straps over his shoulders and hop on his motorcycle before taking off down the driveway.

The smell of the ocean wafts into my nose, inviting a chilly breeze along with it.

Jameson and Irvin head downstairs with their bags and they both eye us. Irvin drops his bag on the floor, walks up to me, and places his hand on the back of my neck, squeezing tight. I can barely breathe when he bangs my head against the wall.

Lyrical tries to reach for me to stop him, but Jameson holds her back. "Stay out of it, Lyrical."

"If you ever try to kill me again, I promise you, you will meet your maker."

I burst out laughing, so he bangs my head against the wall again, causing my head to throb.

"I mean it. And if you ever threaten to harm Lilac again, I'll kill Lyrical and bury her ass in the backyard. We might not like each other but you will respect me."

He lets me go, and I stroke my face. No doubt, I'm going to have a bruise. "Next time I kill you, I'll make sure you're dead for real."

We stand toe to toe, and I place my hand on the gun tucked into the back of my pants.

Jameson stands between us. "Leave, Irvin. We don't need a bloodbath."

He nods, mumbling "Fucking asshole" and then slams the door.

"What is Irvin speaking about?" Lyrical questions, folding her arms and eyeing me suspiciously.

"Snow tried to kill Irvin by drowning him in the pool because you were seeking him out, but you didn't tell him the reasoning."

Her face pales. "I'm sorry, I didn't mean to get him almost killed. I only told you that to get a rise out of you. I di—"

"It's fine," I cut her off.

"Then Snow threatened to hurt Lilac if he tried to retaliate," Jameson adds, rubbing the back of his head.

Lyrical punches me in the arm. "Snow! You will not hurt my friend. We're not pawns to be used between you and Irvin for your guys' pissing contest."

I shrug. "I had to do what I had to do."

"Well… I'm off. I'll see you after the holidays."

"Wait," Lyrical murmurs.

She wraps her arms around him but pulls back quickly, and

awkwardness settles between them. "I'm sorry for your loss as well." He gives her a puzzled look so she goes on. "Bailey. Snow told me you were in love with her. I'm sorry you didn't get the chance to love her the way you wanted to. I understand how you can have feelings for someone, and you couldn't let them know."

He glances at the marble floors, inhales deeply and exhales. In all of the years I've known Jameson, I've never seen him so broken. He was robbed of his happy ending, and if Bailey had survived, he would have gone behind my back and tried to marry her, and I wouldn't blame him because if the roles were reversed, I would have gone behind his back and married Lyrical too if she were his sister. Nothing would have stopped me.

He clears his throat and his gaze drifts to me. "I'll be fine. It hurts like a bitch, but everything will be okay. I'll try my best to cope." He runs his fingers through his hair. "I'll take it one day at a time."

"I'll see you next semester, Jameson."

"You too. Stay out of trouble and don't burn my mansion if Snow pisses you off again," he jokes.

Sighing, he leaves too. We have the entire mansion to ourselves, and I grab her hand and lead her out to the backyard, straight to the forest.

She smiles at the bare trees and the inky sky.

"Run, Blue."

"What's going to happen when you catch me?"

"It's a surprise. Five…" I start.

She kisses my cheek and takes off, running deep into the forest.

"Four… three… two… one."

I chase Lyrical.

The girl I can't ever live without. The girl who has had my heart since I was seventeen. The girl I will kill and die for.

Please leave a rating for *Ruthless God*.
I really, really, appreciate it.

The Next Story is *Treacherous God* (Lilac and Irvin Story)
Tropes:
Revenge
Tricked into marriage
Dangerous Past
Stalker
CNC
Dubious
On Screen Murder
Antihero
Coming up 2025

STALK ME

J.m.stoneback (@j.m.stoneback5) | TikTok

J.M.Stoneback (@j.m.stoneback) • Instagram photos and videos

www.goodreads.com/book/show/197305912-ruthless-god

ABOUT THE AUTHOR

J.M. writes dark new adult and contemporary romance. When she is not reading and writing about hot guys, she is spending time with her boys and husband. Travel, food, video games, and anime are her hobbies.

OTHER BOOKS

Heartless Boss

Arrogant Boss

The Deal With The Playboy

The Villain Collection
Devious
Villainous

The Natural Born Killer Series.
The Viper

The Gods of the North Haven University
Ruthless God

Made in the USA
Columbia, SC
06 November 2024